THE CERBERUS PROTOCOL

THE CERBERUS PROTOCOL

HARVEY BENNETT THRILLERS
BOOK 14

NICK THACKER

CHAPTER 1
DEMETRI

DEMETRI PUSHED THE THICK, heavy metal door open and heard the hiss of the airlock as it matched pressure with the air from the hallway. He stepped in, careful not to catch his hazmat suit on the sharp flashing around the doorframe.

Fully inside, he pressed the red button on the wall to re-pressurize the room to sterilize and kill anything that may have hitched a ride on his suit. Above his head, a countdown timer began at 28 seconds.

Apparently, 28 seconds was the magic number for fully stabilizing and sterilizing a lab.

He turned and peered through the tall rectangular window that led deeper into the laboratory's main space. It was late; no one would be awake. That was how he liked it.

Ever since starting at the Russian laboratory, he had felt increasingly ostracized. It wasn't the others — they were all good people, good scientists. It was just how he was. Clinically introverted, Demetri preferred working through the night. Not a night owl like Pablo, but a true nocturnal worker. He felt his best science and focus were achieved when there was no chance he would be bothered by human intervention.

The others didn't exactly appreciate his schedule, of course. They were a team, and their team leader suggested more than once that they should work as one — implying that Demetri should maintain a more "regular" schedule.

But what was regular to *them* was not regular for *him*. He preferred working at night; they preferred working during the day.

He chuckled as he thought of it. What did it matter what time they worked? They were half a mile underground, inside a Russian military laboratory on the side of a mountain, deep in a national park surrounded by nothing at all.

That his coworkers chose a schedule that matched that of a typical office job was arbitrary. The hours here were all the same.

The countdown timer buzzed, and the door to the interior chamber was unlocked with another slight buzzing sound. This door slid to the right, and he hoisted it in that direction with a glove-covered hand.

He felt his heartbeat quicken, his excitement rise. His life's work lay inside, the very thing he dreamt of as a boy.

Back then, it was a common dream: what boy didn't dream about digging up dinosaurs, finding their bones and piecing them together, and creating a narrative of what their life must have been like? What boy didn't want to be a paleontologist, even before they knew what the word meant?

He had been giddy with excitement when he won the bid to be the station's fourth and final researcher. There had been a skeleton crew of helpers working in the installation as well, early on. Cooks, cleaning crew, admin, IT support. But recently they had all been reassigned, leaving the scientists alone in the base. He was one of only four people allowed to continue working at the clandestine research lab.

It wasn't that the work they did was terribly important — it was still just research, after all — but his government loved to cover up anything that might one day lead to progress and military advancement.

If it could possibly be used as a weapon, it needed to be top-secret.

The joke was that because dinosaurs had turned into oil after millions of years of compression and heat — and oil was used to power tanks — paleontology was, therefore, a military endeavor.

So far, nothing they had found around their site, and nothing that had been brought to them from elsewhere, even remotely suggested a practical military use. But rules were rules, and he got to do what he had always wanted. Studying the animal life that had once roamed the earth was his passion, and he was quite good at it.

He walked forward, wasting no time moving toward his destination. The Block sat in another, smaller room, one chilled to below freezing. His hazmat suit was lined internally with wool, and he also wore a merino wool sweater and thick sweatpants beneath it. Working in a subzero environment was an annoyance, but it was worth the discomfort. Their hands would often chill past the point of being useful, so during working hours the teams usually ran shifts of 30 to 45 minutes only, taking turns warming up back in the larger laboratory space.

It didn't help that "The Block" was literally a block of ice and that everything they touched was frozen. The block had been discovered at the very site this base had been built on, and was thus the reason for the facility's construction in the first place. Demetri had come onto the crew last, when the facility was declared finally finished. Building the base had been a monumental undertaking, a Herculean effort from dozens of Army architecture and engineering crews.

And, like most government projects, its purpose had never been disclosed to those who had built it.

But two weeks ago, on Demetri's first day at "the office," they were brought into this internal room and allowed to inspect The Block firsthand.

Demetri remembered the feeling distinctly. It was like a dream come true.

The block itself was nothing noteworthy, literally just a block of frozen water. It was old, likely somewhere in the realm of 100,000 years old, but it was the object inside it — the reason The Block had been retrieved from an underwater frozen lake deep beneath them in the first place — that had captured Demetri's attention.

An animal, frozen in place.

As of this moment, it had not been positively identified. DNA extractions hinted that the creature might be related to the Siberian tiger, but its ancestry pointed back to another creature altogether:

The saber-tooth tiger.

The saber-tooth tiger — or Smilodon — was a species of prehistoric cat that lived during the Pleistocene epoch, around 1.5 million years up to 10,000 years ago. It was named for its long, curved saber-like teeth, which it used to kill its prey. Saber-tooth tigers were native to North and

South America — not Russia — and were one of the largest predatory mammals of their time.

The cats stood about three feet tall at the shoulder and could weigh up to 600 pounds, making them roughly the same size as a modern African lion.

The problem was, their Beast in the ice didn't look much like a tiger. It more resembled a bear, with furry, thick paws that met its body by way of tree-trunk-thick legs. Short and stout, it seemed more strength and power than speed and agility, and it was missing the most distinct part of the saber-tooth tiger: its canines. The long snout of The Beast had no protruding teeth.

But the mystery of it only intrigued the science crew even more. While Demetri thought himself the local expert paleontologist, his team members were quite gifted in paleontology as well, and each of them also had a secondary interest that the Russian government had deemed important to the task. Clive was a chemist, Betany was a cellular biologist, and Fyodor was a paleoarchaeologist.

Together, the crew represented the best Russia had to offer when it came to exploring creatures from long ago.

And this was absolutely a creature from long ago. Perhaps not quite as old as the ice surrounding it — or perhaps older still — the creature looked to be from a time just before the dawning of modern humans.

And it was Demetri's job to determine exactly what it was.

CHAPTER 2
DEMETRI

HE EYED the block with suspicion, a twinkling in his eye. "What exactly are you?" he whispered. "What secrets do you have for me?"

While he truly enjoyed working in the middle of the night rather than when everyone else was awake, bustling around with activity, there was another reason Demetri preferred coming down here when no one else was around: here, he could sit and stare at The Beast within The Block, as if waiting for it to speak to him, to give him answers as to its past, its nature. It was as though he felt the animal could speak to him, if only he could listen intently enough.

Demetri had an almost reverential superstition surrounding ancient Earth creatures. Always fascinated by dinosaurs, he had grown up loving the American *Jurassic Park* movies and the promise they represented. "How much easier would it be to understand life that used to exist if we could simply figure out how to create it once again?"

He had almost majored in genetics, aiming for a career path that would take him down the route of the original *Jurassic Park* scientists, but had opted against it thanks to a wise professor who knew his heart better than he did. They had redirected him to paleontology, perhaps a "stodgier" career field, but one that offered more to a brain like Demitri's. Genetics was fine, but there was little chance he would find work trying to bring a dinosaur back to life — that was pure fiction.

Paleontology, on the other hand, was not limited by such realism. If he wanted to write a story about this creature's life, all he needed to do was study it enough to make some educated guesses about what it ate, where it lived, how it reproduced, and then publish it. It would be received as an academic paper, but to him, it would be as entertaining as a comic book.

Demetri placed a glove on top of The Block and slid it horizontally down to quadrant eight — the top-right cube of ice from this perspective. Inside quadrant eight lay The Beast's back-left foot, his object of study for the past few days. The others had chosen similar quadrants, each focusing on the part of the creature that lived within it, each drawing samples from long drilled bores that allowed them to use equally long tweezers and devices to pry and prod the creature's flesh and fur.

He saw two such holes now, one in the quadrant directly in front of him, and one on quadrant eight's side facing him. Both led down to the foot of The Beast, though one had been used to insert a high-tensile strength syringe through the ice.

From there, they had plucked a few fibers of hair from the top of its foot.

He patted the rear surface of quadrant eight and leaned his head toward it. "Tomorrow's the big day," he said. "Tomorrow, we free you from your frozen fortress. Oh, how I cannot wait to meet you face-to-face without this ice sheath you have been wearing for so long."

He continued walking around The Block, now using his left hand to rub the icy sides of the rectangular prism on the floor of the room. The blast chiller sprang to life, emitting a white smoke-like fog from high above, which filled the air above Demetri's head and began to settle downward. Even through the wool clothes and the hazmat suit he could sense the cooling, refrigerated room.

He saw the tools they would use — hacksaws, a handsaw, a larger device that required four hands. Smaller implements like chisels, ice picks, delicate scalpels. These they would don as soon as they had carved away most of the ice, leaving about a 6-inch gap between them and the creature.

From there, they would break the ice into larger chunks by sawing by hand sections from the creature's ice cage.

Demetri almost wanted to fire up one of the saws now. Surely the levels of this base were insulated enough so that no one would hear him?

He shook his head, waving away the insane notion. So far, their team leader, Clive, had merely hinted at the fact that Demetri should work with the rest of them during "proper" hours. If he were to do something so stupid as to actually start cutting into The Block, Clive would begin to insist on it, and Demetri would be forced to act like a normal, well-balanced adult, working during the day.

He continued his path around the creature, not wanting to start in on the mountain of research paperwork he was preparing in the other room. He had come here to see "The Beast," as they called it, beneath its icy home in the block. Even back in his bunk, he had pictures of it on his laptop, which he would flip through whenever he was supposed to be resting.

The time would come. He had won his bid for the work, and he was being paid handsomely to have a little patience.

Demetri finished examining the block of ice and shook off the snow and water that had accumulated on his gloves. He started walking towards the doorway of the smaller internal chamber but stopped and knelt close to the creature's head, which was split between quadrants one, two, and three. The block was about 8 feet tall and had been cut perfectly to give enough space around The Beast inside.

The effect was that The Beast seemed to be hovering in the center of the room, about a foot off the floor, with the arch of its back ending at eye level.

Thanks to the cold environment in which it had lived and died, The Beast had been perfectly preserved. Tufts of fur seemed to be missing from its body, as if plucked away by another creature just before its death. Its face was smooth, lacking the fuzzy tufts of hair that covered the rest of its body. Its nose resembled that of a bear, upturned at the end and wider than usual. Its mouth was terrifying, almost like a shark's, with rows of teeth that could barely be seen through the icy dust and half-opened mouth.

Demetri couldn't wait to defrost the creature and explore its perfectly preserved eyes, the tiny orbs frozen in time. He was eager to learn about how The Beast saw things and what they could discover about its vision. Based on the spacing, it seemed likely that The Beast had stereoscopic vision like an apex predator's, providing excellent depth perception.

They could learn so much about not just this creature, but also the time in which it lived. What was its prey if it was a predator, as its eyes, teeth, and overall build suggested? Surely there was an animal that coexisted with it that could be cross-referenced, something that had evolved a bit over the past hundred thousand years but could still offer insight into its mysteries.

Demetri was deep in thought, examining the creature's face and trying to imagine what it was thinking just before it died, when its eyes moved.

He blinked in confusion and pressed his face closer to the ice. He thought he must have been seeing things. But as he stared intently at the creature's left eye and held his breath, The Beast twitched.

It was just a flicker, a slight movement, as if the internal structure of its eye had shifted.

Demetri quickly pushed himself away from the block, his back hitting the wall of the small chamber. He sat on the floor, his breath coming out in a ragged and uneven way. He couldn't believe what he had just seen. He needed to confirm that it was real, so he needed to inspect the creature more closely.

The Beast was alive.

CHAPTER 3
BEN

"BEN, TAKE A BREAK."

The voice from the kitchen reached Ben all the way into the living room, which didn't say much considering the size of the space. The brand-new cabin had been constructed quicker than he'd thought possible — multiple crews working what seemed like day and night had knocked out the rebuild in less than two months.

The larger facility going up around the cabin was still under construction, likely because of the strange nature of the project that had been funded.

The cabin build itself had been a simple matter of putting insurance money to work. A few wheels had been greased, and the payout had come only a week after the explosion that decimated the property.

But the Civilian Special Operations' larger facility and headquarters, surrounding two sides of Ben and Julie's cabin, had originally been funded by Mr. E, a strange and reclusive benefactor whom Ben had not seen in over a year. No one knew if the man was alive, but as soon as construction started on rebuilding Ben's cabin, his bank account had been replenished with enough money to rebuild the CSO facility on the property — and then some.

No one knew where the money had come from, but Ben had his ideas.

"I am taking a break," he shouted back.

He heard Julie laughing from the kitchen. "I'm not an idiot, Ben. On the contrary, I'm smarter and better looking than you."

Ben snorted. "Low blow. But if you are really smarter than me, why would you choose to end up with someone not as good-looking as you?"

Julie's head immediately popped around the corner. "Don't think too hard, or you might get a headache." She said. "And I know you're still working."

Ben sighed, rubbed his eyes, and shut the laptop. Work didn't seem all that different from life these days. His wife, Juliet, was his coworker and partner in the CSO, so rarely a day went by when one of them didn't spend an hour or two at least researching.

Hunting.

They were trying to track down Ben's brother, Zachary, to bring him to justice for what he had done in Russia. Ben didn't want the guy to go to prison, but if the US government discovered how he had been conspiring with a Russian farm supply and chemicals company, he would be dragged through the mud, potentially publicly.

The second reason they wanted to find Zachary was that Zack had been running a smear campaign against their organization. While nearly impossible to prove, Ben believed Zack had used his genius to feed Western news outlets with stories of how the CSO was a deeply embedded terrorist cell in the United States, working for their own interests and against that of their nation.

There was enough credibility in Zack's stories that the US military and authorities didn't think they were terrorists, but rather a nuisance. However, this had damaged the CSO's credibility and trust in the government. They had tried to find mistakes in Zack's stories and track him down, but he had been careful and hadn't made any mistakes in the past three months.

The DEA, FBI, and CIA had all come to visit Ben and Julie to follow up on different threads of Zack's stories. Ben had cooperated fully and earned the authorities' trust, but the constant visits from different acronym organizations were frustrating. Ben and his group had always worked on the side of what was right, but Zack's smear campaign had worn them down.

Now, Ben and Julie's main goal was to clear their name, find Zack, and bring him to justice.

He was one of the good guys. They all were. For his brother to tarnish their names and reputation was unforgivable. Eyes closed, he lay on the couch with the laptop on his lap, trying to slow his mind enough to rest.

He opened his eyes and slid the laptop off his lap just as Julie wheeled around the corner and placed their infant daughter, Hope, on his lap.

"Here, since you're not doing anything," Julie said, smiling.

"It was a trap all along!" Ben exclaimed. "You didn't want me to stop working; you just wanted me to hold Hope."

"You *wanted* to hold Hope," Julie answered, "you just didn't know it yet."

Ben held his daughter out in front of him with both arms, making a goofy face.

Hope immediately smiled, her eyes lighting up.

"Yeah, you're not wrong," Ben said, pulling her close and tickling her under the armpits. He got a quick, sharp giggle out of her before she burped.

"Oh, that was a good one," Ben said, laughing along. He tucked her head into the crook of his elbow and rubbed her belly as he looked towards the kitchen. "Want me to cook dinner?"

Julie laughed again but didn't reappear. "No, I don't want chili again."

"How'd you know I was going to cook chili?" Ben asked.

"In the years I've known you, what else have you ever cooked?"

Ben feigned a pouty expression and looked down at Hope. "But my chili is really, *really* good," he said.

At that, Hope turned her head to the side and spit up all over Ben's left arm and chest.

CHAPTER 4
REGGIE

"WHILE YOU'RE UP, mind getting me another drink?" Reggie asked.

He winced, anticipating the smack on the top of his head before it came.

It did, but not nearly as hard as he would've thought.

"Get up and get your own damn drink," Sarah responded. There was a playfulness in her voice, but Reggie knew she wasn't kidding. "I can't believe you waited for me to get up. You've been nursing melting ice for 10 minutes now."

Reggie leaned back in the lounge chair so he could arch his neck up and see his upside-down girlfriend standing behind him in the sand. "10 minutes isn't that long!" He argued. "Who drinks a drink every 10 minutes, anyway?"

She shook her head. "You do, Reggie. That's literally what you do."

He pulled himself up out of the lounge chair, stretching and making a groaning sound as if preparing to do an incredibly difficult and physically demanding thing Sarah had requested of him, but she just rolled her eyes. "I'm just going to run up to the room and grab a book," she said. "But feel free to grab me a drink if you go up there to get one."

"A trap. Always a trap with you women."

Sarah was already turned the other way, but she whirled around and stopped. "What women? How many other women are there?" The playfulness was back in her voice, and she raised her hand again, preparing to smack him once more.

He smiled sheepishly and began walking toward the outdoor bar. It had been decorated to look like a hut, complete with palm fronds hanging from its sloped roof on this side of the cabana. The long, open rectangle forming the bar countertop had swivel chairs mounted directly into the sand, and a stereotypical Hawaiian shirt-wearing bartender worked over the Acacia wood countertop with a white dishtowel.

"Yeah, yeah," Reggie said. "You and I both know you're the only one on the planet who can put up with me."

"I don't like the implication that I can actually put up with you," Sarah shouted behind him.

Reggie laughed, continuing his arduous trek through the sand. The sun was baking his skin, and since he had spent most of the morning beneath the wide expanse of a hexagonal umbrella by their lounge chairs, he hadn't bothered to put on sunscreen.

The problem, of course, was that he had made this trip to the bar more than a few times already that day. The umbrella side service had ended two hours ago as if the resort's waitstaff was trying to tell them they had been there too long. For the last two hours, Reggie had had to fetch his own drinks from the cabana bar 50 feet away.

He sidled up to the counter, and the bartender gave him a wide, pearly white smile. "Two more Mai Tais?" He asked.

Reggie nodded. "Add a Bahama Mama as well, for the lady."

Reggie dropped his hotel card and credit card on the counter and patted them. "Better close up as well," he said. "The missus and I will have to start heading back for dinner soon."

The bartender frowned as he scooped ice into the metal shaker. "Dinner? It's only one in the afternoon. How long do you think it will take to get back through the resort?"

Reggie shrugged, doing his best theatrical impression of someone well past their limit of alcohol. He swayed left and right on the chair. "You know," he began. "We might have to meander around a bit first."

The bartender laughed, continuing to mix the drinks.

"Plus, I'm hoping if I can get showered off and presentable enough, the missus might actually take an interest in me again."

The bartender smiled again and winked at him as he threw the combined shaker contents over his shoulder and began work.

Reggie watched the master at work, then grabbed the three drinks and took a careful grip, bringing them all back to their umbrella side table. Sarah was already there. Stunningly beautiful, she was now holding the book she had gone back to retrieve — the latest Kevin Tumlinson novel. She was wearing a large, floppy hat, and her long legs poked out from the bottom of a thin, sheer fuchsia top that was tied around her belly button. Her two-piece swimsuit lay just beneath that, and Reggie had to do his best not to trip and spill their drinks as he approached.

But as he got closer, examining his girlfriend's face, he realized that she didn't appear to be in a good mood. He saw that she was holding her phone in her other hand.

"Oh," he said, setting the drinks on the table. "Is everything okay?"

She shook her head, holding out her phone so Reggie could see the text message she had just received. "Looks like we're cutting our vacation short, babe," she said.

Reggie frowned, trying to move the phone so it was under the umbrella and not in the direct light. "What are you talking about?"

"It's Ember," she said quickly. "She found him."

CHAPTER 5
REGGIE

THE SUN WAS JUST BEGINNING to go down over the mountain to their left. Long, deep shadows flowed over the grounds, crisscrossing the resort and pool area and stretching to the shoreline. Reggie was sitting next to Sarah at a table near the same cabana they had been drinking from before. This time, however, the drinks sat idle while they video-conferenced with Reggie's best friend, Harvey Bennett.

"She says she found him," Reggie said. Julie was also on screen, both their heads tiny on Reggie's smartphone. It was resting diagonally against the stand of the umbrella that shot down through the center of their table.

Harvey nodded onscreen. *"We got word, too,"* he said. *"Apparently, she thinks my brother is still somewhere in Russia."*

Next to him, Sarah stirred. "Could be that he has to run things in person," she said. "Perhaps he wants to be more hands-on with his little project."

Heads nodded. *His little project*, Reggie thought, *is going to change the world. And not for the best.*

They had narrowly escaped death in Russia only three months prior. Harvey's brother, Zachary Bennett, had been conspiring with a man who ran a large seed and fertilizer company in Russia. All across the Siberian Plateau, where temperatures were often too low to sustain crops, Venelov Manufacturing planned to plant fields of wheat. Their seed, laboratory-created, boasted the possibility of being able to grow in conditions and elevations previously impossible. It would usher in a new era of wheat production, and — their assumption was, at least — eventually, other crops.

It would increase Russia's output of wheat at least twofold, if not more. It would be enough to make Russia a dominant world power and control the world's supply of wheat.

That part of Venelov's plan made sense; no one could fault him for wanting to try. The man was a genius, someone who wanted to save the world.

But that's where the altruistic intentions ended. Venelov's plan involved knowingly killing millions of people to fix the issue he most deeply cared about: overpopulation. He wanted to ensure that the world's resources would not be consumed by an out-of-control population growth, and he wanted to do it by literally controlling who got to live.

And who got to die.

Reggie fumed, remembering how they had discovered Venelov's true intentions back in his office in Russia.

Just before Ben had forced the man to jump out his own office window and plummet to the concrete far below.

It seemed Ben's younger brother had taken up the mantle and wanted to continue Venelov's plan. He had made a case, passionate though misguided, that world population was in fact the biggest issue facing the planet in the next decade, and if left unchecked, billions could die rather than millions. It was a utilitarian approach, one that Reggie understood had more than one side.

But they weren't battling the issue of overpopulation — they were battling the issue of one man trying to play God.

It seemed there were other ramifications, as well. The way Venelov's plan had been structured was such that Russia would seem the victim — that others around the world would rush to their aid, ensuring that the poorest of the poor in Russia — the farmers themselves — didn't die of starvation while they tried to plant a strain of wheat that could be fully controlled by Venelov.

Everything he had created could be controlled by a chemical trigger:

a slime mold that changed the wheat seed's properties such that it would not respond to water, food, sunlight.

The very thing that could *save* the world was the very thing that could *end* it — with the flip of a switch.

The world would watch in horror as Venelov quietly and secretly ensured that no wheat crops could be grown but his own. A famine would set in, killing hundreds of thousands of people over the course of a single growing season and the subsequent winter, at which point he would be able to effectively turn on his slime mold-infused wheat seed and show the world that it *could* be saved.

But only with *his* product.

It was a sinister proposition, and it was amazing that Venelov had nearly pulled it off. Zack had been infatuated with the man's genius, his scientific ability and unlimited resources. While Venelov had never assumed he would die at the hand of Zack's older brother, it was clear Zack was trying to take the man's place as quickly as possible.

"Or it could be that he doesn't think we'll look for him in the most obvious place," Reggie added.

"Either way, how does she know it's him?" Julie asked.

Ember Clark, Zack's ex-girlfriend, had partnered with the CSO to find the man responsible for what could be an unfathomable amount of deaths in Russia and around the world. She was busy putting plans together to travel to Russia to track her ex-boyfriend down.

"She's a pretty capable hacker," Reggie said. "I've seen her skills at work, and Zack always spoke highly of her ability to get into computer systems she wasn't supposed to be in."

More heads nodded on screen and next to him.

"I suppose we could just trust the data, but she seems to think she found something from a hidden laboratory in the Russian Kodar mountains."

On-screen, Ben rolled his eyes. He let out a deep sigh. "Another *secret laboratory?*"

Reggie smiled. "Hey, at least it's not a cave."

Sarah spoke up. "Actually, I was looking through some information about the location online. There's obviously not much — the Russian military wants to keep this installation secret — but there were some images of the area before this military base popped up.

Seems like the whole thing was built into a massive, ancient cave system."

Ben groaned.

"Where exactly is this place?" Julie asked.

Ember had only given them the name, and so far, only Sarah had had time to research its location. She described it as a place high above the tree line in the northernmost tip of Zabaykalsky Krai. About an hour from Chita as the crow flies, with only a few tiny villages scattered around the plains surrounding the mountain. Getting to the location unseen would be simple, but navigating the region's rugged terrain might be tricky.

"I've had Freddie put together some satellite imagery his old man gave us a while ago, but..."

"But we've been sidelined, and General Rollins isn't going to play ball."

Sarah nodded.

Freddie Rollins was the CSO's newest member, the son of a US Army general. They had received help from Freddie's father before, but thanks to Zack's smear campaign, even General Rollins was on thin ice due to his son's association with the CSO.

In short, finding Zack would be a nightmare — and not just because they would have to fight their way in.

"If we want to do this right, we're going to need a much better plan than we've had in the past," Reggie said flatly.

"You got any ideas?" Ben asked.

Reggie smiled. "I'm not really a *plan* sort of guy, Ben," he said. "I was hoping *you* had something."

CHAPTER 6
LUCIA

LUCIA VERGOTTI PULLED her parka on over her clothes as she prepared to leave her apartment. It wasn't the coldest night of the year in Moscow, but she had been feeling chilly all day. As she took the elevator down to the underground parking garage, she checked for her keys, purse, and wallet. She couldn't believe that going out for a last-minute meal had become such a chore.

Vergotti was a 38-year-old Italian-born microbiologist working in Moscow to help the National Parks program. She was interested in anything related to animals and the cells that created them, and her particular area of expertise was microevolution. She documented small changes in species, particularly those tied to human interaction.

Human beings were changing not only the world they lived in but also the creatures they shared it with.

This had been a passion of Vergotti's for as long as she could remember. Growing up in a wealthy household, her parents had provided her with every academic opportunity. Through private tutoring and the best schooling available, she excelled and earned an undergraduate degree at an Italian university at the young age of 17. She quickly completed two master's degrees and was working on more postgraduate studies whenever she had time.

But time was something she rarely had. She threw herself into her work at the national parks system and often found herself so deeply involved in whatever she was studying that she forgot to eat.

Tonight was no different. She had a scheduled call with some of her coworkers, a brief catch-up to keep everyone on the same page, but she had decided to cancel at the last minute to go out for takeout.

There was a Chinese place around the corner that had become a personal favorite, not because it was particularly good, but because it was cheap and fast.

The elevator dinged as it reached the lower level of her apartment complex, and she stepped out onto the concrete walkway. It was dark, and she wondered why places like this didn't invest in a few more light-bulbs — the cheapest security possible.

Due to her appearance, Vergotti had grown accustomed to attracting attention from the opposite sex, but she had also learned that her looks could attract others as well. She was small, thin, and with a youthful face, she gave off an air of naivety.

Women like her made easy targets for petty thieves and small-time criminals.

Lucia had learned to be cautious when out and about in Moscow. She had spent most of her adult life on college campuses, studying and conducting research, and had had to earn her street smarts the hard way. She knew that her looks could attract attention from both men and women, and she had learned to keep a can of bear spray in her purse for protection.

She felt her heart rate rise — was that just her nerves talking, or was it multiplied by the fact that she was starving?

Her car was parked near the elevators, the third space in the row directly to her left. She made a beeline for it, careful to watch her peripheral vision for any movement.

The garage was empty, aside from her. She reached her car safely and pulled the door open, closing it behind her and immediately locking it once more. She let out a breath she hadn't realized she had been holding, then laughed.

"No one wants to steal your purse, Lucia," she told herself. "No one cares about it."

Aside from her physical appearance, there was no reason a thief might target her. She wore no fancy clothes or jewelry, her shoes were off the rack at a big box store, and on nights like these — when she had nothing planned other than meetings and research while holed up in her apartment — she wasn't even dressed for business.

As she smiled to herself and put the car in reverse, she heard her phone ding. She frowned; it was the same sound that used to inform her that one of her cameras inside picked up movement. Her only room-mate was a cat, and he slept 23 hours out of the day, and it was nowhere near time for him to eat.

She pulled her phone up, swiping at the screen to load the app that would tell her what was going on. Sometimes shadows from the busy street down below set the thing off, so she quickly read the information on the screen, satisfied to note that the alert label was: *motion detected.* While she waited for the app to load, another alert came in from the top of her phone at the top of her screen. She frowned.

Person detected.

She felt her voice catch in her throat, still waiting for the camera to load.

When it did, she let out a deep breath. There was nothing on screen; the camera had just captured a shadow, thinking it was a person and sent the alert.

She shook her head, pulling out of the space a bit farther and preparing to put it into drive to head down the street.

She caught a glimpse of the screen while mounting the phone to its magnetic connection on her dashboard.

What the hell?

The shadow passed across the screen again, this time its shape was unmistakable.

The app told her that a person had been detected inside her apart-ment again.

Her breaths came faster, and she watched as two dark shapes zigzagged across her apartment's living room.

How did they get in? she wondered. She had a security system installed on the front door that would inform her of anyone trying to break in or if it detected the sound of windows breaking.

One of the shapes turned and noticed the camera then. Terror spread through her entire body as she locked eyes with a man, staring at her from behind the camera. He flicked his head sideways, intrigued as he approached.

He stepped close to it, reached out his hand.

The camera feed cut to black.

CHAPTER 7
LUCIA

HER PHONE SAT PROPPED against a heavy salt and pepper shaker at the center of the café table. Lucia had considered calling the police, but she wasn't sure she could trust the local Russian authorities. Perhaps they were working with the intruders? Perhaps they were colluding with whoever was trying to kidnap her?

She shivered, still wearing the parka and clothes she had on before. After leaving the parking garage, rather than looking for food, she had headed straight for a favorite little shop near the university, a 10-minute drive from her home but a place that would put hundreds of stores and restaurants between her and the people who had broken into her apartment.

She sipped a cup of tea she held between two palms, waiting for the terror she had felt to subside into a dense ball of fear that settled in her core. She didn't understand what this was all about, but she knew who she wanted to talk to. She had planned on reaching out to the group after uncovering some information on the government research network. It was a forum of sorts, meant to keep researchers and scientists in touch with one another who were working on similar goals.

And though it was very likely watched by the Russian government, most of the information sent back and forth was tame, just the excitement of new discoveries and findings.

She waited for the phone to connect, preparing her thoughts. She needed to tell them what she believed the manufacturing company was doing and how it was related to her own work. The implications and potential ramifications were staggering, so she wanted to get ahead of this the only way she knew how.

A week ago, she had put things in motion by posting on the forum that she wanted to speak with the CSO group, as she believed her work and theirs might benefit each other. No one had responded on the forum, but about 15 minutes after posting it, she got a call from a woman named Ember Clark, claiming to have been the ex-girlfriend of Zachary Bennett, whom she believed had been working with a company called Venelov Manufacturing and was still at large somewhere in or around Russia. The CSO was very interested in speaking with her, she'd said, and they exchanged a few more details via email.

Ember wanted to brush up on the situation a bit, so they had set up a time to chat tomorrow when two of the group's members would return from vacation, but she had been given a phone number in case anything else came up.

Breaking and entering certainly counted as something 'coming up,' she figured.

The call connected, and Lucia saw on the screen the face of a younger woman, fit and composed.

"*Lucia Vergotti?*" The woman asked. "*I'm Ember Clark. Nice to meet you.*"

She smiled, but Lucia could see the stress and tension on her face even through the tiny screen.

She didn't have headphones; those were back in her apartment and she wouldn't be returning. She had to hope no one else was listening in, either snooping or just offended that she would take a call in the middle of a busy café. She brushed the feeling off. Lucia was wired to please others, to oblige and accommodate.

She croaked out a few words. "Hi... I'm sorry," she stammered, her face flush.

"It's okay," Ember said, "is everything all right?"

She shook her head quickly. "They — someone tried to break into my apartment. They *did* break into my apartment."

On screen, Ember's eyes widened a bit. *"Hopefully you were not there."*

She shook her head again. "Thankfully, I was just leaving to grab food. It happened 15 minutes ago. I was in my car, watching the cameras in my apartment. I have recordings of them — "

"Send them over," Ember said suddenly, cutting her off. *"We can get a head start on trying to cross-reference anyone's faces or figures through an artificial intelligence system I've been working on. If we're lucky, we can get a match before they try to scrub it from any servers."*

She swallowed, then nodded. "Yes, right away. I know we had a scheduled call, but I'm afraid this all may be related."

Harvey's face appeared on screen now. *"First of all, just try to relax. Keep your head. They're still going to be looking for you, but it's possible they don't have your phone tracked just yet."*

She shuddered again. She hadn't considered that — were they tracking her even now? Perhaps they were already on their way to this very café. She glanced around, the terror once again growing.

Onscreen, Harvey Bennett smiled. *"Listen, you're in a public place, right? They came to your apartment because they thought it would be easy to get you when you weren't paying attention. You're hyper-vigilant now, paying attention to your surroundings. That's good. We can help each other, I think. If you can trust me, trust us, we can hopefully get you somewhere you can lay low for the next couple of days until we get there."*

"You're coming here?" She asked, surprised.

Ember took over once more. *"We have to find his brother, Zachary,"* she said. *"It seems you've stumbled onto something we've been dealing with for months now. And it's going to have an impact on the entire world if we don't stop it."*

"We'll tell you more, but we'll do it in person," Bennett said. *"For now, we're going to send you a location via text message. It will be a real address, but you'll need to change it a bit, just in case someone has already hacked your phone. Reverse the order of the numbers, and use the exact opposite word for the other two words in the address. Like 'up' becomes 'down,' that sort of thing."*

She frowned, but nodded.

"It will make sense when we send it over. Give us some time to put it together. Are you safe now?"

She nodded. "For now."

"Good. We are on our way — keep your phone close, for now. Once the address comes through, figure out where it is and see about getting a ride there. And do it with cash, if you can. Leave your phone at the café, preferably in a car or something that will move around a bit in the next few days. Got it?"

She was doing a terrible job keeping her fear at bay, but still she nodded, forcing herself to push forward. This was not a situation she had ever been in, and her terror was combined with excitement and confusion. This was all new to her, something she never would have imagined getting involved in. For a moment, she regretted posting anything about the CSO on that forum.

But her intelligence got the best of her. If there was any way she could truly help, she wanted to. Whatever they were talking about, whatever they were afraid of, she would know if it were real. These people had been working nonstop to try to find someone like her, someone who could help them connect the dots.

She agreed, then ended the call. Once again, she gripped her tea and lifted it to her lips, closing her eyes for a moment and taking a deep breath, doing as Harvey Bennett had instructed and forcing herself to try to relax.

CHAPTER 8
DEMETRI

"READY FOR SECOND INJECTION," Dr. Clive Donahue said.

Demetri blinked a few times, trying to get the grogginess out of his eyes. He had only slept for a few hours, but didn't want to let the team remove The Beast from the ice without him. He had made an exception to his preference of working through the night rather than during the day, all because today would be the day.

Today, they would free The Beast.

Most of the ice had already been removed from around the creature's body, leaving about an inch-thick padding through which they could see the details of The Beast's scars and scrapes from hitting against rocks or fights with other animals. It was like looking into a time machine, watching the world unfold through the stories told on this creature's body.

Demetri hadn't told anyone what he had seen the previous night, either. He knew what they would say — that he was exaggerating, seeing things where nothing existed.

He knew the scientific explanation, as well. 'Flutter' was the proper term for it. The eyes had fluttered, the ancient cells inside not reawakening but simply shifting, moving, creating a sort of apparition due to the chemicals injected inside the creature's thawing body by the scientists.

Demetri had the next two injections ready, both the same cryostabilizer product that they had used a thousand times before. The company behind it was a provider of stabilizers, cryogenic compounds like antifreeze-enhanced proteins, and this — a compound that would loosen animal cells' adherence to structural elements, as if reversing the effects of rigor mortis. It allowed teams like Demetri's to move specimens, to literally shift their limbs around without snapping them off.

Because the near-perfect nature of this creature's state meant they were working with a never before seen opportunity, they wanted to do everything correctly. Once thawed, even in a super chilled room like this one, The Beast would begin to decay almost immediately. It would decay faster than a typical body, thanks to its unique frozen state.

They needed to run tests, to extract bigger and better samples of the different bone cores, muscle mass, and body matter from around the creature. Some of these they would send away to other labs for support, while some they would study here, in the presence of the very creature they had taken the samples from.

Demetri was beyond excited. He couldn't wait to get started and uncover the secrets of their shared past. Some previous iteration of *Homo sapiens* had walked the earth with this very creature. Had they ever met? Have they ever interacted? Was this a predator for early humans? Or the other way around — had this creature hidden in caves to disappear from the two-legged hominid that hunted it?

He knew they would find answers to these questions, all in good time. This was what he wanted more than anything in the world. He lifted the syringe, its foot-long needle steady in his hand. He watched where it was pointed, then nodded. The same hole they had drilled through the ice block before was now covered by shards of broken ice and melting water. Someone leaned down and brushed away the hole so Demetri had easier access to it. He thanked them, then he held his hands tightly around the large syringe as he poked the needle down into The Beast's fur.

Still frozen solid, they had had to drill an inch into the creature's fur to get through the frozen, matted texture and to the skin. From there, though still frozen, the needle would do its work for them, poking through another inch into its hide, where Demetri would slowly inject the fluid inside.

The liquid compound would melt through the skin, spreading in a localized area inside the frozen specimen. It wouldn't go far, which was why they had to be careful yet consistent. Three more injections were planned on the other side of the creature, as it slowly thawed. The entire process would take hours, and they would be working well into the night.

Demetri hoped he would be able to maintain his stamina until then — he needed a nap, but he pushed weariness away.

This work was too important. Waiting for Clive's nod of approval, he then hoisted the end of the syringe and slowly began injecting the fluid. He watched as it filled the frozen area inside the hole they had drilled, watching the fluid spread into deep pockets between ice crystals, microscopic and invisible to the human eye. It melted the ice as it spread, the compound delicate enough to not damage the animal's cells but instead reinforce them while pushing away the dangerous shards of ice that could harm those very cells.

A bit of fluid poked out the top of the hole, and he slowed. They would take turns, moving half a millimeter at a time, waiting for the fluid to do its job on its own. If they forced it, all of the fluid would simply squirt back out the hole and dribble down the side of the block onto the floor. That would not do — it would be a waste and would only require them to start over.

He looked around at the other scientists as he applied pressure on the end of the syringe. Behind their masks, behind their suits, he knew they were smiling. They shared this, at least. Their love for study, for discovery. Each of them had come here their own way, their own expertise leading them to this shared path. Now they were on it together, taking this journey as a group.

Demetri couldn't be prouder. He was happy to share with them, happy to have people who understood the impact this situation had.

He couldn't believe this was real.

CHAPTER 9
ZACK

ZACHARY BENNETT RUBBED at his temples, trying to ease the pain in his head.

It didn't work. "We need this to go away, Victor," he said to the man on the video call. He was seated at his desk, a wooden table he had found near a trashcan behind his small home. The single bedroom house had a small kitchen and bathroom separate from the larger living space where he had set up his office.

It wasn't much, but it was enough for his needs. He was working, and the house offered a way to stay hidden.

"I agree," Victor said onscreen. "And we have... observed her. We do not believe she knows more than what she posted on the forum. What would you like me to do?"

Zack sighed. He pulled the curtain behind his desk closed, feeling like he was being watched at all times. Even though he was in a small neighborhood outside of Moscow, surrounded by civilians and middle-class workers, he couldn't shake the feeling of being under surveillance. *How did it get to this point?* he wondered. *Did I get too deep into this project?*

His partner and mentor — Jakob Venelov — was dead, and Zack felt he had been passed the baton. He was supposed to carry this charge and finish what Jakob had started.

Right?

He believed that what Venelov had started was good, that his work would change the world for the better. But he couldn't convince others of that until he achieved his goals. This was the driving force behind his work, why he kept going.

His eyes returned to the screen, staring at the camera rather than the man displayed on it. "I hired you to make sure this woman isn't coming near me or my work. I need you to make the whole problem go away," Zack said, speaking through clenched teeth.

"Just make it go away," Victor repeated.

Zack didn't like Victor's tone, and though they had worked together for over two months, he felt that the man had no respect for him or his authority.

"I didn't say *kill* her," Zack said. Did he need to clarify that to the mercenary? Was that the expectation here? That he had hired these men to simply execute anyone who was too close to his work?

He rubbed his temples again.

He had never worked directly with mercenary crews before, so he wasn't sure if this was normal. Victor was ex-military, special forces, and ran a small team of close-knit troops from different branches and even different countries, mostly Peruvian. He was both the leader of the main unit and the owner of the security company. Zachary had hired him as an insurance policy, one that he had used more often than he would have liked. He had given them their charge: *keep me safe and keep any prying eyes away.*

And Lucia Vergotti was prying. A week ago, she had posted a message on a research forum, looking for help from the CSO — the Civilian Special Operations team that Zachary Bennett's brother and sister-in-law had started. She claimed that Venelov Manufacturing had begun live testing of their latest product in the Kodar Mountains, fewer than 100 miles away from the northeastern tip of Lake Baikal.

Zack had investigated, finding that Vergotti in turn was responding to *another* post on that forum — one from a researcher working in an undisclosed facility, their identity kept secret. Apparently, she made the assumption that they might be using Venelov product *in* their lab, which the poster claimed was a little-known research station in the mountains built above an elaborate, ancient cave system.

"I can't find any research station, or facility of any kind, in that region."

"There has to be *something* there. Look harder. Even if you can't find anything, I need you to go there anyway, to check out what Ms. Vergotti was responding to," Zachary said. "If that station exists, if what she's claiming is true..."

"There's no way it can be true, Zack," Victor said. *"You said your product won't have an effect on the human population, right?"*

Zachary squeezed his eyes shut. He didn't feel like giving the man a biology lesson. Yes, it was *technically* impossible. But nature somehow always found a way. He knew all too well that microbiology and the chemistry that made up the molecules inside every living thing was a convoluted mess of functions, hundreds of thousands of different mechanisms all vying for survival.

And Lucia Vergotti was not just some Internet keyboard warrior with a passing interest in animals. She knew her stuff, judging by the research on her Victor had turned in. If she truly believed it were possible for the slime mold-enhanced wheat fertilizer product they had delivered those farmers was dangerous...

The political ramifications would be staggering. It could end his experiment before it even started.

He shook his head, knowing that this wasn't even the biggest problem he was dealing with.

If they're planning on using the product in the lab... studying its effect on whatever animal specimens they might have there...

"Just go find the base; see what you can find. If it's there, it's there on purpose. That region is hell as far as terrain goes; it's a great place to hide. Whatever they're doing out there, it's likely they're trying to do it in secret. That means the Russian bigwigs won't want us poking around."

"Agreed," Victor said.

"And I can't have this coming back on Venelov Manufacturing, or me. We are live-testing the first batch of fertilizers near this region, so if there's *is* a negative side effect on humans we didn't predict, I need to know about it."

Victor didn't speak.

"I want you to get there before the Russian government gets wind of it and figures out Venelov product is around. The last thing I need is them pinning all of this on me before I'm finished."

The man nodded. *"It might be... difficult. Even if that base is kept under wraps, the forum Vergotti used isn't exactly top-secret."*

"I know," Zack said. "Which is why we need to hurry. Get a team together and plan to leave here tomorrow night. And you know my rules."

The man nodded again, a slight look of disappointment on his face. *"Don't hurt anyone unless it's absolutely necessary, and don't attract attention to yourself."*

Zack smiled. "These are scientists who have been locked inside the facility for who knows how long. It shouldn't be too hard to make them play by the rules."

"And what if we do find anything... strange? If they've been studying something they want to keep secret?" Victor asked.

Zachary let out another breath. "I wouldn't worry too much about it. I just need you to get there and make sure that Venelov's product is nowhere near it. It will be easy enough to claim self-defense, though, if things get hairy. If you or your men do find something unexpected, be wary, but don't hesitate to remove them from the equation."

Zachary was saddened by the words. He was no killer. "Get to the park first, put a plan together for getting to this secret research station, and we can go from there."

Victor confirmed, then left the video call.

Zack stood, once again rubbing his temples. Finishing what he had started seemed so simple at first, but now it had become a lot more complicated. Why did he get the feeling he had bitten off more than he could chew?

His thoughts returned to his interactions with his brother three months ago. The Civilian Special Operations group had become a larger thorn in his side than he'd expected. His goal to silence them through negative media campaigns had worked to keep them off his tail, but he knew it was only a matter of time before Julie — as capable a computer scientist as anyone he had met — was able to track him down digitally.

And if his ex-girlfriend, Ember, was working with her...

He stood, walking to the kitchen. He rarely drank, but he felt today necessitated a glass of something dark and strong.

CHAPTER 10
FREDDIE

FREDDIE RECLINED the plane's seat all the way back. *I can get used to this*, he thought.

He had flown with the CSO team multiple times before, but this was the first time they had booked a private charter jet. It made sense, as the trip would involve almost a full day of travel. He had flown to Anchorage and met up with Ben and Julie earlier that morning, leaving shortly after.

He put his hands behind his head, closed his eyes, and smiled.

"Don't think you're going to get away with falling asleep on us," a voice said.

He opened one eye and stared up at the looming bear of a man, Harvey Bennett. Ben was the same height as Freddie, but where Freddie was built like the corn-fed Midwestern farm boy-turned-soldier he was, Bennett's build was leaner, crafted from years of exertion and practical use. He was no trained fighter, but Freddie didn't want to poke the bear. He knew Bennett's superpower was resilience — the ability to take a hit — sometimes dozens — before calling it quits.

He respected Ben, and was pleased to be involved with the group. It was unfortunate his father, General Rollins, had severed ties with him and his new employers due to political pressure, but he knew it would only be a matter of time before the CSO group could right the ship and get back in the good graces of the US military.

Freddie knew what everyone else knew — this was a game, and the CSO was currently the weaker opponent on paper. Their US-based allies had gone to ground, but no one actually believed the group was harmful.

The media liked to portray them as a cancerous thorn, but Freddie had learned to trust the media even less than politics.

If they could find Ben's kid brother in Russia, they might be able to put an end to his smear campaign and begin working toward making amends.

Either way, he was in it for good. He had left the military to join this group, and he was pleased to be able to travel with them now.

Freddie opened his other eye and smiled wider. "I figured you'd put me to work right away," Freddie said. "No worries — I learned to sleep in 15-minute intervals wherever and whenever I could."

"We'll have plenty of those intervals in a bit," Bennett said. "Julie and I just wanted to talk through everything before we caught some Z's. Figured we could work through what we know now and let our subconscious handle the rest of the problem later."

"Works for me," Freddie said, pulling his seat forward and standing. He followed Bennett to the front section of the plane, where Julie was sitting in a chair facing him.

She waved. "Glad you could be here."

"Wouldn't miss it for the world," Freddie said, letting a bit of his accent slip.

Ben took a seat next to Julie and saw the table in front of them covered with news articles and translated documents. It was everything they had on Zack, which meant it was everything they had on themselves. He was looking at news reports, media articles, and printed Internet filings blasting the CSO.

"We've been through these a thousand times," Ben started. "I doubt there's anything new here, but in light of recent developments, I wanted to bring them along just in case."

"New developments, as in hearing from Lucia Vergotti?" Freddie asked.

Ben and Julie nodded in tandem.

"This could be quite the breakthrough, assuming she is who she says she is," he said.

"She is," Julie said. "I was able to get into her university's servers to find your transcript. No reason she would go that far back to craft a story. Plus, she's got plenty of published papers under her own name. She's the real deal."

"But that doesn't mean she found Zack," Freddie said.

"Doesn't mean she didn't," Bennett said. "We've got nothing better to go off of, so we're going to follow this one. Besides, even if he's not in Russia or we can't dig him up, there's more to look into with this potential Venelov stuff she found."

Freddie nodded as Julie continued. "Zack told us point blank he was going to continue what his old boss had started, what Venelov had been working toward. He most likely used his time wisely, keeping us occupied with one hand while continuing the plan with his other. Shipments went out, farmers processed their wheat and prepared next year's seed, and it's very likely the slime mold he created is already out in the wild."

"According to Lucia, it is," Ben added. "She's looking into it, at least. This may not be wheat-related at all, but when we told her there was a slime mold involved, she seemed to think it could have gotten released into the water system somewhere, which of course could affect plant and animal life in the region."

"I thought the stuff couldn't affect animals?" Freddie asked. He had read the briefings Ben had sent over, even going so far as to research the slime mold they had found a few months ago. It was nasty stuff, potentially. It was a reminder that the power a single organization — or one man or woman — could have was staggering.

As altruistic as Zachary Bennett had wanted Venelov Manufacturing to seem, Freddie knew the truth: absolute power corrupts absolutely. If given the opportunity, the power potential would be too great for even a good person to ignore forever.

Zachary Bennett was poised to change the course of human history in one fell swoop, just by coordinating who got to grow what, and where.

Now, to learn that the slime mold and its technological underpinnings could potentially affect animal life as well... That had even more unlimited ramifications.

They needed to stop him.

CHAPTER 11
DEMETRI

DEMETRI'S back was beginning to get sore. He was beyond tired, and they were only on the second injection. The first had taken over an hour, swapping once with someone to give his hands some relief.

But the injections were working as expected. Even now, ice was beginning to melt from around The Beast's form. What had been an inch-thick layer was now less than half an inch, and his three counterparts took turns wiping down the surface of the ice with warm cloths, the gentlest way they had found to melt these layers of ice that were in contact with the creature.

A deep groan emanated from within the block, and Demetri paused. He looked up at the others.

"What was that?" one of them asked.

"Just the ice shuddering as it warms," he said. "Nothing to worry about, but let's check the integrity of the underside."

They nodded and together disappeared underneath The Beast. They had decided to leave the bottom of the block in situ, supporting the weight of the creature as well as the particular way it lay in the ice. They didn't want to melt the underside of the ice block just yet, for fear that it would damage the creature.

While they inspected, Demetri continued pressing the fluid into the microscopic cavities within the ice. He focused intently on keeping his pressure steady, letting the fluid do the work.

Just then a loud *crack* reverberated through the small room, and one of the scientists shouted something unintelligible.

He held fast, not wanting to upset the integrity of their research by pulling the fluid out too early. Still, he looked around, trying to examine its side to see what had happened. Had the animal thawed too fast? Had a fissure formed under its frozen skin and expanded outward?

Another crack, followed by another groan.

This time, Demetri pulled the syringe out. He assumed the sounds were emanating from the quadrant he was working on; perhaps he was forcing too much fluid into the creature's side.

The others looked up at him, their eyes wide. He wasn't sure what the protocol was, but he wanted to finish the injections today. He was tired of waiting and wanted to see the majesty of this creature up close.

Demetri backpedaled away from the block and the creature inside, watching as larger shards of ice began falling from its side.

"What is happening?" their leader asked, his voice frantic. No one answered.

Demetri stared at the animal's side, watched as its chest began moving, convulsing. His heart caught in his throat. If he wasn't mistaken, it seemed as if the creature was —

"It's alive!" another scientist screamed. "It's waking up!"

"Impossible," came the immediate reply. "It's been dead for thousands of years. There is no way..."

Ice shifted beneath The Beast, and its head fell downward. Just as quickly, it snapped back up, as if recoiling in shock. It slid forward, no longer captured by its icy prison. Demetri dropped the syringe, letting it shatter by his feet. Two scientists ran for the exit, but Demetri held up a hand to stop them. "We cannot open the door," he said quickly. "The warm air could harm it."

"Demetri, we cannot stay in here. Are you mad?"

He didn't meet their eyes. Instead, he was watching those of the creature lying in front of him.

Only, now it wasn't lying down. It seemed to be moving on its own accord, though not quite... alive. There was something uncanny to its movements, as if it was governed not by its own mind but that of something else. Perhaps something they had injected into it.

"Come on," Donahue said, moving once more towards the door. Demetri moved to the left, sidestepping one scientist and standing directly in front of Donahue. Putting his body between them, he said, "No one leaves."

This was the opportunity of a lifetime. This was something unheard of. If there were any possibility that this creature was actually *waking up* — that it had been alive all along — this discovery would be sensational.

As far-fetched as it seemed, Demetri knew it was possible, at least in theory.

Demetri had studied the effects of the wood frog, which was able to freeze and thaw every year. He also knew of the woolly bear caterpillar — *Pyrrharctia isabella* — which was capable of freezing for long periods of time. Even the Greenland shark, capable of living 500 years, posed incredible genetic possibilities for researchers who were willing to take a leap of faith.

This animal, moving around in front of them, represented such a leap.

Rather than make assumptions about what it was not, Demetri wanted to allow possibilities for what it might be. Whatever this was, it was miraculous.

There was a scream, and Demetri watched as one of the scientists cowered in the corner of the room. The Beast eyed him, dead eyes still flickering with telltale signs of flutter — millions of molecules and cells interacting, breaking apart, and congealing at a frenetic pace, as if the interior of the creature was made of nothing but liquefied glitter.

And yet, it *moved*. It reached and pushed up on its hind legs, steadying itself, as if learning to walk for the first time. Its front legs extended as well, and for the first time Demetri saw that the front of its foot was segmented into three massive toes.

Large claws extended from each of them, slowly protruding.

The whole scene was horrifying — yet incredible. There was no way this creature could be standing here in front of them — no way it could be alive. There had to be something in the compound they had been injecting into it that caused this effect. *Something* that created the appearance of life from something long dead.

Whatever it was, they could research it later. Right now, they needed to make sure the creature didn't —

It suddenly lurched forward, then darted to the right. Directly at the young biologist on their team. She screamed, but the creature cut the shout short with a clamping of its jaws, covering her entire throat and the bottom portion of her head. It wrenched its neck sideways, ripping away flesh and bone.

And blood.

The dark liquid spilled out over her chest, and she fell to the side, dead.

Donahue screamed loudly, directly in front of Demetri. He ducked, stepping once again to the right as the creature jumped over the remainder of the ice block and landed on top of the team leader.

This couldn't be real. This couldn't be happening.

And yet it was.

No longer worried about the creature's safety, Demetri pulled the handle open and let the door fall inward, the rush of warm air feeling good on his face.

But nothing else felt good. Everything was chaos, terror. He heard the gnashing sounds of The Beast's jaws open and close as they worked in tandem to rip his coworkers to shreds. Demetri slunk through the door, crawling on his hands and knees, hopeful that the creature was unaware that he was escaping.

He didn't dare look back.

Once inside the warmer laboratory room, he stood and ran directly to the side, diving for cover through the airlock door 20 paces away. There was no way to secure this room, no way to prevent anyone else from entering. There were no locks on this laboratory door, considering they were already inside a secure facility.

Demetri paused, panting. He was in the airlock now, looking out through the rectangular window. He stared wide-eyed, imagining the carnage inside the smaller chilled space.

The only reprieve was that the airlock would remain secure for the necessary 28 seconds until whomever was inside had been sufficiently sterilized. This time, the 28 seconds was excruciating. Demetri stared through the rectangular window, waiting for The Beast to emerge into the larger room.

He thought of his friends and coworkers, lying dead or dying in the refrigerated space. He blinked a few times, still not willing to accept that what he had seen was real. He looked down at his hands, spatters of blood there he wasn't aware had landed. His hazmat suit was slick with the stuff as well, and he realized it must have been from his boss, the leader of their group.

He began crying, almost convulsing and trying to hold back vomit. Still, he stood steady at the window, once again looking back up and through the rectangular glass.

That was when he noticed the door to the interior room was still standing open just a crack.

And that crack was widening slowly.

CHAPTER 12
VICTOR

FOR THE PAST NINE YEARS, Victor had been looking for a retirement plan. As the leader of a small but successful private security firm, Victor was growing tired of the mundane tasks and day-to-day administration. He had started the company because it was the best situation for a discharged Army veteran with 15 years of experience running missions in all corners of the globe. He was good at that job, and moving into private security was a natural step for a lot of soldiers. He proved to be good at this as well, though he disliked the office work.

And lately, most of the work he had been doing was nothing *but* office work. There was always somebody else to hire, someone else to promote or review, always another mission to draw up.

As a smaller firm, Victor did not have the luxury of setting parameters and issuing demands. That was for the larger security forces, the ones that had a veritable army of paramilitary troops at their disposal. These companies were the security firms hired by multinational corporations, oil companies, banks, world sports organizations, and the like. Wherever there was dirty work to be done or any work that leaned over the line between clean and dirty, these firms were available.

While Victor performed the same sorts of activities for his clients, his firm was considered a newcomer in private security. Rotating between 15 and 20 contractors at any time, Victor's force was far smaller than even the next level up. But he had to start somewhere, and had excelled for the clients he had had in the past.

Those clients were becoming more and more demanding, it seemed. His latest, Zachary Bennett, was smart enough to know he needed Victor's services, but not smart enough to just let Victor handle everything on his own. Bennett was a sole proprietor, with no company name offered. According to research Victor had found, Bennett was a scientific genius with a black hole in the middle of his career. Upon further investigation, Victor discovered that Bennett had worked for some shady organizations in the past, likely working with individuals unscrupulous enough to warrant keeping their names hidden. Most recently, that employer had been Venelov Manufacturing, though Victor was not sure exactly what the nature of that relationship was. All of this proved to Victor that Bennett was a top-notch scientist and researcher, someone easily headhunted from one organization to the next.

And that should have been enough — Victor's job was to make sure Zack could do his work. He hated babysitting and handholding, and lately, it seemed that his clients all wanted some form of either. Zachary Bennett, in particular, wanted to meddle in all of Victor's affairs, micromanaging how he performed his duties for his client.

Victor sat in his office now, letting out a deep sigh as yet another email from his overbearing client hit his inbox. He didn't bother clicking it, hearing instead the click of the door as his right-hand man, Ortega, entered.

Ortega was a career soldier like Victor, reliable, capable, and talented. He had joined Victor's team five years ago and quickly proved to be a crucial asset on just about any mission. Victor had even sent Ortega out on his own to lead small teams.

Victor held his arm out, palm up, indicating that he wanted Ortega to sit. Ortega nodded quickly, walked across the room, and pulled out a metal chair.

Victor had not planned for comfort in this small office. It was meant to be used only as an official address for his business, a place where he could answer a few emails and make a few calls when needed. Lately, he found himself sitting here for hours at a time, communicating with clients about nitpicky things.

"You called?" Ortega asked.

Victor rubbed his temples. "Yes, I was just thinking about our current assignment."

"That Zack Bennett kid?"

"Yeah, specifically, I was thinking about retirement."

At this, Ortega raised an eyebrow and smiled. "I thought you were like 25, man," he said.

Victor laughed. He had what others referred to as a "baby face," looking years younger than he truly was. Still, he had the beginnings of a five-day beard and mustache, with some spots even speckled gray. He knew it was his sharp, piercing gray eyes that somehow made him look younger than he was.

Certainly younger than he felt.

"I don't necessarily *want* to retire, Ortega," Victor continued, "it's just that when there's an opportunity..."

Ortega shifted in the chair. "You think Bennett's contract presents such an opportunity? It's not like he's paying us our weight in gold."

No, he's certainly not. Victor had even lowered his price a smidge when approached by Bennett, simply because the kid seemed nice enough, wanting a little extra protection. "I just want someone watching my back," he had told Victor.

Yeah, turns out you want that 24/7, while you also *want me running around the world chasing your pet projects down and making sure no one gets too close.*

"Not Bennett directly, but something he's involved with," Victor said. "Seems there are some interesting scientific developments out east in Zabaykalsky Krai."

"I didn't take you for the science type, boss," Ortega said.

"I'm not, but when these nerds get all hot and bothered about something, there's usually a way to turn it into an income stream. He wants me to send a team down to the Kodar mountains to check it out."

Ortega whistled. "That's pretty rough terrain," he said.

"Which *also* means it's going to be sparsely populated," Victor answered. "The kind of place someone could, you know... get lost in."

Ortega nodded, looking down as he contemplated what Victor was planning. Neither man considered themselves thieves — they weren't pirates or marauders. But Victor would absolutely describe himself as an opportunist — he played by the rules, as long as those rules suited him. It was the same sort of characteristic he appreciated in Ortega. The ability to follow orders, think on his feet, and not ask questions.

"Whatever it is, I'm in," Ortega said, as if needing to explain his position to Victor.

Victor laughed again. "Brother, I never had any doubt. I guess I just wanted your opinion on the matter. Is it something we're ready for?"

"Well, I guess we need to hear the details first," Ortega said. "I trust you, though. If you're even bringing it up to me, you've already done enough research to know it's possible."

Victor nodded, frowning. "That's just it — I've tried to do the research, tried to figure out what exactly this kid, Zachary Bennett, has gotten himself into. He's been covering his tracks pretty well, especially for a civilian. I think we'll crack it, but I want to get a head start on it all. He seems to think a third party is after him as well. He's pretty paranoid about it, actually."

"I remember you mentioning that. The Civilian Special Operations, or something like that?"

Victor snickered. "Yeah — the guy's older brother is the founding member. Apparently, it's a little bit of a family spat between them, and we are supposed to play defense."

"Okay, it's starting to make sense. You want to get down there before this other group arrives, poke around a bit, see what's going on. You've already got the blessing of Bennett, so nothing will look strange."

"Precisely. If there's a way to profit from this without Bennett sniffing it, I want in. Get the unit together — five total. Typical loadout for recon — but a few packs of C-4 into Perez' pack. I don't want to mess around with trying to break into an old bunker or whatever it is that's waiting for us with just grenades." He paused. "And, obviously, I want you there."

Ortega nodded once. "You got it, boss. Wheel's up?"

"0400," Victor said. "Get some sleep if you need it. I want to get there in the morning tomorrow."

CHAPTER 13
LUCIA

LUCIA SAT in the booth next to the large American soldier. He had introduced himself as just "Freddie." Next to him sat Julie, and across from her in the opposite booth were Harvey Bennett and Reggie — Gareth Red. Gareth had a prosthetic arm, but to Lucia, it was almost indistinguishable from his other arm.

He didn't mention it, and when she glanced at it, he slid it sideways, turning his wrist so that the tiny USB port on the underside of it was face-down. She had never seen anything like it, and assumed it was cutting-edge technology, a way to update the arm and its firmware as needed.

It was surreal that she was here now, in the back corner of a small Italian restaurant in a seedy area of Moscow. No one was eating, a fact Lucia felt grateful for. She could tell by the smell that this place cared less about the quality of their Italian cuisine than they did about... well, everything else.

She didn't have to order something to know this would not be her grandmother's home-cooked Italian. This restaurant was likely a front for the mob — not a place she was going to experience the flavors and nostalgia of home.

Reggie and Ben had ordered a drink — a local Russian beer — mostly to ensure they wouldn't get angry looks from the waitstaff for not ordering and taking up space.

Even though the place was empty, Lucia assumed they needed to at least appear to be patrons in order to not earn them undue scrutiny. Still, she was drinking water, as were Freddie and Julie on her side of the table.

It was strange being here with them now. She had seen pictures of Ben and Reggie online, and though they were not necessarily celebrities, their association with scientific endeavors had led to her seeing articles about their projects.

She knew the man they were trying to find, Zachary Bennett, had worked to drag their names through the mud, so most of the things she had read about this group lately she knew not to trust.

Julie had made the introductions, her voice soft and kind, and Lucia immediately liked her. Harvey was a bit more firm, his face wearing a permanent frown, his mouth a thin smile. He had been cordial enough, but he clearly wanted to get the pleasantries out of the way as soon as possible. She didn't fault him for that — this man was stressed and wanted to get his life back on track. His own brother had tried to take him down, and he was trying to pull his career out of the sewer.

"And you have a daughter back home?" Lucia asked Harvey.

She saw his eyes twinkle then, lighting up a bit at the mention of her. "Hope," he said, stealing a glance over to his wife. "She's with Julie's parents now."

Lucia smiled.

"We really do appreciate your willingness to meet with us on such short notice," Ben continued. "I hope you'll excuse my rudeness, but the sooner we can figure this out and find my brother, the sooner we can get back to her."

Lucia nodded. "Of course. And I appreciate you all coming all the way here to meet with me. I hope this leads somewhere — I would hate you to make the trip for no reason."

"Knowing my brother, he's probably still neck-deep in this, and since Venelov Manufacturing is in Russia, it's a good bet he's here, too."

"Russia is a big place," Reggie added.

"I've been gathering data for the past couple of days, continuing to analyze the results I'm getting from other researchers in the field."

Heads around her nodded for her to continue.

"I can't predict the accuracy of my findings without seeing some of that fieldwork firsthand, but if what I've collected proves to be true, I do think I've narrowed down a good starting location for your brother."

"Can you explain how you got to that conclusion?" Julie asked from beside Freddie.

"Of course," Lucia said, clearing her throat. "I work with other researchers around Russia, all of us tracking certain key data points of the environment — pH levels in soil, temperatures, that sort of thing. Basic stuff, and we share it on a forum as part of our regular job duties. All of this helps us identify any trends that are out of the norm. It's like crowdsourced environmental research. Anything outside of typical seasonal environmental changes is something we will notice."

"And you noticed something in the Kodar Mountains?" Freddie asked.

She had sent along a brief snippet of her findings, as well as a rough hypothesis for the group to read while traveling here. She wasn't surprised that they had done their homework.

She nodded again. "It's not an area I've studied extensively — but my colleagues at the national park have found some disturbing trends in the soil content, not to mention the initial report from the unidentified scientist claiming to be inside the lab. It's all hard to explain without seeing it firsthand, but the levels of certain elements are extremely high, and it's not something that can be explained by natural causes."

"Disturbing?" Ben asked, raising an eyebrow. "In the report you sent us, you just mentioned it was strange that some of these levels were high this time of year."

"Yes, but I've come to believe this is something indicative of foreign involvement. Anomalous results pop up every now and then, even the earth likes to play games and throw things out of balance once in a while. But because what we're seeing is so isolated to a very specific area, and the results are growing more and more consistent the longer we're looking at them, I've come to believe that this isn't mother nature causing a problem."

"You think it's human-caused."

"I do. We see these sorts of results when there's an accident — chemicals leaked into a river, affecting shoreline downstream. Concentrated particulates from pollution falling over areas of forest because of winds."

"I see."

"With the report from the lab that I found first, and then noticing the environmental data points surrounding the area they claim to be in... it has to be related."

"And Venelov Manufacturing fits into this somehow?" Julie asked.

Lucia shrugged. "I don't know much about them, but sure — if they're creating any sort of production chemicals, they could absolutely have an effect on the environment, at least in a contained area."

"Okay then," Ben said. "I think we're onto something."

CHAPTER 14
VICTOR

VICTOR FOCUSED on the crunching sound his boots made as he followed behind Ortega. Three team members followed behind, a straight line of mercenaries on a short day hike.

They had landed that morning in Chita, Zabaykalsky Krai, and then flown north to the tiny Chara airstrip where Ortega had arranged for two ATVs they had picked up and driven to their drop zone. Ortega and Victor had chosen an entry point to the northwest. From there, they had set out on foot, hoping not to alert any national park security forces or rangers sprinkled around the area.

One interesting feature of this particular park, however, was its very off-limits station built by the Russian government, designated simply as a 'research facility.' The land the facility sat on stretched from the far edge of the park to the north-central quadrant and backed up to the southern banks of Lake Nichatka — often referred to as 'Little Baikal' for its proximity and similarity to the great lake. The base appeared on no public maps, and the only signifier it even existed was a demarcated area on the local information maps found on the national park's website. None of these maps were publicly accessible online, but Ortega had done a fine job providing reconnaissance for the area.

Upon further examination of the demarcated region and the discovery of the base that sat on it, Victor did more research. He'd discovered that the facility was built for research of some scientific flavor

57

unbeknownst to him, complete with a level 3 biohazard-equipped laboratory.

There was no other information about it. But it didn't matter what was inside — it was the only building standing in a 50-mile radius. Bennett had been paranoid about the results from *some* laboratory Lucia Vergotti had found.

The exact research station reporting the data was also still unknown — it was clear to Victor that the scientists had been ordered to keep their location secret and personal details. Yet one of them had asked for help, simply stating that their facility was somewhere in the northern region of Zabaykalsky Krai.

Victor was not in the business of believing in coincidence — this facility was in the exact place Vergotti's scientists had claimed to be, which meant that it *had* to align with his client's work. Bennett may be paranoid, but he wasn't stupid. If he wanted to make sure his work with Venelov Manufacturing hadn't spilled out and gotten the attention of some nearby Russian researchers, Victor would look into it. They had been sent to recon the area situated at the northern edge of the national park, so when Ortega had uncovered the existence of a top-secret Russian science station that might be there, it seemed too good to be true.

They were now making a beeline for that very base, coming in over one of the steep mountains just from the south. With any luck, they wouldn't have to use the rappelling gear or any crampons their men carried, but they were certainly far away from the nearest hiking trail.

The going was tough and treacherous. All of the men were trained soldiers and survivalists, trained to handle just about every environment and region on planet Earth, and none of them complained when he explained how they would be arriving at the base's backdoor. The mountains formed a perfect rear gate to the facility, so Victor's assumption was that if there were any active guard patrols around, they would not be focusing their attention on the mountains, but on the lake and plains beyond.

But Victor was not in the business of relying on luck, either. They were armed to the teeth with assault rifles — easy to find in Moscow, but certainly not easy to acquire legally. Getting in a sticky situation in

Russia would cause him too many setbacks, so Ortega had called in a few favors and gotten them outfitted through one of the back-alley channels he kept in communication with. Technically, Victor wasn't operating a business in Russia — he had no interest in getting in bed with Russian clandestine services and FSS. He officially operated his paramilitary organization out of his home country of Uruguay, though he hadn't been back in over a decade.

Ortega slowed, and Victor watched as the man bolted over descending rocks, each time landing softly on his boots and coming to a crouched position before jumping to the next. Ortega had always been athletic, and Victor was suddenly jealous of the slightly younger man's smaller frame.

There was a thin layer of snow which gave their boots purchase on the rocks, and Victor was pleased with their progress. He could see the roof of a small shack in the distance, likely a guard booth or shed full of maintenance gear. A large outcropping of rocks stretched from one side of his vision to the other, about a hundred yards past the tiny building. Interspersed amongst these larger boulders he saw flat, concrete structures.

This confirmed what Ortega had claimed. From satellite imagery, it seemed as though this base had been built into the side of a mountain itself, most of the facility completely underground.

"Why put a building above ground when you can spend ten times more and put it underground?" Ortega had joked.

Running his team from Russia for the past four years, Victor had learned just how paranoid the country's military was. Mistakes were punishable by death, or, technically, *disappearance*. He knew multiple government officials who had simply ceased to exist, their names and faces wiped from official records as if they had never been born.

He hoped they wouldn't run into any overzealous government types, looking for an easy score by bringing in the foreign mercenaries. It was just the sort of thing Victor could imagine an agent getting excited about. Russia was in its own Cold War, one against the rest of the world. They had been focusing their efforts on improving their military might through technological innovation and working to assuage the fears of their neighbor to the east, China.

Most assumed the two mighty nations were in bed with one another. On paper, this was true. But they were, without a doubt, two very distinct nations with two very distinct goals. While Victor knew Russia and China had their interests aligned on the world stage for the time being, it was only a marriage of convenience and efficiency. As soon as one country asserted dominance over the United States and the rest of the Western world, the other nation would immediately revolt against them, to keep the power balance in check.

Victor did not need to get caught to know that trying to explain himself to a government *looking* for spies and crooks would be a losing battle.

With any luck, they could poke around, gather some intel for his boss, and be back in Moscow in a few days.

CHAPTER 15
VICTOR

"SHOTS FIRED!"

The call came from one of Victor's men, hiking behind him. He turned just in time to see Joaquin Benavides fall to the ground, clutching at a gaping wound in his side. Only a split-second after the man had shouted, the sound of a rifle crack echoed through the air.

"Sniper," Ortega whispered.

Instinctively, Victor and his team hit the ground, taking cover.

They were positioned on a rise above a large, open clearing. At its edge, a small hut had been constructed, one they had spotted from near the top of the mountain peak. It had taken them an hour and a half to make their way down the mountain, finally reaching the final 50-foot descent over rocky soil. The plan was for Victor, Ortega, and their other three men to make their final run to the hut, then use it for cover while they assessed the situation and identified any guards in the area.

However, what they *hadn't* anticipated was that there would be guards already waiting for them. Victor's mind raced as he thought about the implications of this discovery. If this was just one guard post, there likely would be others hidden around the compound, guarding against more obvious approach routes like the lake to the north.

No matter who they were, they were smart, having placed at least one man facing towards the mountains, equipped with a sniper rifle.

This told Victor that they were not dealing with a low-level security force, but with trained soldiers.

Victor crawled over to the injured man and assessed the situation. The wound was through-and-through, and he could already tell it had pierced organs.

Benavides was not only unable to continue fighting, he would die here.

Perez spoke softly as he assessed the injured soldier. "I'll wrap it up, then I can..."

He was quickly silenced by the injured man. "I know what this is. Keep going; I'll be fine."

Victor knew he was just trying to keep his men engaged in the mission, not wanting them to dwell on the fact that they were already down a man and they hadn't even entered the base.

He nodded. "Be our eyes and ears up here. Call us once we're through the open space past the hut."

Benavides nodded in understanding, frustrated but in pain, and Victor watched as the man silently wrestled with his fate. Perez gave him his medkit, while Garcia tore off a length of his shirt for Benavides to use as a tourniquet.

Benavides, for his part, accepted that this was the best course of action for the team, and began wrapping his side. He would likely try to fight it, try to staunch the blood and close the wound with the adhesive bandages in the kit, but Victor knew he saw the truth of it.

Victor didn't want to raise the alarm by turning on their close-range radio communications systems. If they had guards, they might have someone listening to open channels.

Perez and Garcia had now taken cover behind a small boulder, where Ortega and Victor now kneeled, watching the open space.

"You get a direction?" Ortega asked.

"Negative," Victor replied.

Shit, Victor thought. *We are under attack, and we can't even see our attacker.* Benavides and his two other soldiers remained out of sight. Still, Victor and Ortega had crept up to a boulder, watching the scene down below and letting their peripheral vision detect any movement at the extremities. All they needed was a flash, a sign that —

"There," Ortega said, mumbling the word almost silently, his face unmoving. Victor's head remained still as well, hoping not to invite another shot from the sniper down below. He moved his eyes to where Ortega was pointing, then squinted out into the valley.

He waited a moment, then saw it. Just a shift, something subtle against the trunk of a tree. A ghillie suit, hidden behind a tree trunk at the edge of the field to the northwest. The sniper was lying prone, the long barrel also covered in camouflage. But it was the telltale triangle at the end — the stand for the sniper's barrel that sat on the ground and lifted the rifle to the proper angle — that gave it away.

"He's out of range," Victor said.

"We will have to lay cover fire while we slide down the hill. Once we're behind the hut, we can proceed into flanks, working around the field."

"It's not ideal," Victor said. "I would have much preferred to walk straight up to the back door of the facility unmolested."

But they needed whatever cover they could find, and whoever had built this place had made sure there was little of it. Despite this, there were a few trees scattered sparsely around the facility grounds. If they could run and maintain their cover fire, they might have a chance.

"As long as there's only one sniper," Victor added.

"He's going to tell his friends we're here," Ortega said.

If he didn't already. Victor nodded. "All the more reason to move quickly."

Victor looked over his shoulder at Benavides, who was now sitting up, his stomach and side bandaged and tightly wrapped. He had his rifle out and was ready to place it on top of the same boulder that Victor and Ortega were hiding behind.

He was sweating with pain, his mouth a thin line. There was blood seeping out around the bandages, dripping and pooling beneath him.

"He's got five, maybe ten minutes, I'd guess," Ortega said softly.

Victor's eyes fell. *We haven't even stepped foot inside, and already I've lost a man.*

He had lost men before, on a handful of occasions. Every one of them had been gut-wrenching, terrible experiences. Every one of them left him with memories — nightmares. Every one of them had caused him to reassess his actions that day. Had he done something wrong? Not something necessary to keep them alive? How had his leadership failed them?

He pushed the thoughts away for now; he needed to compartmentalize. There was no time for distraction, for feeling down. He still had three men with him, three men who needed him.

He waited for Benavides to steel himself once more, giving him a slight nod when he was ready.

He nodded back. "On my count," Victor whispered.

CHAPTER 16
VICTOR

"ARE THERE SUPPOSED to be soldiers here?" Ortega asked.

"Supposed to?" Victor responded. "No. But we are prepared for anything."

"Are we?" Ortega asked, gripping his rifle tightly. "I didn't think we'd hit resistance *before* we even got inside."

Victor ignored Ortega, knowing he was just frustrated about losing Benavides. But there was nothing he or anyone else could do about it other than continue on and push through. He, Ortega, Perez, and Garcia had made it successfully down the mountainside to the back of the hut. There, Garcia and Perez had found a door that was unlocked, leading into a small 8' x 8' space. They stood on either side of the back of the hut, guarding the open space beyond, while Victor and Ortega ran in.

Inside, Victor found that it was indeed full of maintenance equipment — lawnmower, fertilizer, and all sorts of equipment that looked as though it hadn't been touched in a hundred years.

But it was what hung on the opposite wall he was most interested in.

A window.

Next to the front door opposite the door they'd come in through, a window had been built into the wall. Not surprisingly, the glass had long since broken away from the small frame, providing Victor not just with a clear shot outward, but also a way to get his gun situated without having to break glass and alert anyone nearby.

The rest of his men stayed at the back of the hut, curling around its edges to prepare for any newcomers. So far, they'd seen only the sniper, and Victor thought they had taken him out already — they had fired down on the sniper and had not seen him pop up again.

But at least the one enemy combatant had known their exact location — whether or not he had signaled the rest of his team, wherever they may be — and Victor's men were now known entities.

The sniper had either remained hidden or had already been hit while Benavides laid covering fire, allowing Victor's team to descend the hill. As planned, they had not yet turned on comms, so Victor had no idea if Benavides had seen the sniper was still in his spot behind the tree trunk or if he had decided to move back to the copse of trees at the northwest side of the facility. They were running deaf and blind, with no way to know where the enemy was or how many they were — not a situation Victor liked being in.

Victor watched out the window, careful to keep his head away from the center of the open space. The valley grew up around him, but he was focused only on the area just ahead. What seemed like a large pile of massive boulders, pockmarked with lighter-colored concrete walls and roofs, was their next target. The destination they had come for.

And it was clear now that this destination was a popular one. Whatever Russian entity governed this facility, it was of primary interest to keep outsiders away.

Victor noticed movement from one of the concrete walls. A darker shape passed in front of it, then crouched behind a boulder nearby.

Ortega was next to him now and had observed the same thing. "Movement dead ahead. 1 o'clock."

Victor nodded, gripping his rifle with two hands as he watched silently.

"Did you expect company?" he asked.

"No, I didn't," Victor replied. "You knew what I knew. Bennett seemed to think this place would be either entirely abandoned or just a skeleton crew of researchers. I wonder if Zack knows more about this place than we do."

"You think he could be withholding information from us?"

"Not sure what good it would do," Victor replied. "We're supposed to be his security, his protection. If he expected us to run into hostile forces and didn't tell us, how would that help him?"

Ortega shrugged. "Well, we didn't exactly wait for his stamp of approval on this one, either. We rushed over here — maybe he was going to tell us later. Maybe these guys were planning to leave later today, and Bennett was waiting until then."

Victor smiled, glancing sidelong at Ortega. His right-hand man shrugged again.

"Let's check comms, just in case there's an update."

Victor nodded. It couldn't hurt. If anyone was listening in, it was not like their progress had been made under cover of darkness — it was broad daylight, and at least one hostile soldier knew exactly where they were. It was very likely the guy directly in front of them was simply waiting for them to reappear.

Victor reached to his side and turned on the walkie-talkie. It immediately squawked to life, Benavides' dying voice finding a bit of energy. *"Inbound RPG... I repeat, RPG inbound!"*

His voice was shaky, wobbly, and he was breathing heavily. Victor knew the man would bleed out and die within minutes, and this was his final act — helping his teammates.

Ortega's eyes widened, but Victor pushed him aside and ran directly for the door at the front of the hut. He didn't have time to give specific orders to his men, so he relied on them to react quickly. He fumbled with the walkie-talkie, turning up the volume as Benavides' alert was repeated.

Victor barreled through the door, its rusted keyed lock blasting apart with the force. Ortega was at his heels as they both tumbled out the front of the hut.

The world erupted in front of them, gunfire coming from all sides.

Behind him, Victor saw his men diving away from the edges of the hut they had just been hiding behind. As he rolled away as fast as possible, careful to stay beneath the rounds sizzling over his head, the hut exploded in a fiery blaze.

CHAPTER 17
BEN

AFTER LEAVING the seedy Italian restaurant, the CSO group drove to a private airfield south of Moscow and caught a flight to the Kodar mountain range. Finding a small town in the Kalarsky District of Zabaykalsky Krai, Ben was able to rent a midsize SUV with enough traction to get over any rough dirt roads they might come across on their way to the national park.

Established in 2016, Kodar National Park was one of the newest national parks in mainland Russia, created to preserve wildlife, offer places of rest and refuge for tourists, and catch up with similar programs in the West.

But there were still some wrinkles that hadn't yet been ironed out. Lucia explained on the way that these parks were often staffed by skeleton crews of rangers and park staff, sometimes as few as one employee for every 500 tourists. There were no souvenir shops or gift shops, few restroom facilities or playgrounds, and the only way to tell if one was in a park was if they happened upon a sign declaring as such.

They reached the park entrance a half-hour later, and true to Lucia's word, they were met with no resistance upon entering. Not even so much as a check-in stand, though Ben saw a small building still under construction off to the left side of the road. It seemed the intent was there to create a full-fledged national park, but for now, the place was just a wild sanctuary encircled by a handful of Russian-built fences and marked on a map but little else.

It was quite literally in the middle of nowhere, and Ben was once again glad for his wife's ability to navigate computer systems around the world, as well as Lucia's ability to uncover the IP address of the forum post she had read, allowing them to find it on a map.

He only hoped it hadn't been obfuscated behind a layer of VPNs and other encryption. Not that he knew what any of that meant, just that Julie had described their ability to find this place 'a potential crapshoot.'

But up ahead, he saw the road opening up to a wide valley with a river-fed lake off to the right. Directly in front of them sat a pile of large boulders, with what appeared to be buildings interspersed with them.

"That's it," Lucia said. She sat in the front seat next to Ben, acting as part guide, having the most knowledge of this region.

Ben nodded and aimed the SUV for the edge of the woods they had been traveling through. After cresting a small hill, he found himself driving downhill into the valley. He pulled the SUV to the right, descending toward the river and lake beyond, keeping the outcropping of rocks and buildings on his left. As they drove around the facility, they examined their surroundings. No one was outside, and they saw no vehicles.

"Over there!" Reggie snapped his finger, then jabbing a thumb against the rear window. Ben felt the man's knees digging into the back of his seat. He shifted, squinting through the side window of the driver seat. After a few seconds of searching, he saw what Reggie was pointing at.

Two vehicles, parked side-by-side, with a camouflage net hastily thrown over them. The camouflage was the wrong color, not mixing well with the snow-speckled terrain. Still, it hid the vehicles better than if they had been allowed to shine in the morning sun.

"Two SUVs, probably able to carry 6-7 guys each, with loadouts," Reggie mumbled.

"And it looks to me like they don't want anyone to know they're here," Julie added from next to Reggie. Freddy sat in the third row, his legs stretched out over the seat next to him. He said something, but they couldn't hear the man's reply.

Ben continued driving, wanting to glean as much information from the scene as possible before making a decision to park and try to get inside. As this facility was on no maps or public databases, it had been extremely difficult to even discover its presence here. As such, they had no idea what to expect. Were the doors sealed tight like a bank vault? Or was this just a glorified gift shop that was kept unlocked 24/7? Would there be guards or rangers waiting for them?

He felt a bit unsettled knowing that whoever had driven the SUVs here had tried to camouflage them, and even more unsettled when he realized they had done it hastily enough not to be terribly concerned about anyone coming.

"I don't see any guards; whoever was in the SUVs is probably already inside," Julie said.

Ben was about to respond, but Reggie cut him off. "I don't know about that. Check it out."

Ben used his peripheral vision to see where Reggie was pointing and then followed his finger again to see what his friend was looking at.

Ben pulled the car to a halt, put on the parking brake and opened the car door.

"Ben, are you sure it's smart to get out? If there's anyone watching..."

Ben didn't answer. Instead, he kept the door open and started walking the twenty paces toward what Reggie was looking at.

He heard the passenger door open, and his friend was beside him in a moment. Together they walked, side-by-side, toward...

The scene of a massacre. Bright red streaks of blood screamed through the delicate whites of the taiga snow. It seemed there had been some sort of fight, jostling at least.

There was a weapon sitting in a pile of dirt and snow off to the side, but blood was sprinkled over everything in sight. Tracks ran from the spot to the pile of boulders nearby. Ben frowned down at them. They seemed like bootprints, but they lacked the lines and markings found on the soles of shoes.

"Jesus," Reggie muttered.

"Tell me about it. Whoever this was, it didn't end well for him." Reggie walked over and retrieved the weapon, examining the rifle. Ben saw its long-range scope affixed to the barrel, identifying the weapon as a sniper rifle.

The realization sent a shiver down Ben's spine. He hadn't been able to shake off the feeling that they were not alone out here, and this scene confirmed it. The sight of the massacre in front of them only intensified his feeling of dread.

The bloodstains on the snow were still fresh, and the SUVs parked nearby made it clear that whoever was responsible for the violence was still in the area. Ben glanced around, trying to assess their surroundings and figure out the next move. It was a risky situation, but they had come too far to turn back now.

He took a deep breath, steeling himself for what lay ahead.

CHAPTER 18
BEN

BEN FOLLOWED the tracks the forty feet or so with his eyes, where they then disappeared into the boulder pile and toward a concrete wall. Ben and Reggie stood silent, Reggie now holding the loaded rifle as they watched for any movement. He checked the barrel, magazine, and sight, playing his finger over the brushed steel stock. Satisfied it was in working order, he nodded at Ben.

Together, their eyes fell back down to the bloody circle on the snowy ground.

"Blood's still warm," Reggie said. "I reckon they went down twenty minutes ago, maybe even less."

A chill landed on the back of Ben's neck, reminding him that even though it was summertime, mornings in this region could be downright cold. If the bloodshed at their feet was still warm, it would have had to have happened very recently.

"They left the rifle but pulled their man inside. Why?" Ben wondered.

Reggie shrugged. "Must have been in a hurry. Guy was all shot up, bleeding out."

Ben squinted as he looked down at the scene of the crime. "I don't know. Seems like an *awful* lot of blood for just a couple of gunshots."

"Maybe it was more than a few gunshots, then," Reggie suggested. "Or a few *big* gunshots."

Ben nodded, not really believing his friend. He knew a large weapon, not unlike the sniper rifle Reggie was now holding, could take massive chunks off of a man. It would no doubt leave bloody residue, evidence of a brawl. But this still seemed like too much blood.

And where did they take him? Surely the guy isn't still alive...

Reggie turned and pointed at the concrete wall protruding from the top of a section of boulders, where the tracks ended. "They built this place on top of an existing cave system if those geologic surveys we found can be trusted. All these little concrete walls must be the edges of the buildings, the upper level. And I see a door."

The unsettled feeling Ben had was still there, but he felt a bit more comfortable knowing they wouldn't have to do any spelunking today. He didn't like the idea of being underground at all, but at least they could descend through a facility's subterranean levels instead of through a winding, dark cave system.

Besides, Reggie was now armed, and even though it was a long-range rifle, the man was a trained Army sniper, and the weapon would be better off in no one else's hands.

They walked back toward the car. Julie was standing outside of it, walking in place to stay warm, but she reentered the SUV when Ben arrived.

"What is it?" she asked.

Ben answered through the open window. "Someone had a bad day," he said, shrugging. "Reggie found a toy and an entrance. I think we park here and head inside."

Lucia snapped her head sideways and looked at Ben. "You think there are other people here?" she asked, eyeing the long rifle barrel Reggie held. "People who are armed?"

"There was definitely *someone* here," Ben said softly. "And they were armed. Not anymore, though. We can't know for sure until we get inside if they were alone or not. But I need you in there, Dr. Vergotti. I need you to figure out why this place is suddenly so popular."

He saw her swallow a lump in her throat, but she didn't respond at first. Finally, with a timid voice, she turned back to Ben and the others. "Okay. I trust you. And I really want to know what is going on here. Whether your brother is involved in this or not."

In the SUV, Julie nodded.

Lucia continued. "Let's get inside and find something that tells us what this place exists for. If it has anything at all to do with your brother, I suspect I'll be able to find it. And if we're really lucky, I might be able to figure out what he was doing here."

Ben smiled at her, hoping it looked more reassuring than it felt and entered the car again. Reggie started walking toward the rock outcropping while Ben drove the SUV over to a thin peninsula of boulders poking out from it. He parked on the other side of the strip of rocks, hiding it from the other vehicles, then turned off the ignition and opened the door.

"Once more into the breach," he mumbled.

CHAPTER 19
VICTOR

THE PLACE FELT LIKE A FUNHOUSE, minus the fun.

Victor and Ortega led Perez and Garcia deeper into the facility. The corridors were tight, the stairwells narrow. The ceilings were lower than they should have been, and Victor got the sense that this place had been built hastily, using as few materials as possible. He felt as if the entire place would collapse on their heads just because they were marching around inside. It seemed like the slightest vibration would set off a chain reaction, collapsing the pile of boulders above their heads.

After the hut had exploded outside, the team of four, aided by their eye in the sky, Benavides, watched from high above, had taken out two Russians hiding amongst the boulder-riddled area. The man who had fired the RPG toward them had fallen first, the second soldier shortly after.

Just as quickly as the attack started, it had ended. They weren't shooting at an army, they were shooting at a few guards. The intense battle was over before Victor could even figure out *why* they were shooting at each other. It was obvious that he and his men were seen as hostile intruders, but he couldn't figure out why they were so intensely guarding the space.

But they had been able to proceed unopposed after that.

Victor had taken his group around the far perimeter of the boulder outcropping, eventually finding the Russian team's SUVs and a doorway that led into the facility. It had been left open, lending more credibility to his theory that the Russians were still inside.

He didn't know what was going on here, but it was clear to Victor that there had been activity inside the facility very recently.

Victor wanted to push through the entire facility quickly, both to find the Russians and to figure out what it was they were working on here, but he did his due diligence as they traveled. He poked into a few rooms as they passed, seeing only the same thing every time: tables and chairs upturned or broken, files and papers spread haphazardly over the floor as if they had been tossed from the ceiling. Someone had ransacked the place, and it was unclear as to why. Items weren't just taken out and thrown on the floor — they were broken. Fluorescent lights sputtered, if they were even still in one piece.

It had been difficult to keep track of their progress through the dark base with only their gun-mounted flashlights, but it was enough to get a feel for the place.

Someone had come through and decimated this station. Was it the Russians? And why? Why was it necessary to destroy each room after not finding whatever it was they were looking for?

When they reached the third subterranean level, there were no more working lights. They rounded the staircase and came onto the hallway floor, and Victor cautiously pressed forward.

They were in pitch darkness, doffing their mounted flashlights in order to maintain stealth.

He frowned. Victor heard the sound of... scraping. He paused, placing the back of his hand against Ortega's chest to slow his progress. Perez and Garcia stopped behind them.

He made a shushing sound. "You hear that?"

Beside him, Ortega whispered in response. "Yeah, sounds like footsteps. Slow."

Victor realized Ortega was right — it wasn't scraping, but slow, steady footsteps, each one barely lifting from the floor. It was the sound of boots sliding on concrete.

And each step was getting louder.

"It's coming from right in front of us." Ortega's voice was almost inaudible. Victor could hear the breaths from the men behind him. If he had known they would be descending into a cave-like maze underneath this concrete bunker without *any* lights on in the place, Victor would have opted for light-enhancing vision kits. Standard night vision goggles wouldn't do the trick — there wasn't an ounce of light down here to amplify.

Victor held his breath and whispered. "Hold your fire."

The team stood together in a tight square, with Ortega and Victor in the lead, straddling the narrow corridor on this level. He wondered if the space in front of them was similar to the floor above: just a short, narrow hallway with only a few doors leading to rooms on either side. If he had to guess, he figured they were likely twenty or thirty feet underground now.

The air was chilled and grew colder with each step, and Victor could swear he felt a cooler breeze coming from farther down the dark hallway.

The scraping sound was directly in front of them now. Victor wanted to fire, to simply spray the darkness with rounds and take care of whatever terrifying thing was sneaking up on them. But instead, he held his ground, and his men waited, well-trained and trusting of their leader.

With slow, calculated movements, he moved his left hand over the flashlight and placed his thumb over the button on the back of it. He gave himself a silent countdown, and then the scraping stopped. It was as if whatever had been sneaking up toward them had sensed their presence.

But it was pitch black here — not even a pinprick of light emanating from upstairs reached this level.

He flicked the beam on and illuminated the entire hallway in front of them.

Victor wanted to scream.

CHAPTER 20
FREDDIE

BEFORE THE SUV had even stopped, Freddie was in motion. He climbed back over the seat, popped open the hatch, and fell to the ground awkwardly. Without missing a beat, he stood and ran to the passenger-side door, opening it before Lucia could exit.

She frowned at him as he yanked her door open but eventually accepted his hand as she stepped out of the vehicle. She stretched, reaching her arms up over her head.

Freddie tried not to notice her thin figure but immediately felt his throat constrict. There was no conscious mind that could subvert eons of male wiring and programming.

He coughed, suddenly feeling very exposed.

"You must be what they call a 'southern gentleman,' yes?" Lucia asked.

He cleared his throat to no avail, feeling his cheeks flush. "Yes, uh, that's right. It's just being polite, you know?"

Lucia was smiling, trying to hold back laughter when Julie jumped in. She exited the rear passenger-side door next to Freddie and Lucia, glaring up at Freddie. "You know what *isn't* polite? Running past one perfectly good female just to open a door for another one."

Freddie's cheeks flushed redder. He stammered a response, but Ben called them over before he could finish. "Freddie, stop flirting with my wife. I want to get inside and start scoping things out."

Freddie nodded quickly, then walked around the front of the vehicle to join Ben and Reggie in front of the concrete wall they had seen from below. There was no walkway leading to it, just the bloody path of footprints that led over stone and snow. Reggie held the sniper rifle in a firm grip and led the way.

As they neared the door, they saw it was standing open a crack. "Looks abandoned," Freddie said. "That door is ancient."

"Whoever died back there was definitely pulled inside, or at least into the rocks nearby," Ben said quietly. "But I'd *love* for this place to be abandoned — it would make our jobs that much easier — but I have a feeling we won't be alone in there."

Freddie followed behind Reggie as the man pushed the doorway open and stepped through. It was quiet inside, but it was anything but abandoned.

"Holy hell," Reggie muttered, stepping over a fallen filing cabinet.

The place, if it had been abandoned, had been abandoned very recently. There was stuff everywhere. Chairs and tables overturned, paper cups and napkins strewn about, and reams of paper spilled out onto the floor to their left. None of it seemed dusty or old.

"Someone was definitely here recently," Julie said from behind Freddie. "They ransacked the place."

"Probably looking for the same thing we are looking for," Freddie said. "On that note — what exactly *are* we looking for?" He turned around to find Lucia standing in the doorway, her small frame dwarfed by the large bunker door.

She stepped fully into view. "If this place is a research facility, we will know soon enough. There will be a lab of some sort — equipment, computers, test chemicals, that sort of thing. These lights above our heads could be solar-powered, but there's probably no power on deeper in the facility, so we won't be lucky enough to get into the computers to see exactly what they were studying."

"You think this could be where your colleagues posted messages from?" Julie asked.

Lucia nodded. "Of course. I didn't know there was any such facility in this region, and certainly not in the national park. Though the park probably came later. It would make sense this place was hidden here, kept secret by the Russian government. Even if their research was mundane, the Russian state likes to keep its scientific initiatives hidden away from the world, at least until they are certain it can't be used for military purposes."

Freddie understood exactly what she meant. The last time his team was in Russia, they discovered this to be the case. Many countries engaged in secret scientific research, looking for advancements in chemistry and physics that could be used in military applications down the road. No one wanted to let the cat out of the bag before the scientists figured out exactly what they were dealing with.

The group followed Reggie and Freddie forward to a descending set of stairs on the other side of the room. If he had to guess, Freddie assumed this room served as some sort of antechamber for the rest of the facility. Perhaps it was used as storage or like a room-sized closet when the weather outside got rough. There were no other doors in sight, and this room had no windows, being three-quarters of the way beneath the rocks around them. As Lucia had said, it could be that this room was the only one lit by solar lamps, and that deeper in the base, they would have to use their phone flashlights to see.

He checked his, not surprised to find it powered on but without service.

"Seems a strange place to build a research facility," Reggie said. "Expensive, too. Why not just put it above ground and use more common — cheaper — construction materials?"

"If they were studying something related to the Earth's crust, or one of the many underground water systems that feeds the rivers and lake nearby, it might be helpful to have their research set up at the source."

"That, and it's a great way to keep the research out of sight if they *are* doing something a bit more nefarious."

"Don't be pessimistic, Ben," Julie said, smiling. "For all we know, we're about to stumble onto a bunch of soil geeks on their lunch break."

Ben chuckled, muttering under his breath. "We could only be so lucky."

CHAPTER 21
VICTOR

STANDING DIRECTLY in front of Victor was a man taller than him. Russian. He wore black fatigues and a long-sleeved black turtleneck. Neither article of clothing was in good shape. They were in tatters. Ripped, and shredded, white skin poking through both torso and legs.

The man's face was bloody. Not streaked, not dotted, but completely covered with slick black liquid. It dripped from him, down around his shoulders and neck, cruelly seeping back into the open tears on his sweater.

The Russian man carried an assault rifle, which Victor immediately recognized as one of the same weapons that had been used against him and his team back outside. But the man carried it loosely in one hand, its barrel pointed down at the floor. It was not a weapon now, but simply a prop, a part of the man's character he had already forgotten how to use.

His eyes told Victor everything. They were stunned, wide, unknowing. They stared at Victor's light as if it was the eternal calling him home. His face twitched, eyes blinked.

He focused on Victor's light. Trudged toward it, the scraping sound beginning once again. He mumbled something in Russian. The words were short, broken and repeated.

Perez spoke the language, but if he understood this man, he didn't offer a translation.

Victor inadvertently took a step back. He felt the barrel of Garcia's rifle behind him, then the pressure released as he, too, took a step back. He kept the light steady on the man's face, on the blood.

What the hell happened to this guy? Victor wondered.

The wounds on his face looked like they could have been burn marks. Had this man been in an explosion? He and his team had grenades and C-4 packs with them, but they hadn't used any explosives on the Russian attackers up above.

Whatever had gone down, it had happened down below. Beside him, Ortega let out a breath.

"Who — who are you?" Victor asked.

The man faltered. His eyes blinked again, then grew wide. They had taken him by surprise, no doubt.

But he would not stop staring at his light. Was this man looking for death? Did he think this was the proverbial tunnel?

It was impossible to assess the man's wounds with so little light, at least without putting him and his team in danger of attack. It was safe to assume this guy was on his last legs. He was swaying now, trying to move forward. He continued encroaching on their space, crawling one sliding boot step at a time.

It was horrifying to watch, as if every second of life was severe pain.

Ortega made a snap judgment, running forward and kicking the Russian's rifle to the side. The man dropped it without fighting and allowed Ortega to grab his elbow and armpit. Ortega grunted with the sudden exertion as the man nearly collapsed into his hold. Garcia ran forward from behind Victor as well, cradling the man's left side.

The man's eyes blinked a few times, still in shock, then fell to his knees. Victor stepped up, faced him, still holding the rifle's flashlight on his face.

"Do you speak English?" he asked slowly.

He kicked himself for not paying more attention to the language during the last few years he had been here. He mostly spent time with his team — all of whom spoke fluent Spanish and English, but not Russian.

Except for Perez, who had a passing experience with the Russian tongue. He turned to him now, waiting for either the Russian soldier or his teammate to respond.

The man whispered, "No." Perez spoke to him; a question. The man looked up at him, surprised, then whispered a few words. Perez answered. "He says he does not know."

"Doesn't know what?" Victor asked.

The man muttered again. Perez translated, "I'm sorry, it's hard to understand. He's barely able to speak. It sounds like he's saying he didn't know, or they didn't know."

They didn't know what? What was waiting for them downstairs?

Victor's blood ran cold as he realized this Russian soldier was no longer afraid of the mercenary intruders from outside — if he ever was. The terror on this man's face said everything. He was afraid, but it was not of Victor.

There was something far worse than mercenaries or soldiers waiting downstairs.

Something that Victor knew he would soon find.

CHAPTER 22
BEN

THE STAIRS TWISTED to the left, descending another story before leveling out to a narrow corridor. Reggie reached the first door on his left and nudged it open with the end of his rifle. He stayed at the doorway, allowing Ben to enter first.

"Looks like a laboratory in here," Ben said. "Maybe. It's too damn dark to see anything."

Ben was holding his phone's flashlight, which lit a bubble of space about five feet around him. He saw a room not terribly different from the one through which they had entered this station. Papers were scattered on the floor, file cabinets and computer terminals knocked over and all sorts of equipment he didn't recognize. It could be a laboratory... or just some old garage. It was impossible to tell without any light.

"Smells like a bathroom," Julie said from behind Ben.

He turned around, the others squinting as his light blinded them. "This is going to be a lost cause unless we get some lights turned on," Ben said. "I guess the good news is that if there are generators somewhere on-site, and they haven't been turned on yet, it means we're alone. Nothing to jump out at us, no one here to scare us."

"Yeah, maybe our buddy from outside got attacked by — "

A deep snapping sounded as lights above Ben's head began to buzz with electricity. One by one, lights transformed the hallway they had just been in from a dark crypt into a brightly lit corridor. The room Ben was standing inside came to life, now fully illuminated.

"What was that you were just saying about us being alone here?" Freddie asked, a grin on his face.

"I guess that answers that question," Ben said. "Okay, everyone on high alert. Don't be stupid, but there's no reason we should assume whoever's down here with us is hostile..."

"No reason we shouldn't assume they *aren't* either," Reggie added.

Ben turned back to examine the room they had stepped into. He changed his initial assessment. It didn't look like a laboratory as much as just an office room. He could see its general shape, though most of the items inside had been destroyed or strewn about the room. A table had been smashed in half, splinters littering the floor in the center. An archaic phone system lay in a pile of cables and wires on the floor next to it.

"Conference room?" Reggie asked.

Ben nodded. "Either that or an office."

"What the hell happened down here?" Julie asked softly. "All of these rooms look like the aftermath of a cage fight."

"Yeah, and I'd hate to see the other guy," Reggie quipped.

Ben stepped forward, walking around the broken table and splintered chairs. An empty water jug sat crumpled in the corner of the office, and still more reams of paper slid beneath his feet.

"Should we be picking up all this paper?" Julie asked. "If the printouts are of what they were working on, they might clue us in." She knelt to grab a handful of white printer paper that had fallen.

"My guess is that everything is going to be in Russian anyway. The only one here who speaks it and reads it fluently is Lucia, and it will take too much time for her to go through it all."

Julie nodded but handed the stack to Lucia anyway.

"These are just schedules," Lucia said, confirming. "Maintenance, cleaning, that sort of thing. There's nothing indicative of any research — or anything useful — here."

As they made their way down the narrow hallway, Ben couldn't shake the feeling that they were walking through a hastily assembled space. The walls were made of thick concrete, but there was a sense of unease that permeated the atmosphere, as if the builders had cut corners or rushed through the construction process. He couldn't quite put his finger on it, but the hallway felt more like a bunker than a lab or office space.

Ben couldn't help but wonder about the people who had built this place. Were they the same ones who had conducted the research he and his team were investigating? If so, what kind of work had they been doing down here? The more he thought about it, the more he realized that the layout of the space made it difficult to get a sense of the overall purpose of the facility. It was as if the design had been intentionally confusing, perhaps to keep outsiders from understanding what was happening inside.

Reggie took the lead as Ben trailed behind, his thoughts turning to the design of the hallway. It was far narrower than it should have been, which only added to the feeling of claustrophobia that had been nagging at him since they had first entered the underground facility. He wondered if the builders had been limited by the available space or if there was some other reason for the cramped conditions. Perhaps they had been trying to save on materials or cut corners to save time.

Then, he had an idea — what if the builders of this place had used the underground cave system as a rough outline for the design of the space? It would explain why the hallways were so narrow and why the whole facility seemed to be carved out of solid rock. It would also explain why the place felt so claustrophobic. The builders had been constrained by the natural shape of the cave system and had had to work around it, resulting in a cramped and confusing layout.

Ben knew that they were in a dangerous place, and the design of the space only added to the sense of foreboding that hung over the group. He wondered what kind of security measures the builders had put in place to protect their work. Were there hidden cameras or traps waiting for them at every turn? He couldn't shake the feeling that they were being watched.

With a deep breath and a nod toward his best friend, Ben once again led the way forward. He knew that the next few hours would test their skill and courage, but he was determined to see the mission through to the end. The truth was out there, and he was determined to uncover it, no matter the cost.

The hallway ended in a T-intersection. Peering around to the right, Ben could see another doorway on this level. The door was closed, and no lights spilled out from the crack underneath.

There was Russian text scrawled on a metal plate on the front of it, and Lucia read it aloud. "Cleaning," she said.

"Just a closet," Ben confirmed.

To the left, there was another set of stairs. Ben wanted to get a read on how the rest of his group was feeling, knowing that by continuing downward, they were making it that much harder to get back out if something were to go wrong.

Before he could open his mouth to speak, however, he heard three quick patters, the impacts reverberating loudly through the tight space.

"Were those gunshots?" he asked.

Lucia's eyes widened, but Ben focused on Freddie and Reggie — the two men here who were military-trained. Both of them nodded at once, just as two more rounds rang out from down below. They echoed easily, carrying from downstairs into Ben's ears.

"Well, I guess that settles it," Reggie said, as the gunshots subsided. "We're *definitely* not alone."

CHAPTER 23
BEN

BEN EYED Reggie from across the room as he stood near a metal table that surprisingly remained untouched amidst the chaos. He leaned against it, half-seated with his arms crossed, his eyebrows raised as if already asking a question.

Ben nodded to his friend. "Reggie, with me. Freddie, stay here with the ladies. We'll go down and see — "

"No."

Ben whirled around and saw his wife staring up at him. She stood on messy pages of printer paper that had fallen out of an upturned printer, its power cable sheared in half.

Ben frowned. "What do you mean, 'no?' Jules, we need to figure out — "

"And we *will* figure it out," she said sternly. "That's what we're doing, figuring things out."

Ben felt the tension of the moment rise. They were running out of time, having heard the unmistakable sound of gunshots, and he wanted to know who was shooting and who they were shooting at.

"We're going to figure this out together. One step at a time, remember?" Julie replied.

"Those were *gunshots*, Jules," Reggie said from behind her. "Don't you want to know what's going on? We could be in danger here."

"I'm going to save us all the time," Julie answered. "We *are* in danger here. We are *always* in danger, guys. Remember who we are? What we do? For *years* we've been trying to pretend like we're just snooping around, playing detective. You all know damn well that nothing we ever do ends without shots fired."

Ben chewed the inside of his cheek. He wanted to argue, but how could he? It's not like she was wrong. "We've all been hinting at changes we want for the CSO, for our group. All of us, either privately or out loud. We've been frustrated, beaten-down, exhausted. We've lost friends, *family*." She turned and faced Ben again as she spoke these words. "Why do you think that is? We are a good team, but only when we're *forced* to be one."

Reggie met Ben's gaze, and Ben was reminded of how he had met his best friend. Brazil, in the Amazon. They had been in a hotel lobby, pinned down by a group of trigger-happy mercenaries who were ready to destroy anything and anyone in sight. Broken glass surrounded Ben and Julie, pinning them into their defensive positions, which were entirely impossible to defend since they were unarmed.

The mercenaries closed in, one of them lobbing a grenade into the hotel foyer. Then flashes of light, bright and targeted, like multiple searchlights honing in on their location. Ben had been blinded by the lobby's sudden shift to bright daylight, and even the mercenaries seemed to stop for a moment, confused. That apparently had been the moment Reggie was waiting for.

Gareth "Red" Reggie had slipped in behind them, taking out the mercenaries methodically, using his skills as a soldier in the United States Army to serve up his own brand of justice. He had saved their lives that day and many days after. Ben and Reggie had quickly become friends, forging a bond through one impossible circumstance after the next.

Yet, Julie wasn't wrong in her assessment. They were reckless and rash, excelling purely because their adversaries often outthought and outsmarted them, and Ben and Reggie relied on luck, something entirely unpredictable. He had built the Civilian Special Operations to model his own leadership, one that relied on individuals doing their part, operating as autonomously as possible. It was an alliance formed between men and women who were willing to push forward *without* a proper plan.

But his wife was right, and he knew it. That 'without a proper plan' had worked against them more than he cared to admit.

Ben smiled and nodded. "Okay, you're right."

Lucia flicked her eyes from Julie to Ben, obviously trying to assess the leadership dynamic she was witnessing. The tension between Ben and his wife had not subsided, but Ben knew better than to argue against Julie. He was alive not just because of Reggie's rash aggression, but also because of Julie's calculated and strategic deference.

"I'm *not* losing any of you... not this time," she continued. "Lucia, as much as I want to find out what's going on here, I won't do it unless we are all working together."

There was a long pause, the air in the room seemingly gone as Ben waited for Lucia's response. But even before she spoke, he knew her answer.

"Of course," she said. "I thought that was the plan all along."

CHAPTER 24
VICTOR

"CAN YOU TELL ME YOUR NAME?" Victor asked.

Perez, now playing the part of translator, did his best to parse the words. Victor understood a few of them, as most of the exchange was entry-level Russian.

The man's eyes rolled around in his head, each controlled separately. It seemed as though he was going to pass out. Still kneeling on the concrete floor of the corridor, held up by Ortega and Garcia, Victor looked down at the Russian soldier. It was hard to tell where exactly the man was wounded. It seemed as though he had scratches and gashes across his face and arms where his clothing was torn, but upon further inspection, it didn't seem like there were many wounds beneath the torn fabric. The blood covering his face was either not his own or remnants from wounds the man had received prior.

But in that case, why was this blood still wet? He couldn't see any overt cuts or scrapes, even though it was clear the man seemed to be in agony. The whole thing was more terrifying to Victor than he cared to admit.

He was *obviously* injured, but it was not an injury he had seen before.

"Do you have a name? What is your name?" Victor repeated, altering the question to make it even easier for Perez to translate.

The soldier sputtered, then coughed. He fell forward, jerked upright

97

by Ortega and Garcia. Blood landed on Victor's boot. He didn't wipe it off. Whatever was afflicting this soldier, he didn't want it on his hands or any open skin on his body. He reached forward, using his rifle's barrel to lift the man's chin. The man looked up at him with those same wild, terrified eyes.

Is he neurotic? Going insane? Victor thought. He looked to Perez, but the man shrugged. "Sorry, boss. Russian is pretty tricky."

Victor nodded, frustrated but understanding. He looked at the kneeling man again and delivered the main message he wanted to get across to the Russian soldier. "Ask him if he has any partners here. A team. A unit. Any word that you know. We need to find out if he's alone. We found his friends upstairs, but I need to know how many more there are in here."

Perez's eyes widened, and Victor watched as the man delivered the words in Russian. He thought he understood the word for team, and the Russian soldier's eyes seemed to steady and lock onto Perez's face as the question came. The man nodded once, quickly, then collapsed deeper into Ortega and Garcia's grip.

"Great!" Victor said. "Where? Down below?"

There was a bit of back-and-forth, and the Russian soldier finally mumbled a few words.

"He says there are more," Perez answered. "About a dozen total. But then he said there are fewer now. I don't... I don't exactly know what that means. Sorry, boss."

"No need to apologize. That's helpful," Victor said.

Ortega made a face at Victor and then motioned with his head. *Should we continue?*

Victor nodded. They were exposed here. Garcia's and Ortega's backs were to the corridor behind. He told Perez what to translate next. "We need to keep going, to keep getting deeper into this place. Whatever the hell... *this* is — whatever happened to him — we need to know if it's something Bennett wants to get his hands on. I want to know what he was doing here. If these soldiers were part of the research team, or guards. Perez... just figure out the best way to get that information."

While Perez fumbled for the correct Russian words to use, Victor changed his mind. "Actually, countermand that. We need to keep moving. Perez, Garcia, you two push ahead. Keep your flashlights on in case the lights go out again. I don't want you running into anything that takes you by surprise in the dark. We need to know what we're getting ourselves into, so stay alert but keep moving. Don't get pinned down, and don't get cornered."

He thought he saw a flash of trepidation, no more than a shake, pass over Garcia's face as he let go of the Russian soldier's elbow, but his men were good. Neither would argue, and both would understand that the mission was more important than their fears and worries.

Garcia stood, waiting for Perez to check his weapon. Once ready, Victor and the two men set off, continuing down the corridor toward the next set of winding stairs.

"Ortega, let's get this guy inside one of these rooms. I want to stay out of sight, just in case."

Ortega grunted in confirmation, pulling the Russian back to his feet. The soldier seemed about ready to throw up, but for the moment he had worked back the unsteadiness and drunken behavior. He stood as well, allowing Ortega to guide him down the hall.

Victor sent off a silent prayer as he walked behind the two men. He hoped this was the last strange encounter they would have today, but he knew better than to let his guard down.

CHAPTER 25
VICTOR

VICTOR, Ortega, and the Russian soldier were making their way painstakingly slowly toward the end of the corridor. The Russian was moving even more slowly than he had on his own, a fact not lost on Victor. Was he trying to compromise their progress? Was this all just a ruse?

Victor couldn't help but assume the worst — it was part of his training, part of his survival instinct. He wanted to get their trio to the room at the end of the hallway, where hopefully there was a place to sit down inside. But he assumed that room would be like the others — in a state of complete chaos.

He held the Russian soldier's elbow and armpit just as Ortega and Garcia had, careful not to accidentally trip the man. If he *wasn't* toying with them and was truly in as much pain as he looked, Victor didn't want to upset him. This man may know more information about where they were and what they would find downstairs. Even in broken English and Russian, they had already been able to figure out that the man was not alone — there were about a dozen in his cohort somewhere down below.

They reached the room, finding the door closed. It was unlocked, and Ortega reached out, twisting the handle and pushing the metal door inward. Victor held his assault rifle in his left hand, in the crook of his armpit, waiting for anyone inside to open fire.

The room was empty. Even more surprisingly, the room was not in ruins. It seemed to be a bunk room of sorts, the same that might be found belowdecks on a Navy ship. It was small, with four beds, two sets of bunk beds straddling one corner of the room. The opposite corner — to Victor's right — had two desks; on one sat a small foldable vanity with a mirror. All of it was in fine condition. Whoever had come through and damaged everything in the rest of the rooms had not made their way into this one. Three of the beds were made, one of them with the sheets pulled back and the pillow smashed in the center as if someone had recently laid there and gotten up without fixing it.

Clearly not military, Victor mused.

The Russian soldier let out a groan, and Victor nodded to Ortega. Together, they carried the man over to one of the beds on the left wall, where they sat him down. He began falling backward immediately, and Victor put the pillow on the bed behind his back.

The man lay awkwardly on the bed, his feet on the ground and his head against the hard concrete wall. The blood had mostly congealed, but bits of it fell off in globs onto the comforter.

"Let's hope whoever was sleeping here doesn't come back for a nap," Ortega said quietly.

Victor ignored him, standing now and walking over to the desks on the opposite side of the room. If there was any information here about what this station had been studying, he might find it in this room. This was obviously where some of the researchers had lived, and it wouldn't be surprising at all for some of them to bring home some paperwork after working downstairs.

He ignored the desk with the vanity, assuming it would be full of toiletries and bathroom essentials. He focused on the other desk, pulling open the two drawers that sat alongside the opening where a chair would sit. The drawer on his right was empty, but the one on his left had a stack of papers neatly arranged and clipped together.

He pulled this out, then looked up at Ortega and rolled his eyes. "It's all in Russian," he said. "I don't know why I assumed it wouldn't be..."

"Here, let me see," Ortega said. "I can read it better than I can speak it. I might notice a few keywords."

Victor handed his friend the stack of papers and waited impatiently. Ortega's eyes flitted over the top page, a slight shake of his head. He pulled the page back and began examining the second page.

"Anything?" Victor asked.

"Sorry, boss," Ortega began. "It's all gibberish to me — "

Ortega was cut off, and Victor heard the telltale sounds of gunfire rising up to greet them, reverberating from outside the room. He wasted no time. He whirled around and ran out the same door they had entered, stopping in the center of the corridor. He swung the assault rifle down on its shoulder strap, cradling it in two hands now, ready.

He waited, not moving.

Three more shots rang out, not in a burst but from two separate weapons. *Were they shooting at each other? Or were they on the same team?*

It was clear the shots came from beneath his feet, ringing out from the narrow set of stairs just to his left at the end of the hallway. So far, all of the activity seemed to be coming from down below.

Down where his men had gone.

Victor shuddered, hoping he had not just sent two of his best soldiers to the slaughter. They were good men, loyal. He enjoyed their company when they were off-mission.

Ortega was in the hallway now, pulling the door closed behind him. A smart move — it would give them a few extra seconds to prepare in case the Russian inside had been playing them the whole time.

"From down below?" Ortega asked.

Victor nodded. He gripped his weapon tighter, checking the magazine and putting his eye through the Aimpoint red dot as a test.

"Should we go?" Ortega whispered.

He waited for an excruciating three seconds. There was no more gunfire, but Victor thought he heard the sounds of voices. *Screams? No, not loud enough.* Talking or whispering, perhaps. Maybe the same sound he had heard before — the Russian's boots scraping against the dusty concrete floor.

Victor shook his head. "Yes, but no reason to rush," he said. His eyes reached the floor, not wanting to believe it, but knowing it was true. No more gunfire could only mean one thing... "Care is our best option now.

With the lights on, we won't be able to move unseen, so let's go slowly so we don't alert anyone down there to our presence."

Ortega confirmed the order, prepared his own weapon, and stepped forward. "If that Russian soldier is playing us, I would still rather find Garcia and Perez and link up first," he whispered. "But I don't think he's going anywhere."

Let's hope not, Victor thought. *All we need are more surprises.*

CHAPTER 26
VLADIMIR

VLADIMIR WAITED SILENTLY in the darkness, his breath ragged. He tried to control his breathing and lower his heart rate.

Can it sense fear?

He gripped his knees, trying to work his blood through his limbs, needing to stay active, to stay moving. And yet, he didn't dare move, didn't dare call attention to himself.

Down here, five levels beneath the surface, it was nothing but darkness. The lights were broken, and the power from the generator in the cavern section on this level still disrupted by fits and starts. The old machine hadn't been used in decades, it seemed, and the fuel was likely no good. Two of his teammates were working on it, but it seemed the going was rough for them as well.

At least they didn't have to deal with *this*.

As part of the 14-man group sent to patrol the mountain range two days ago, Vladimir was the second youngest soldier, and the youngest one still alive. Fresh out of training, he had been assigned to this unit as an honor: his father was a high-ranking official in the Russian government, and this detachment was supposed to be an easy gig. They were a patrol group meant to support the edges of national parks and open spaces that bordered hostile nations, playing watchdog in regard to civilian security teams.

Unfortunately, the hostile forces down here were like nothing Vladimir had ever seen.

And, to be fair, he hadn't exactly *seen* the hostile forces yet. Whether one or many, he didn't know.

He just knew there was someone or something down here with them. He had watched one of his teammates get mauled by the thing, the sickening crunch of bone snapping and blood squealing out against gnashing teeth as he was dragged away in the darkness. Illuminated only by a flashlight, the terror was unending. His mind had pieced together the remnants of what he had seen in the blink of an eye, and it was far worse than what he would have seen had the lights been on. It seemed to be a monster of some sort, a bear perhaps, but it moved like a cat, far more agile than its enormous size should allow.

They had been patrolling this fifth level, the one that connected to the longer cavern system surrounding the subterranean complex. Typically, groups of two would be sent on patrol, a half-hour at a time. Vladimir had come along as a learning experience, opting to gain insight into how his older counterparts operated.

It seemed his overzealousness had cost him his sanity.

He had watched as the sergeant had been carried off and his partner, a private like Vladimir, had attempted to retrieve their friend. Vladimir had dropped the flashlight then, the light forming crazed shadows as the beast destroyed their higher ranking squadmate, then turned to his friend.

Vladimir had waited in the darkness for as long as he could bear, finally hearing slow footsteps. They were just slight scraping sounds, heading the opposite direction down the hallway. If his partner lived, Vladimir was not about to find out.

He was not going to cross the section of hallway that he knew the beast remained in, eating their friend.

So he waited. Silence had fallen over him. The darkness consumed him. The lights in the rest of the facility remained on, but he was plunged back into darkness, feeling safer in the room with no light.

He sobbed silently, careful to make sure his breaths measured evenly as possible. He didn't know what they were dealing with — if it could see in thermal or infrared, measuring the heat signature of Vladimir in the corner. He assumed it could.

And yet, he was so cold. Surely he had to be disguised enough to make a run for it? Could he go the other way? Could he head back down to the cave where the remainder of his men waited?

Another patrol would be up to replace Vladimir's group of three in a few minutes, and their commanding officer, a brutal slab of a man, would not be amused that they were late. He would send the second patrol after them, unknowingly sending even more men to the slaughter.

Vladimir *had* to make it back. He *had* to alert his men.

With a sudden surge of courage he did not know he was capable of, he stood, wiping the tears from his cheeks. He felt around for his weapon, which he had leaned against the wall next to him as he sat. He found it, gripped the cold metal and held it tightly, knowing it was his only lifeline.

Even that felt futile.

He slowly turned, squaring his shoulders toward the direction he knew the doorway to be in. He had to do this completely silently, completely in the dark. If there was any chance this creature could not see his thermal signature, perhaps it was as blind now as Vladimir. That might give Vlad the slight edge he needed to get back down to the caverns safely.

He sniffed quietly, then sucked in a breath. He had his mission now, his goal. He had little experience in matters of war, but he was a good student. He needed to keep his objective front and center, to move toward his men and commanding officer with as much speed and stealth as possible. The only way they could possibly win against whatever they were fighting was to do it together.

With one careful, precarious step, Vladimir began his arduous journey back down the hallway toward the cavern.

CHAPTER 27
ZACK

ZACHARY BENNETT NEEDED to get away, perhaps on vacation to a beach somewhere far away from Russia. He wanted a break, to relax for the first time since...

He couldn't remember when. He was driving around Moscow, heading to a restaurant in a shopping district he and Ember had frequented back when they were dating.

He missed her most of all. Their split had been hard on him, compounded by his isolation and the constant barrage of work-related nuisances.

Some of these nuisances were morphing into full-fledged problems. Victor's team had left for the Kodar Mountains far sooner than he would have liked — sooner than he had told Victor to leave. Likely because the man was finally willing to play by Zack's rules and wanted to please him.

Whatever the reason, Zack had been surprised to discover that Victor had left almost a day earlier than they had discussed, taking a small group of men with him to investigate what might exist at the national park research facility.

He parked the old car in an empty spot near the restaurant when his phone vibrated. He picked it up, noticing that it was a number he didn't recognize, local. He pressed to answer the call and lifted it to his ear. "This is Zack Bennett."

"Bennett, it's Igor Schwartz."

Schwartz was one of the security men who had worked for Venelov Manufacturing. Zack had confided in him early on while working in and around the labs and facilities, and their paths had crossed enough for Zack to eventually come to trust the man. Ex-military, the security employee was like Zack's eyes and ears when he wasn't around. He was an ally working inside Venelov. Russian politics was a new game for Zack, one that required stealth over strategy. Schwartz, German but born and raised in Russia, was a master at this game.

"Schwartz," Zack replied. "Good to hear from you." Zack felt a sigh of relief as some of the anxiety subsided. He suddenly felt less isolated — was he that lonely? He wanted nothing more than for Schwartz to invite him to get a beer. Hell, he would drive across the city to do it.

"Wish I was calling about good news, Zack," Schwartz began. Zack's heart sank once more, and he gripped the phone tighter. *"I've heard about some maneuverings that may interest you."*

"Maneuverings? Government?"

One of Zack's major battles was with the Russian government — not necessarily in working *with* them but in keeping the right information *from* them. The Russians weren't as tightly wound as their Chinese neighbors, but the heads of state here in Moscow enjoyed having access to the flow of information. They preferred keeping their privilege of knowledge to themselves, and any Russian company allowed to do business in the nation and on their soil was required to have a good rapport with their closest government agency oversight agency.

Venelov, a shrewd man himself, had done his best to maintain the facade that Venelov Manufacturing dealt only in farming tools, equipment, and chemicals. But it didn't take a genius to see that the massive profits Venelov had reinvested into research and development had gone into chemicals and products quite unrelated to farming and agriculture. It was these research facilities that Venelov had established over the years, all around the world, that needed to be watched carefully in order to prevent prying eyes from discovering their existence — or worse, their reason for existing.

Government types — overt agency personnel and spies alike — trawled the country trying to uncover any organizations or companies working against the Kremlin. Subterfuge of any sort was not allowed and was punishable by death.

Venelov himself had 'disappeared' certain employees for their lackadaisical efforts to keep their research hidden. The man had been paranoid, but he had no choice. This plan required getting to the finish line — half measures would not do.

It seemed Zack had adopted some of this paranoia after Venelov's death. Or maybe he was wired this way all along and just had never experienced the extreme pressures required to surface it.

"Military, actually," came the reply. Schwartz's voice was cool, smooth, his Russian having no hint of a German accent. Zack had picked up the language quickly, even thinking and dreaming in Russian now. *"I heard there's an Army detachment that's been deployed to the Kodor mountain range."*

Zack's blood ran cold. *That's where Victor is headed.* "Why? Why there, specifically?" Zack hoped it would just be a fluke, a coincidence.

But Venelov had taught him the mistake of trusting too heavily in coincidence.

"Seems there was a post on some forum — some scientific community, I guess."

Zack knew what the man would say even before he finished.

"I guess there's a research facility there run by some backwater office of the government. No idea what they're studying, or how many personnel they have, but seems like one of the scientists asked for help identifying the effects of some chemical stuff."

"I see."

"Gotta be honest — this seemed like it was right up your alley. What with the chemistry nerd stuff and all."

"Yes, this is definitely something I need to be aware of. Thank you, Schwartz."

"I couldn't get any information about the size of the detachment deployed, or if this went any higher in government or not. Chances are this is just a little scout troop sent out to do some investigation before the higher-ups file a report."

"Who told you about it?" Zack asked, curious.

"No one told me," Schwartz said, *"it's just sort of a hobby of mine... A*

talent, *if you will. I see one thing and then another, and my subconscious makes the connection. It's as simple as that."*

Zack frowned. Nothing was ever 'as simple as that,' but he knew better than to pry. *Gift horse in the mouth and all that,* he thought.

Surprisingly, Schwartz laughed, then continued. *"I've got a friend of a friend who was deployed there, actually. Pulled off their cushy patrol duty and sent to the corner of the country, posthaste. Seems to think it was a bit strange, so I did some digging around. That's when I made the connection — the ones who sent the patrol of Army personnel are the same ones who claim to control this research facility."*

Zack frowned. This was new information. And it *had* to be connected — he just didn't know how.

He thanked Schwartz, ending the call and leaning back in his seat.

He needed to make another call; one he had been putting off for some time.

CHAPTER 28

VICTOR

THE PAIR HADN'T MADE it as far as the stairs before Victor heard footsteps again. He stopped Ortega at the stairwell, his eyes darting left and right, looking for any cover the place might offer. But this stairwell was like the others they had come down, save for the one that featured a closet to the right. It was narrow and low-ceilinged, the walls made of concrete. No design features had been added, not so much as a nook to duck behind or a soffit to use as an obstruction.

In other words, they were sitting ducks.

The footsteps were moving quickly, the person in a hurry. Victor and Ortega simultaneously pushed their fingers over their rifle's safeties, wanting to be ready for anything.

While it could be one of the Russian soldiers come looking for his friend, Victor wanted to believe it was one of his men.

But then, that would mean...

It was one of his men. *Only* one.

Garcia rounded the staircase and stopped on the landing between the two subterranean levels. He looked up, the dim, single bulb hanging above them the only light. Long shadows cast his body off in all directions, strange angles. He looked like a character from a film noir, his eyes looking sunken, hollow...

And he was absolutely terrified.

"B — boss," he stammered, "Perez... he's..."

Victor lowered his rifle and held out a hand. "It's okay, brother. Slow down."

As he spoke, Ortega began descending the stairs towards Garcia, rifle at the ready as he rounded the corner. Suddenly, Garcia reached his hand out and grabbed Ortega. "No!" he shouted.

Ortega jumped back, startled by the volume of his teammate's voice. "What the hell, Garcia?"

Victor stepped forward. "Where's Perez? Are there any other Russian soldiers still alive?"

Garcia swallowed. He shook his head. "It wasn't... it wasn't Russian soldiers."

"But we heard gunshots. They were yours?" Ortega asked.

Garcia nodded again. He started walking up the stairs again, his head dancing to the side as if looking over his shoulder. Something had the guy completely freaked.

Once Garcia was on the top level where Victor waited, he seemed to relax a little. His eyes were still frantic, moving quickly, surveying their surroundings every second. Waiting for something.

"It came out of nowhere," Garcia whispered. "Something... I don't even know how to — "

He lurched forward, nearly falling, but Ortega was there. He held up their partner, steadying him.

Victor frowned. He was acting like the Russian soldier they'd met in the same corridor. He seemed confused, wild-eyed, unsure.

Victor wanted to smack the guy, to get him to focus and deliver whatever words he was trying to form. Instead, he waited as patiently as possible for his team member to explain.

Finally, he regrouped. "It wasn't... the Russians."

"You're *sure*?" Victor asked. "You didn't see them? We heard gunfire."

"Something... I don't know what... took Perez. One second we were walking down the corridor — it's another one just like this one, but with a lot more doors. Laboratory rooms and chambers, that sort of thing."

"I don't understand," Ortega said. "Who were you shooting at if it wasn't the Russians?"

Garcia steeled himself again, as if holding back a bout of nausea. He shook his head, swallowing. "No, I don't — I don't think so. We... there was *something* in one of the rooms. It was dark, pitch black in there. We heard it moving, and — "

"Heard *what*? What sound did it make?"

"Some kind of animal, I don't know," Garcia said. "We heard it bumping against tables and chairs, knocking things over. It was huffing a lot, like it was having a hard time breathing."

"So you just started shooting at it?" Victor asked.

"Perez went first. Just poked his head in. I stood by the door. The lights weren't working in there for some reason; maybe it knocked them out."

"This thing was tall enough to knock lights off the ceiling?" Ortega asked.

Garcia looked pained. "I don't *know*," he emphasized. "It just — we were standing near the door, Perez a little bit in front of me, and then everything went quiet. We waited; I even held my breath, counted to four. And then... Perez was gone. Just... disappeared."

"Keep going. How do you know he was gone?"

"Before it happened, we had our flashlights on, tight beam. We were making little arcs around the room, trying to figure out what made the noise. My light swept over it for a split second, and it just... disappeared from view as soon as it was in the light. I kept moving it, trying to find it again, but I heard Perez next to me yelp, then the sound of air."

"Air?" Ortega asked.

Garcia nodded, tears in his eyes now. "Yes, *air*. Like... *whoosh*. And he was gone."

Victor didn't believe what he was hearing, but he let his man continue.

"That's when I started firing. I put some rounds straight forward before I realized what I was doing, before switching to single-fire. I thought I saw it — nothing but a giant shadow in front of me then — so I fired twice more. I — I don't know if I hit him, but I didn't want to. I didn't want to hit Perez."

"Did you hear anything after that? Did he scream? Call out for help? How do you know he wasn't just playing tricks on you?"

Garcia glared at Ortega.

Ortega put his hands up, palms out. "Okay, okay. Sorry, just had to ask. I believe you."

I don't, Victor thought, his frown darkening, but he kept his mouth shut. It seemed his man was afflicted by the same strange thing that had affected the Russian. Something had both of them spooked.

He shook his head. He hated superstitions — they always led one astray.

"I've never seen anything like it," Garcia continued. The wave of nausea seemed to have passed, but he was now looking down at his hand. A tiny pinprick of blood was on his wrist, and he picked at it. "It was so fast, one second in front of my light at the other side of the room, and then all of a sudden, it was directly in front of me. Smelled like rotting flesh, like death. I — I didn't even see it happen, I just... sensed it. Felt it. After I fired three rounds, my nerves got the best of me. I started running. Made it all the way down the corridor before I heard anything again."

Victor's eyebrows rose. This was interesting information. "You heard something else?"

"Can't be sure exactly, but it sounded like voices. Like someone... whispering."

Victor let out a breath. He smiled. "I understand." He reached out and patted Garcia's shoulder, comforting him. "You're in shock. It happens — it was dark, weird, and they caught you off guard."

Both Ortega and Garcia stared at their commander.

"It's obvious, isn't it?" he continued, laughing now. "These Russians — they're playing with us. Taunting us. I think it's time we go and have a chat with our friend in the room back there."

Ortega pondered for a moment, then nodded.

Victor felt satisfied that they had reached the bottom of the situation, and he led the way down the corridor to the room they had left earlier, where the Russian waited inside.

But he got the sense that Garcia wasn't buying his interpretation of the events. The white shock of terror was displayed openly on his face, as if he had seen a ghost. Before they reached the door, Garcia grabbed

Victor's elbow and pulled him aside. He spoke in a low whisper, his eyes still crazed.

Victor frowned, looking at his man. "What is it?"

"I know you don't believe me, but..." his voice trailed off.

Victor urged him on. "But *what*? What is it?"

"It's just... you're wrong, and I'm afraid there's only one way to prove it to you."

CHAPTER 29
ZACK

"COME ON, PICK UP," Zack muttered as he looked down at his phone. After thirty seconds with no response, he hung up and tried again.

Again, there was no answer.

Frustrated, he ended the call and slapped the phone down. He hadn't left his car since arriving at the restaurant. After his call with Schwartz, Zack had contacted one of his contractors back in the States. The man slept all day and worked all night, so he knew he would be awake. It was possible Zack could have done enough research on his own, but it was uncomfortable working in the driver's seat of his vehicle. Plus, his contractor could work much faster in front of his wide bank of monitors.

It hadn't taken the man long to confirm everything Schwartz had told Zack — there was a Russian contingent headed to the Kodar Mountains, if they weren't already there. The man had passed along the official orders to Zack as well, hacked from a private military network — and Zack had read them while on the call.

Details were sparse, but that seemed to be no coincidence. Somehow, the Russian military was also interested in whatever was taking place at this science facility. He had his man do a little more research on the facility, digging up anything he could find about it. Unfortunately, the contractor had not been able to find anything Zack didn't already know.

It was a research facility established long before the national park had grown up around it, and the area was patrolled by park rangers and a part-time security force. The facility itself had a skeleton crew when it was active, but no one knew if research was still being conducted at the base or if it had been abandoned decades ago.

He had ended the call and immediately sent Ember Clarke a text message.

> *Ben might be in danger. Call me, please.*

He knew his ex-girlfriend was his best hope at contacting his older brother — they never answered their cell phones anyway, and both his and Julie's had gone straight to voicemail.

He feared the worst, that Ben and his group had journeyed to Russia once more, eventually getting into contact with Dr. Lucia Vergotti, the scientist who had posted on the forum asking for their help.

If she told them about the research station...

Zack shook his head, not wanting to admit to himself the truth. He knew his brother — he knew him to be hardheaded, stubborn.

He had joked that Julie was even more so. This was a group that had been successful in uncovering conspiracies and plots all around the world; why should this be any different?

He couldn't convince himself otherwise: he knew his brother well enough to know that Harvey was either on his way to Russia right now, or already at the facility.

They could be walking into a trap, marching right into the Russians' hands.

The phone vibrated next to him, and he snatched it up quickly. He didn't bother looking at the number, pressing to accept the call. He put it up to his ear and heard her voice immediately.

"Zack?"

His heart fluttered, and his breath fell faster. It was really her. "Ember, hey, I just want — "

"What do you mean, Ben's in trouble?" she interrupted.

He squeezed his eyes shut. *Of course* she wasn't calling to make up, to ask him to apologize so they could continue where they had left off.

Of course she was still upset about his betrayal, even though she didn't understand...

Of course she wasn't calling to try to understand. This wasn't about them.

"Ember, you need to contact them. If they're planning to come to Russia, they're — "

"What do you know?" she demanded.

Zack almost smiled in spite of himself. This was certainly the girl he had come to know and love. She was shrewd, trained in the dark arts of killing, espionage, and intelligence gathering. She wouldn't budge, wouldn't give an inch. If she wanted to extract information from him without giving him any, that's exactly what she would do.

And he wasn't going to fight it.

"Ember, they might be in danger. The Russian military knows about the research station in the Kodar Mountains. They're sending a team there. They might already be there."

There was a long pause. He wondered if it had worked — if Ember had been caught off guard by his admission that there even *was* a research station. Did that mean she already knew about it as well?

"Okay," she said. *"Keep talking."*

He breathed a sigh of relief. At least she hadn't hung up on him. "Look, I've got reason to believe the Russian army sent a group out to investigate. To poke around this weird little research base. I don't even know what they were studying there, but if the CSO guys are planning to come, you need to call it off."

Another long pause. *"I can't just 'call it off', Zack,"* she said. *"We've got reason to believe you've got your fingers in the research station as well."*

"I don't; I swear, Ember. You have to — "

"What? Believe *you?"*

He sighed. He should have seen that one coming. "I mean you have to trust me when I say I don't know why this place is suddenly a hotbed of activity. We are still testing the first round of Venelov product, and — "

"And Venelov Manufacturing chemicals are being used in that region," Ember finished.

Zack frowned. *How did she know that? Is she just guessing?* He didn't feel like playing games, however. "Yes," he said softly. "I know for a fact the chemicals are safe, that they won't harm the environment. Ember, I'm a microbiologist, remember? This is what I *do*. It's what I've always done."

"You used to be a scientist, Zack. Not a terrorist."

"Terrorist? Ember, you've got to be kidding. I know you don't understand the full breadth of all of this, but — "

Ember screamed. *"Then tell me, Zack! Tell me now! You had all the time in the world to tell me before, to tell all of us. To try to prove to us that you weren't working with the terrorists to try to affect population growth. Tell me that's not true!"*

Zack paused. How could he tell her that wasn't true? Sure, it wasn't the full truth, but it was the ugliest part of the truth. "Ember, I can't explain it all right now, but trust me. I will — I *want* to. Can we meet in person?"

"You know I can't set foot in Russia," she said.

"Ember, you're... you're something else. You know what you are as much as anybody. If you wanted to sneak into the country, you could do it."

"Zack, you know the risks. Don't even try to tell me it's worth it. You know what they do to people like me there. If I'm caught..."

"You *have* to stop Ben and Julie," he pleaded.

"As much as I want to help you — if only to help them — I can't. My hands are tied, Zack. And I don't think I need to remind you that all of this is your fault. If you want to make it right, make it right. You go fix it. You're there, aren't you?"

"Moscow," he mumbled.

"And there's no target on your head. You're free to move about the country. I suggest you do exactly that. Go help Harvey. Get him out alive, and then we'll talk."

He was about to protest, about to argue, but the line disconnected.

Still, what would he have said? What argument could he possibly make? He smacked his head backward on the headrest harder than he'd intended. He rubbed at the sore spot and reflected.

She was right, of course. She was right about all of it.

CHAPTER 30
BEN

THE WALLS SEEMED to roll and move as they walked past. Nearly microscopic fissures acted as pores where water seeped out, trickling down the concrete and hitting the floor where it mysteriously disappeared into another invisible crack. Hairline fractures surrounded him on all sides as Ben pushed his group forward.

After discussing it a bit more, the team had decided on a plan that everyone seemed satisfied with. It was simple, and perhaps elegant in its simplicity: they would stick together, no matter what.

After descending yet another set of stairs into the third subterranean level beneath the surface, the CSO team, walking side-by-side in two pairs of two with Reggie running point, reached the third floor and found the space even more constricting than the upper two levels.

Ben nearly had to stoop, and Reggie and Freddie, a hair taller than him, actually did. He trudged behind Freddy and Lucia, walking by Julie. Reggie led the team, holding his newfound sniper rifle.

It seemed these corridors acted as hallways to stairwells rather than hallways intended to house offices and rooms. While there was a room at either end of this corridor, the entire rest of the length of the concrete chute featured no doors or windows. It was as if the builders of this place had dug a stairwell, run a length of concrete to frame the walls, ceiling, and floor, and then dug another stairwell at the opposite end.

Ben wondered if by building this way it balanced the structure a bit, helping with the integrity of the cavern system and caves around them.

He shuddered as he thought of the caves — he hated tight spaces. He wasn't exactly claustrophobic, but having had one too many bad experiences in such places, he preferred to be above ground and outside.

While technically a facility, the space they were traversing now seemed no better than a cave. A water drop hit the top of his head, reinforcing the thought.

He was holding hands with Julie, but neither spoke as they followed behind Freddie and Lucia. Julie seemed as equally amused by their conversation as Ben.

"So you've been, a scientist for a while?" Freddy asked Lucia.

Lucia nodded and answered quickly. "Yes — ever since I was little. I mean, I've always wanted to be a scientist, since I was little."

Ben glanced at Julie, who had a huge smile on her face. It seemed the pair in front of them had reverted back to high school versions of themselves — the butterflies of a crush growing inside them.

Seems like our boy Freddy has a thing for Ms. Vergotti, Ben thought.

"And you've always been a..." Lucia wasn't sure what to say.

Ben listened to Freddy stumble over the words. "Uh, soldier," the younger man said. "I mean, that's technically what you call someone in the Army. I don't mean I'm a soldier like... uh, like a *macho* guy or anything."

Lucia looked up at the huge man, repeating the word slowly. "What is ma-cho?" she asked. "This sounds like an Italian word."

Ben couldn't help but smile.

"I mean, my old man was military, and both his dad and grandfather before him," Freddy continued. "It was sort of like going into the family business."

Lucia continued their slow walk, looking up at the bigger man as he spoke quietly. "I enlisted after high school, after 9/11."

Up ahead, Reggie held up a fist, and the group stopped. Ben heard voices spilling out from the room at the end of the corridor. Beyond this room, Ben saw the other stairwell, leading deeper beneath the surface. *How deep does this place go?* he thought. *How many levels do we have to search?*

The voices were English, two distinct males. It seemed they were arguing about something, yet their voices were hushed. *Scared?*

Ben released Julie's hand and walked over to his friend at the front of the line. Neither man spoke, each already knowing the plan. Ben and Reggie had worked together so often now that they were like one mind.

Reggie gave Ben a nod, though he saw a hint of trepidation in his friend's eyes. He was the only one armed, but it was a sniper rifle. It would be effective close range, but far more difficult to aim. Bigger, slower, and while it packed a punch, Ben would have preferred for his friend to have something lighter and capable of putting a lot of rounds through at once.

They would have the element of surprise on their side, but if the two men inside were armed...

Or if there were more than just two people inside...

Ben rushed forward, Reggie following suit. He ran through the door, knowing their best bet was to take them by surprise. He had to believe these men wouldn't just shoot before taking stock of the situation.

Still, he held his hands up as he ran in. "Don't shoot!" he shouted.

Both men whirled around and stared, wide-eyed, at the newcomers. Both men were armed, assault rifles slung over their shoulders. Ben felt Reggie's presence behind him, holding the rifle out to his left, aimed at the two men.

"Who the hell are you?" the man on the right — slightly older — asked. He had dark curly hair, cut short over a furrowed brow. His ears were small, his face round. He probably stood a head shorter than Ben, shorter even than the man next to him.

Both men wore packs, belts with gear clipped to them, and held weapons. Ben saw both also had a sidearm — some sort of pistol — on their sides.

The man to his left looked younger, but Ben knew it was a trick his eyes were playing. The man had steely gray eyes that seemed to assess everything in an instant. Specks of gray shot out from his wavy hair, hinting at his age.

"I'm — " Ben cut himself off. *Good question,* he thought. *Who are we pretending to be?*

Ben hadn't thought they would run into hostile forces — or even anyone armed beyond a security guard or two. He had assumed this place was a research station only, one staffed by nothing but scientists, researchers, employees.

The assault rifles swung around in the men's hands, reminding Ben that he and the others had just stumbled onto something going on here beyond benign research.

The younger-looking man frowned. "Do you not *know* who you are?" he asked, the beginnings of a smirk on his face. His eyes remained passive, calculating. "Let's start with names. My name is Victor. Who might you be?"

Ben swallowed. Next to him, Reggie stepped forward and answered for him. "We are here to figure out what the hell's going on in this place."

"Seems like we have similar goals, in that case," Victor said. "This is my man Ortega, and behind us on the bed is Garcia."

Ben hadn't even noticed the third man in the room. His eyes shot over to the corner, where a dark shadow shifted on the bottom rack of a bunk bed. He was seated on the mattress, looking straight down at the floor, rocking quietly back and forth.

"Name's Ben," he said. "This is my man, Gareth — "

Victor cut him off. "Gareth Red — but you go by 'Reggie,' right?"

Ben couldn't help it. His mouth fell open. *They know who we are?*

"Yes, I know you. Or, rather, I know *of* you. You are the team that gets themselves into quite a bit of trouble. What is it? Civilian Special Operations?"

CHAPTER 31
ZACK

ZACK WAS EXHAUSTED. After a day of flights, haggling over car rental options, and driving another 200 miles, he was able to get into the national park without more fuss. He pulled up to a narrow, flat valley slightly sloping down towards the river. The road he had come in on was hardly more than a hard-packed path, trodden only by the vehicles of whoever worked at this facility. Even then, it seemed no one had traversed this route for months. Grass grew up through the frosty ground, making it difficult for him to tell where the road ended, and the forest began at some points.

As much as he had wanted to rush in and figure out if his brother was already here, Zack knew caution was in order. He could already see the tops of two black vehicles parked near the massive pile of boulders. Individual buildings seemed to poke out from between the boulders as if the facility had been built directly into the rock itself.

He frowned as he slowed the vehicle, taking in the surroundings. A destroyed structure sat far in the distance on his left, still smoking from an explosion. There had been some sort of fight, some sort of battle here. He shuddered as he let his mind collect the evidence. All evidence suggested his brother was in trouble.

"Please don't be here," he willed out loud.

He had wanted to keep the Civilian Special Operations far enough away from his work with Venelov Manufacturing in order to finish the job. There was no way to explain the full picture to anyone unless he had completed the job. He knew his brother was uncannily good at piecing together individual components of the larger puzzle, and that was the very success the CSO also enjoyed. As such, they were the biggest threat to his progress, to his success. *If they stop us before we finish,* he remembered thinking, *all of this will be for naught.*

He looked around at the devastation now, and remembered the devastation — and death — at Venelov Manufacturing headquarters. *Was it worth it?*

He knew it wasn't his fault the Russian military had sent an army patrol here, likely the cause of the explosion nearby. But he couldn't help but feel responsible for anything that had befallen his brother or his team.

I didn't want any harm to come to them...

He had worked hard to ensure the CSO would only be sidelined temporarily. Media cycles followed a narrative until it was no longer profitable, until the unsuspecting public latched onto the new topic du jour. *"Sweetheart Civilian Group Goes Bad"* was just such a narrative — one that had all the underpinnings of being a media darling for a time but also one harmless enough that Ben and his friends could resume their work in short order, eventually returning to the good graces of the US government and military organizations that had previously supported them.

Besides, even if they no longer wanted to support them, they had always existed at arm's length from the government. Ben had set up the company in such a way that there was enough plausible deniability for any trouble the group might get into.

When Zack had first learned of the organization, he had been stunned and surprised at his brother's wit and strategic thinking. His brother certainly wasn't dumb, but he lacked the brainiac cerebral skills Zack and his mother had. He took after their dad, Johnson Bennett, more of a rough-and-tumble 'shoot first, ask questions later' sort of guy.

He assumed Ben had had help setting up the CSO and the organizational administration. Surely Julie would have played a large role in this, but he also knew that Ben and the others had a silent benefactor, someone they rarely talked about. Perhaps this person was the real one pulling the strings?

Thoughts of his brother, his wife and their new daughter, and the others associated with Ben's group bombarded Zack's mind as he tried to focus on the present. He wasn't sure what he would do if harm had come to his brother's team. It wasn't fair that they were involved in this, even though they were the ones who had poked their noses in the first place.

He parked the rental car, which was somehow a worse ride than even his old beater, next to another vehicle he discovered. The car was parked oblong near a thin line of boulders that stretched about ten feet high, separating this spot from the other two SUVs. He noticed that it was large enough to be able to support potentially seven or eight adults. Was this the ride the CSO group had come in on? Did this mean they were already inside?

At the thought of going inside, he glanced up as he exited the vehicle. The cold mountain air hit him first, causing a chill that started at the back of his neck and ran down his spine. He was ill-prepared for this in every way. He had not packed specific clothing, had no weapon, and no plan of attack.

And if he had to defend himself, what did he hope to do? Flail his arms wildly to scare them away?

Another memory played at the back of his mind, causing pain.

His father, his older brother Harvey. Camping. Zack was nine years old. The bear and its cub somehow ended up on opposite sides of Zack. He had stumbled into the woods, on a trip with their family, reckless and curious, just like the bear cub next to him.

A gunshot, the loud crack deafening his senses and dulling his reflexes. Zack remembered the fear, the palpitations as his heart seemed to rise in his throat. He couldn't tell why until it was almost too late.

And then his father stepped in between him and the mama bear.

Zack shook his head, not wanting to resurrect these long-dead memories.

He swallowed, steeling himself. There was no reason to suspect foul play here. He tried to remind himself that anything could have caused the explosion — chemicals, ignited fuel, someone messing around.

He saw a door, a stone pathway hewn from the rock leading up to it. Was this the main entrance of the facility? He had read that it had taken an enormous amount of excavation to create this base, but the plans and blueprints had been long since lost, likely never having been uploaded to any server in the first place since the place had been built so long ago.

In addition, there was an ancient cave system beneath his feet, deep down in the mountain, sharing a water source with the very river that lay 200 paces to his right, downhill. He wondered if the space had been situated here purposefully, not just out of the way from prying eyes but also because of the natural resource of the open caverns down below. He wondered if it stretched from the surface all the way to the caves, if they had used the structure of the caverns as a foundation for the facility.

He approached the door, surprised to see it standing half-open. He had to force it open further, realizing that the frame had shifted on its hinges over the years, becoming stuck if he pushed far enough back.

He entered, pulling it all the way closed and hearing the latch click before turning around to see what exactly he had just walked into. He checked the handle, satisfied that it was still unlocked — the last thing he wanted was to be stuck down here with an unknown enemy force in an unknown facility.

He let out a breath, letting his eyes adjust. As he took one step forward over debris and clutter, he looked up and saw searingly bright lights above his head. They buzzed, the long fluorescent bulbs casting eerie shadows around the room.

He shook his head, laughing to himself. "Get a hold of yourself, man," he said. "You're a grown-ass man. You're a Bennett. Act like one."

And that was when he saw the two men standing quietly in the corner of the room.

CHAPTER 32
VLADIMIR

NOTHING WOULD STOP HIM NOW. Not humans, not animals.

Vladimir ran like his life depended on it — because it did. He had first tried pushing back toward the caverns, where the rest of his team and commanding officer waited. The new patrol would be sent by now, and he had intended to intercept them, hoping their numbers would bolster his courage.

He had made progress, moving slowly, trying to stay against the wall, out of trepidation for what lay inside one of these rooms — and he had almost reached the end of the corridor.

There, the hallway lurched ninety degrees to the right, where it terminated in a concrete archway that led to the open maw of the caverns beyond. His men were there; he had even heard them in the distance, their voices and laughter echoing all the way to his ears. They were only a quarter-kilometer beyond the archway, just around the bend.

But he had not made it that far. As he approached the end of the hallway, one final door was open on his left. Vladimir had felt around, gripping the edge of the door frame with his exposed fingers. They were shaking with fear, uncontrollable.

And that's when he had heard it.

A low, guttural groan. A growl.

It sounded like a cat, if the cat were the size of a cow. It vibrated the hallway, vibrated him.

He shook with a new intensity, literally hearing his teeth rattling together.

He had backed away from the doorway slowly, not wanting to be anywhere near the open doorway any longer but also not wanting to call attention to himself.

Had the beast known he was there?

Whatever it was, he knew it was the same thing that had killed his comrades.

He had swallowed, closed his eyes, and tried to pretend he was somewhere else. In this manner, he had backed the entire way through the hallway, coming once again to the stairwell on the opposite side.

That's when he had turned and made a run for it. He raced up the stairs, taking them three at a time, exiting on the shallow, narrow hallway above, nearly hitting his head as he jumped over the landing. He picked up his pace in the long straightaway, hit the other stairs, and reached the next level.

He raced in this way toward the top of the facility, breathing a sigh of relief when the lights leveled out, and he found himself on solid ground high *above* the level the beast had been on.

Still, he didn't slow down. He knew there was no creature chasing him, knew there was nothing at all behind him, but he was done.

He wanted out. They could punish him if they wanted, remove him from active duty or even kick him out of the Army altogether.

He no longer cared.

Vladimir was going to leave this facility, no matter what.

As he raced down this hallway, he passed a room on his right. He heard more voices emanating from it.

He didn't slow down, breezing past them without even glancing toward the door.

He was at the other end of the hallway, ready to climb the set of stairs before he heard their voices. They had left the room, no doubt startled by the crazed Russian soldier sprinting as fast as possible up and down the hallways.

He reached the top floor, only then realizing that he was out of breath, still shaking but now with the tremors of exhaustion. He felt like he had aged ten years in the past ten minutes. Vladimir pushed the images of the creature he now knew he had seen out of his mind, still not wanting to believe they were real.

But he had heard it. He knew the sound was from the beast itself, from the monster.

On the top level, he stepped over the fallen debris and clutter, finally seeing the doorway that led out. His friend had driven one of the SUVs parked outside, and he knew the man had left the keys inside the vehicle in the console.

He aimed for the door, having slowed to a walk, already working through the route that would lead him far away from this place. He was thinking of the nearest town, trying to remember what it was called, imagining the bumpy dirt road that led out of the park to the small place, when he noticed movement. He stopped, his heart rate accelerating. He frowned, squinting at the corner of the room where he had seen movement.

He let out a breath as he realized he was in no danger. It was just one of his comrades from the patrol.

He stepped forward, and Vladimir saw that his counterpart was covered with blood. Was it his own? He thought he saw ragged scrapes and wounds on the man's face, but in the darkness and with black liquid covering his entire body, it was hard to tell.

The man's eyes were wide, ghost white. He stepped forward still, coming further into the bright light of the room. No longer camouflaged against the dark wall, Vladimir was able to assess his fellow soldier. He seemed to be okay, obviously shaken. He knew what this man had seen — he, too, had seen it.

But unlike Vladimir, this man had been attacked. Vladimir saw the claw marks, the ripped clothing where the beast had burrowed its claws into his stomach and flesh, where they had scraped away cloth and Kevlar and skin and muscle. He assessed the soldier quickly, trying to lean on his training. He was no medic, but they were all equipped to clean a few wounds and get their teammates back into the fray.

This was far more than just a few wounds, however. Vladimir didn't need to remind the man of this fact. He stumbled, falling to one knee. Vladimir rushed forward and tried to help him to the ground.

"Sit," Vladimir said, before he could help himself. He felt a sudden bitterness. He was *this close* to getting away, of escaping this hell, but he couldn't leave this man behind. They were not friends, but he knew him well. Seven years older, a career military man, this man would not want to leave before their mission was complete.

No matter, Vladimir thought. *I'm leaving with or without you.*

The man's eyes examined Vladimir, seeming to know this. "I can't help you," Vladimir whispered.

The man shook his head, saying nothing.

Only then did Vladimir notice the semi-coagulated blood gushing from the soldier's side. The gash was deepest here, and he saw three massive claw marks running from his rib cage down to his thigh.

This man was going to die, and it would happen very soon.

CHAPTER 33

BEN

"HOW DO you know who we are?" Reggie asked.

Victor's smile grew.

From what Ben could tell, it seemed genuine yet playful. Ben frowned as Julie, Freddie, and Lucia Vergotti funneled into the room behind them. He shifted, moving shoulder to shoulder with Reggie to form a protective barrier.

"Intel, my friend," Victor said, his eyes widening. "So there *are* more of you. I knew you all liked to travel in packs, but I can't blame you for that — safety in numbers, right?"

Ben's hackles were raised. He was poised for attack — either to attack these two men or to be attacked by them. That his wife — the mother of his child — was standing directly behind him and was equally as unarmed as he was, did not make him feel any better.

Reggie's sniper rifle suddenly felt worthless next to him. He knew the ex-Army sniper was as capable a man as there had ever been with the weapon, but they weren't long-range. On the contrary, he wondered if Reggie would even be able to lift the thing and get off a shot before these two men — clearly trained operatives — fired their own weapons at them.

More than enough firepower to make mincemeat out of him, his family, and his team.

"How do you know who we are?" Ben asked again, letting a little bit of growl come into his deep, threatening tone.

Victor waved it off. "Don't worry; we are all on the same team here. I consider it my job to know who I'm working with or against."

Ben noticed the man didn't specify which of the two the CSO group fell into.

"I studied your exploits on the way here," Victor continued. "Heard of you before that, though. Seems you're quite intimately familiar with my employer."

Ben squinted through one eye at Victor.

"Yes, he confirmed everything we found. Much of what's been written publicly about you is just a media narrative, I presume?"

Julie spoke from behind Ben. "You work for Zachary Bennett?" she asked.

Victor's eyes lit up, and he craned his neck to try to see the smaller woman behind them. Ben didn't budge to make it easier.

"You must be Juliette Richardson Bennett," Victor said. "Julie? Or Jules?"

"Only to those I'm familiar with," she said, biting off her words.

Victor backed away in mock fear. "My apologies. I assure you, we're not here to hurt you or your team. We are surprised to see you here, though I guess it makes sense. You seem to have a knack for being in the right place at the right time. Certainly a knack for intelligence gathering. I suppose it shouldn't be surprising at all that you would end up here, in this backwater corner of Russia, investigating what Lucia Vergotti found online."

Ben tensed more. This man was operating from the exact same information they had, it seemed. Proof that he was most likely telling the truth — that he *did* work for his kid brother.

Of course, Zack was no kid now. While Ben still thought of his younger brother — 10 years his junior — as a kid, Zack was clearly an adult. He had proven to be mature enough to embark on a full-fledged smear campaign against Ben's company, one he had helped build from the ground up. An organization he took pride in.

Zack was university educated, trained and tested with years of experience in microbiology, chemistry, and related fields, and had proven to be nothing short of brilliant when it came to his own unique brand of entrepreneurship.

So he should not have been surprised at all that Zack would hire a private security team.

"He sent you here to do his dirty work, didn't he?" Reggie asked, stepping closer to Victor and Ortega. The third man in the room had not moved from his spot on the bed, though he had looked over at the team as they entered. Ben and Reggie pressed to the side, allowing the three others to gather behind them. They were all in the room now, and Ben appreciated that he and his team were still closest to the open doorway, with Victor and Ortega pressed against the opposite wall.

He intended to keep it that way.

"I'm not sure this is 'dirty work,'" Ortega said, still gripping his assault rifle, though it was no longer aimed at them. "Victor and I were sent here to poke around, just like you."

"And yet armed to the teeth," Reggie added.

Victor shrugged. "'Be prepared,' right?"

Ben couldn't help himself. He chuckled. "Yeah... a phrase I wish I would have paid more attention to over the years."

Victor returned the laugh, suddenly stepping forward. He let his assault rifle fall back to his side, held to his shoulder on its strap. He walked across the room, his arm outstretched.

Victor still wore the smile, though his eyes gave nothing away. Was this man playing them? Was he trying to coerce them into thinking he was on their side? He believed this man was in charge of the mercenary crew his brother had hired. This only intensified Ben's fears as to whether or not this man was going to be outwardly hostile toward them. Surely, Zack hadn't told this man to just kill his own brother and sister-in-law and the rest of their team.

Still, Ben couldn't help but be wary. He had experienced too much over the years to suggest this man was harmless.

Just then, he felt a hand on his arm. *Julie.* It immediately calmed him and reassured him. He trusted her above all else. If she felt safe here, he would lean into that faith and at least reciprocate.

For now.

He stretched out his hand, and the two met a few feet away from where Ben had been standing. They shook, neither trying to crush the other's hand in a show of power.

The concrete room groaned from some unknown pressure down below.

"I hope we can get off on the right foot," Victor said.

Ben didn't reply, though he was no longer scowling down at the shorter man. The time for trying to intimidate one another was over. This was diplomacy now, one group trying to suss out what the other was able to offer — or what the other was hiding.

"You know as well as I do places like this are fraught with surprises," Victor continued. "I hope you will forgive our intensity. You were a surprise to us, as much as I'm sure we were to you."

Ben nodded once. "I think we can work it out."

Freddie flashed a glance at him, and Ben noticed Reggie was also staring at him from the opposite side. Neither man seemed upset by his admission of willingness to cooperate, but more that Ben had been the one to offer it. In the world of subterfuge, mercenary hostility, and conspiracy theories, olive branches were not often part of Ben's game plan.

But he thought of Julie, and of Hope. Of their commitment to sticking together. He felt as though they had turned over a new leaf, established a new MO.

"Glad to hear it," Victor said, his smile wide. Ortega walked over as well now, shaking Reggie and then Freddie's hands. Julie and Lucia stepped forward as introductions were made. Ben kept a wary eye on the men's assault rifles, but now that they were in close proximity and the rifles were pointed to the ground, slung over their shoulders, he felt his team would have the upper hand if things got hairy. He trusted Freddie and Reggie with weapons, but he trusted them even more in closer engagements.

"Your brother sent us here," Victor said. "I've been running his security team for the last few months. Mostly protection in person; bodyguard-type stuff. But he seems to have developed a somewhat paranoid air lately, no doubt due to what he's been working on."

Ben listened intently. Did this man know more about what Zack was working on than he did?

"I'm not sure exactly what he's gotten himself into," Victor continued. "You understand, this really isn't part of our purview. We just... *follow orders.*"

The last of the sentence was clipped, cut off, and Ben thought he detected a hint of bitterness in his voice. Was this man someone who felt relegated to a corner? Someone with career aspirations that had been stunted because of his choice to become paramilitary?

"I can assure you, he's always had that paranoid air," Julie said, smiling.

Victor chuckled. "Very well, it seems he's acting according to his personality then. However," Victor frowned, "I must say, I'm not quite sure exactly what we are looking for here. This place has been a hotbed of activity of late, yet I have no idea why. I'm sure you heard the gunshots earlier?"

Ben and Reggie nodded profusely.

"Russians. Army."

The CSO team exchanged glances.

Victor cocked his head to the side and looked at Ortega as he explained. "Yeah, surprised us as well. Whatever's here — or down *there* — it's apparently worth the Russian military getting involved. From what we can tell, it seems to be about a dozen men."

Ben watched Victor's eyes, saw the flicker as he gave the number. "From what you can tell? How do you know — were those your gunshots?"

"Well..." Victor paused, regaining his composure. "My men's gunshots. We're missing one." He turned and faced the man shaking on the bed. "He's the other. We also took fire outside, leaving our fifth man up above. He's injured, so providing recon and communications, though naturally we've been cut off since we entered the base."

"I see," Ben said, taking it all in. "And these Russians — you don't know why they're here?"

Ortega glanced from his partner to Ben and back again. "They seem to be investigating, like we are. Came through the door up above, but I believe the facility backs up to a deep cave system, where they are now."

Ben nodded. "That tracks with what we know as well. Can I ask —

what's up with him?" Ben tossed a thumb to the man seated on the bed. "Shell shocked?"

Ortega let out a low whistle. "In a sense, yeah," he said. "But he's claiming it's something else. Something he saw."

Victor shook his head and offered a small smile. "My men are afraid of monsters, I'm afraid."

Ortega didn't look convinced, and Ben wondered if this was what they had been arguing about before they'd entered the room. "He — he's not like this. Not ever. Whatever he saw..."

Victor was about to respond when Julie cut him off. "What was that?" Everyone turned to look at her, but she was looking out of the hallway toward the nearest set of stairs. "It was a person — they..."

Ben marched to the door, Victor by his side. Together they peered out of the room and looked both ways. Ben heard the footsteps of the man now, noticed how quickly they were moving.

He turned the other way and saw the back of a thin young man sprinting toward the opposite stairs. He carried an assault rifle, but Ben couldn't see the details of it.

Whoever he is, he's in a hurry.

"Is it Perez?" Ortega asked.

Victor shook his head. "No, but let's go check it out."

Ortega pushed through the group, but eventually the entire CSO team and Victor's man joined Ben and Victor in the hallway.

"He just disappeared up the stairs on the other side," Ben said. "He's moving up, and fast. I want to catch him before he gets outside."

Victor and Ortega were already in motion, so Ben followed suit.

This day was getting stranger by the second.

CHAPTER 34
ZACK

ZACK PLACED his hands behind his head, his elbows out. He stepped fully into the room; the door already closed behind him. "Who — who are you?" He stammered.

One man to his left was covered in blood. Scrapes, scratches, and bruises littered his face and any open skin Zack could see. His shirt was tattered, crusted with dried blood.

He had been attacked. Was it the second man in the room who had done it?

He turned to the second man, the one holding an assault rifle and pointing it at Zack's front. It shook in his hands. Was it fear? Adrenaline? Something else?

Neither man responded. The injured man seemed to wobble a bit, then swallowed and caught his balance. Zack kept his eyes glued to the biggest threat in the room — the man pointing a gun at him.

He tried again, this time in Russian. "Who are you?"

"Army."

Zack made a face. *Well, I guess I should have expected a response like that,* he thought. "Why are you here?"

The man didn't answer, instead flashing a glance at the other person. Zack noticed now they wore the same clothing — dark fatigues. The man holding the gun at him seemed uninjured, his uniform intact. He eyed the guy — no more than a kid, rail thin, tufts of pants sticking out the tops of his black combat boots. He wore the insignia of the Russian army, a symbol Zack had come to know well when he was in Russia.

It wasn't a surprise that they were here — Schwartz had told him as much. But he didn't know *why* they were here now. To his knowledge, this place had been staffed by researchers and employees of the government, and security was provided by Kodar National Park. He hadn't seen a ranger or park employee the entire route from the town to this place.

He knew the government had intended to keep it hidden, but that was par for the course with the Russian government. They tried to keep *everything* secret — anything could be used against their enemies, and therefore was important enough to keep hidden from prying eyes.

But that didn't mean a docile research station like this one should have Army personnel patrolling inside. And it certainly didn't mean they should be attacking each other.

"Who did this to him?" Zack asked, taking a different tack. "Was it you?"

The man's eyes widened slightly. It was exactly what he was looking for. He had caught him off guard, caused him to start thinking of the downsides of insubordination. If this kid thought Zack was in some position of power, he could easily turn him into his commanding officer for reprimand.

"Nyet," he said. "It was…"

The man's eyes flicked to the side once more, fear settling in them. They stayed wide, and Zack frowned. "It was *what*?"

The man shook his head quickly.

"I'm not here to harm anyone," Zack said, stepping another foot into the room. The man's grip on his rifle tightened, but Zack still had his hands above his head. He did his best to look un-intimidating. Vulnerable and innocent.

Still, one wrong move and the man could spook and pull the trigger. At this range, it would be certain death.

"I'm just here to investigate the research facility down below," Zack said, noticing the stairs behind the Russian Army soldier. "You're here doing your job," he continued in Russian. "Just following orders, right?"

The man wasn't sure what to make of that. His eyes danced.

"And those orders are probably to protect this place from anyone who might come snooping around," Zack continued. "People like me. But I assure you, you've got nothing to fear from me."

The soldier squinted at Zack, and he knew he needed to play a card that would buy him some credibility. "Who's your ranking officer here? I might know him. I certainly know who he's working for."

Zack rattled off a list of names as quickly as possible, both real and made up. But the last one he spoke was the name of an actual colonel he had gotten to know during his dealings with Venelov manufacturing.

A colonel who had political aspirations, and was now sitting in a high seat of power in the Russian Ministry of Natural Resources and Environment.

It was a gamble, but Zack had no other option. He needed this man to trust him, and he needed him to trust him immediately. He certainly did not want to be shot.

He had put two and two together — that this army contingent had been sent here to investigate the same thing Zack had sent Victor's team to investigate. They were curious, but otherwise, they had no idea what was happening here as well. But they would have done their homework, or at least been given orders from someone who had. This place was part of the national park — if not officially, at least on paper. That meant they would answer, ultimately, to the Ministry of Environment.

And that meant there was a chance this young man knew the name Zack had uttered last.

The man's eyes stretched so wide Zack thought they might pop out. The kid repeated the name.

Zack nodded, offering a kind smile. "Yes. You were sent here by him, ultimately. Just like I was. I'm a scientist — a microbiologist and chemist, and I'm here to test the very thing that you guys are looking for."

At this, the man to Zack's left reeled. He made a noise that sounded to Zack like the bleating of a pig, and blood dripped from the corner of his mouth. He stumbled forward, coming toward Zack.

Zack acted involuntarily. He reached out, pushing against the man as his blood-soaked arms reached him.

The man was grappling with him, trying to wrestle him to the ground. He heard the man grunting. "Nyet, nyet."

What the hell is this about?

Zack tried to keep the other soldier in his peripheral vision as he wrestled with the blood-covered trooper. He suddenly felt the barrel of a rifle in his gut. He heard the word, the single command. "Stand."

For a kid, the guy's voice was deeper than Zack would have expected. He had found some sort of confidence, had steeled himself against whatever it was terrifying both these soldiers.

Zack complied, standing straighter and facing the soldier once more. Now the guy had a point-blank shot directly into his chest. A single shot would kill him instantly.

"I'm not — I was just trying to — "

Zack wasn't sure what he could say to convince these Russians he was not here to harm anyone. What had he said that had caused the other man to go off like that?

The man covered in blood coughed and spat out a mouthful of bile. He cleared his throat, then wiped his mouth with the back of his wrist. Finally, he stood up to his full height, a head taller than Zack and the other younger man. It was clear he was in pain, and Zack watched his eyes. They rolled back and forth separately, a strange tic.

Zack watched his mouth as he finally spoke intelligible words.

"No one goes down there," he said.

CHAPTER 35
ZACK

"GET DOWN ON YOUR KNEES," the young soldier said.

Zack watched with fascination as the young man seemed to morph before his eyes. Before, he was a young, thin man with a boyish figure, and he seemed to swell up, as if someone were inflating him. His face hardened, his features changed to one of expressionless stoicism.

"Why are you here?" the young man boomed.

"I — I told you," he said. "The colonel sent me. I work for — "

"National Parks is part of the Ministry of Environment," the kid said. The battered, swollen man to Zack's left seemed to be nodding and shaking his head at the same time. "But this facility is now under direct orders of the Russian Federation Army."

Zack squeezed his eyes shut. *Of course.* This facility would not be kept under National Parks. Just because the *land* was part of the park did not mean the *facility* followed suit — especially if there was military-focused research taking place here. Besides that, as soon as this base became a hotbed, of course this place would have immediately come under the Russian Army's purview. As soon as the military got wind of something interesting happening here, it would have been passed off to the military to investigate. Anything that could be used as a potential weapon, scientific or otherwise...

"Listen, I — "

The kid brought the butt of his rifle down against Zack's skull. It wasn't intended to be a killing blow, but it knocked Zack to the side, spinning him around and depositing him face-first on the floor. He groaned in agony, feeling two of his back teeth loosen. Blood sprinkled out from between his lips. He pulled himself up, trying once again to reach his knees. The second Russian soldier loomed over him, fists ready for another blow. He was reeling, trying to stay balanced.

Just then, Zack heard commotion outside the door behind the younger Russian.

Voices.

He heard footsteps pounding up the stairs. He squinted, trying to see in the dim light who it was.

The Russian soldier in front of him didn't move. Zack suspected he knew it was more of his comrades, come up to see what the fuss was.

Zack squeezed his eyes shut, then waited, anticipating the blow.

It didn't come.

"Zack?"

Zack heard a man's voice, and his eyes darted open. He looked up, craning his neck to see around the larger Russian soldier.

"Ben?" Zack asked, incredulously.

Standing in the doorway, side-by-side with his best friend, Reggie, was Zachary Bennett's brother, Harvey.

Zack pulled himself up to his feet, not getting any pushback from either Russian soldier. They seemed to be as stunned as he was, and the younger Russian whirled around and started toward the door.

The injured Russian soldier suddenly fell backward, hitting the wall and crashing to the floor. No one moved to help him, and he stayed on the floor, his eyes still moving around wildly.

Reggie pulled up a long, sick-looking rifle and pointed it directly at the Russian's head. "I wouldn't recommend that," he snarled.

The young Russian stopped. Reggie motioned down toward the kid's rifle, and he finally sighed and let the assault rifle clatter to the ground. Then Ben rushed forward and pushed the Russian out of the way, grabbing Zack by the arm. He yanked him back toward the wall right next to the door.

"Zack — what the hell are you doing here?" Ben snapped.

Zack felt the weight of the emotions. His brother was still alive —

the rest of his team appeared to be so as well — and yet he was here, meddling in the Russians' affairs. Was he working with them?

"Don't make me ask you again, little brother."

Zack swallowed, suddenly sneering. He looked up at his taller, older brother. "Stop with the antics," he said, his voice slow and calm. "You think this is all a game, something you can change. You don't even know what you're doing here, do you?"

Ben's mouth opened, likely to reprimand or insult him again, but then he snapped it shut. Zack saw the sudden shakiness on his face, the same fear he had seen the day their father had been mauled by the bear.

"That's what I thought," Zack whispered.

The others filed into the room. Reggie and another man Zack didn't recognize corralled the Russian soldier to join his comrade in the corner of the room. A woman followed Julie into the room. Zack was about to speak again when he noticed another face he recognized.

His head snapped to the side. "Victor? Is this your man, Ortega? What are you two doing here? Are you working with the CSO?"

Victor seemed frozen in place for a second, likely trying to determine how best to handle the situation. He looked around the room, his eyes landing on each individual before speaking. "It seems all of our interests are finally aligned," he said. "I doubt introductions need to be made — it seems the only unknown variables are your two Russian friends here."

Zack noticed the two Russians in the side of the room watching the interchange. The broken man had started bleeding again, and he was dabbing his face with a piece of crumpled paper he had grabbed off the floor. He sat in a chair that Freddie had turned over for him while the other younger Russian stood to the side.

"They're... Russian Army," Zack said, addressing Victor but raising his voice loud enough for the others to hear. "I just got here. I was trying to figure out what was going on here as well, but they — "

The Russian soldier shot a threatening look toward him. Zack ignored it, repeating his question. "Are you working with them?"

Victor chuckled, then shook his head. "No, we're still in the dark about why the Russians are here and what they're looking for. Seems both of them were pretty spooked, though. We were about to investigate why, but one of them ran past us and headed upstairs. Seems like you got here just in time."

"I was trying to escape," the younger Russian spoke in his native language.

Zack translated quickly, then asked him a question. "Trying to escape from what?" He turned to the Russian soldier.

Before he could answer, a thunderous rattling sound began shaking the room they were all standing in. Concrete cracked, dust and debris and droplets of water spraying from fissures above his head. Zack looked up, pulling his hands up over his head again.

This place is going to collapse on our heads.

Instead, the rattling stopped a second later.

"Explosion," Reggie said quickly. "From down below. What the hell are you guys into?"

He directed the question at the Russian soldiers, but neither of them understood. Reggie walked over to the door leading outside, pushing on it. It opened just a slit, letting in bright daylight. He pushed with everything he had, but it didn't move any farther. He then turned and faced the rest of the group.

"Whatever that explosion was, it sealed this place up tight," Reggie said.

CHAPTER 36

FREDDIE

"WELL, THIS IS AWKWARD," Reggie muttered. He stood by Freddie, who was watching the scene unfold from by the door.

Freddie had been mildly amused upon reaching this top level once more and finding Zachary Bennett inside.

He was less surprised to see the Russians — at this point, they all knew there were other people in the facility.

The only people here who spoke Russian were Zack, Lucia, and the Russians themselves. Zack had been translating for all of them, so he assumed Victor and his other man, Ortega, were just as in the dark about the conversation taking place as he was.

"Awkward or not, we can all work together," Victor said.

A few looked toward Victor in surprise, but Ben and Reggie kept their faces passive. Freddie watched their group's leader as he stood by his brother at the front door. After the door had been sealed shut, Ben had released his brother's arm but remained close enough not to let the younger man escape.

He tried to sense what Ben was feeling. The leader of the CSO group had always done a good job keeping his emotions close to his chest. He had always done a good job keeping his thoughts inside. But then he was not known as a stoic; since Freddie had met him, he had seen on more than one occasion Ben's face twist into a sign of whatever emotion he was feeling.

It wasn't that he was overtly emotional; it was just that he was easy to read.

Harvey Bennett had a strong sense of justice — for better or worse. The trouble with people like Ben was that justice was not something passed down to him by authority. It was justice developed and honed internally, passed up into existence by his own mind.

It was Harvey Bennett's brand of justice. Freddie had recognized early on that Ben was one of the good guys — it was why he had joined the CSO in the first place. He disliked the inefficiencies of military life, disliked the sometimes incredible gap of time between when a threat was recognized and when resources were deployed. The CSO was small, agile. It was able to make change happen quickly.

And it helped that Freddie agreed with Ben's sense of justice and morality.

There were dangers, risks, but either purposefully or not, Ben had structured the group in such a way that his word was not law. His wife and best friend — hell, even Freddie himself — had just as much say in what they did as Ben did.

And he agreed with Ben now, as well. They needed to find out what was going on here. The need to explore the facility. There was a reason Zack sent his own mercenaries here, and a reason why the Russian government had sent their army to investigate. Whatever those reasons were, they lay beneath their feet on one of the subterranean levels.

They hadn't asked Victor if they had explored the level below the one on which they had met, so Freddie assumed that was where they would head next.

"It's not like we can go outside and regroup, anyway," Ben said, his voice a mere rumble. "Whatever that explosion was, it sealed us in tight."

"There's another exit," Zack said.

Ben glared at him. "That cave could be miles away."

Zack nodded. "Doesn't seem like we have any other option."

Heads around the room nodded. Freddie noticed that the two Russian soldiers stood still, unmoving. Their faces were a mask — the younger one simply controlling his emotions, the other covered in blood enough so that his emotions couldn't be seen easily. Whether they understood English or not, they didn't show it.

"What about... what about what happened to him?" Lucia asked meekly.

Freddie turned to the small woman behind him and examined her features, her expression. Was it fear? Trepidation?

"We never got the chance to ask," Ben said. He marched over to the younger man but called back to Zack. "I'll ask you to translate again, little brother."

Zack didn't respond. Ben then addressed the Russian soldier, "This guy over here — what happened to him? Those scratches and cuts, what are they from?"

Zack translated the words as quickly as they fell out of Ben's mouth. There was a long pause, and the younger Russian soldier looked at his partner a few times, as if to gauge whether or not he should respond at all. Finally, he uttered a single sentence.

Zack translated. "There is something downstairs."

Reggie chuckled. "Now that is *news we can use*." He stepped even closer to the Russian soldier, ignoring the young man's balled fists at his side. Freddie eyed the man's rifle that had fallen to the ground, but the Russian didn't make a move for it.

"Care to be more specific than that?" Ben asked.

Again, Zack translated, and the Russian answered, "He says it's some sort of beast. A monster, specifically."

"A monster?" Ben asked.

"Probably a bear or something," Reggie said.

Freddie noticed Ben's eyes flick upward at Reggie when he said the word 'bear.'

Then, Ben turned his head and examined the wounded soldier's body. "This doesn't look like a bear. It's... it's not the way a bear would attack."

Lucia stepped closer to Freddie and spoke, "He's right — I'm no expert, but a bear would attack to kill. It might maul him at first, but it would eventually go for the throat or eyes."

The young Russian soldier seemed to go white as a sheet. He spoke a few words.

All eyes drifted to Zack, but Freddie listened as Lucia whispered the translation next to him. "Not a bear."

Ben frowned, but Reggie suddenly shouted. Freddie watched as the tall, thin teammate scrambled across five feet of debris on the concrete floor. He was all arms and legs, his expression wild.

Ben stepped back in surprise, and Freddie realized what had happened.

The injured soldier, assumed by everyone in the room to be harmless, had suddenly sprung forward and grabbed the assault rifle laying at his partner's feet. Even the young Russian soldier was shocked, nearly stepping on the other man's hands. Reggie reached him first, tackling the Russian soldier out of the way, but the wounded army man retreated just as quickly, sitting in the chair again, now holding the assault rifle.

Freddie started toward the man as well, trying to put as much of his body between the end of his assault rifle and the others standing behind him. He watched as the rifle began to rise in the Russian's hands, his face still darkened with huge swaths of blood.

But he wasn't turning the rifle toward anyone else in the room. Instead, he held the stock awkwardly, his finger stretching up toward...

"No!" a voice shouted from behind him. It was Victor or Ortega. It was repeated by Julie, but Freddie still didn't turn. He looked on as the shot rang out, deafening in the small concrete space.

Freddie couldn't move fast enough to bring his hands over his ears to drown out the reverberating echoes. And there was no way to cover his eyes.

The single shot had removed half of the Russian's skull. More blood splattered the wall behind him and the ceiling above his head. Next to him, Lucia pulled a hand over her mouth, her eyes wide and tears welling.

The young Russian soldier that had been tackled by Reggie began to stand, in a daze. Ben allowed him to move back toward Zack against the wall.

Freddie and the others stood motionless in the room. His ears were finally returning to normal.

The only sound was the dripping of blood from the slumped corpse against the wall.

CHAPTER 37
LUCIA

LUCIA STARED, shell-shocked, as the dead man finally keeled over and fell, half his head missing, to the hard floor. Everyone in the room stared silently for what seemed like an eternity.

Finally, the Russian soldier spoke. Zack translated. "He said he would rather die before going back downstairs."

The Russian kid was looking down at his partner, his mouth half-open. He mumbled a few more words. "Whatever is down there was enough to cause him to do this."

"Whatever is down there is enough for *me* to want to leave," Reggie said.

"Yes," Ben said. "Whatever this is, we are not prepared for it. But we can't get back outside this way anyway. We need to find out what's down there if only to move through the facility and find another exit."

"Ben, it's — "

"What? Insane? Sure. But we're trapped in this place anyway, and something down there is killing people. If it's a bear, we'll kill it. If it's something else, we'll kill it."

Lucia watched as Reggie squinted at Ben, staring at him strangely. The man started walking over toward Ben, still holding the sniper rifle in his left hand, the barrel pointed down. With his right hand, he held it up in a gesture of surrender. "Brother, let's just take a minute and figure this out. We can talk it out, just like we did before."

No one else spoke.

"I know with your... history and all; it's probably difficult to — "

Ben's eyes suddenly glared with an intensity that caused Reggie to stop. Lucia wasn't sure what had triggered this response, but Ben steeled himself, his fists balling, stepping up toward his friend. "*What about* my history?" he snarled.

"Hey, buddy, it's me, Reggie." He snapped twice. "Don't forget that I *know* you." He turned and looked at Lucia, at Freddie and Julie. "We *all* know you. We're with you, man. But..."

Julie spoke next. "Ben, Reggie's right. If we're dealing with a bear, even some sort of genetically modified one, it's probably best if — "

"If *what*?" Ben snapped. "If I don't go down there because my old man was murdered by a bear? Because my brother..." Ben's voice had ratcheted up a few decibels, then dropped toward the end of the sentence. He seemed to sway on his feet, suddenly appearing woozy. His eyes blinked a few times, trying to re-center themselves in his skull.

Finally, Ben cleared his throat and continued. "This is *not* about the bear. It's not about whatever it is down there. It's about what it means." He turned and walked back over to where Zachary Bennett leaned against the front wall. "It's about what *he* did."

Zack's eyes widened. "*I* didn't do this!" he shouted. "I had nothing to do with — "

"You worked with him! You knew everything he was doing because you were his henchman. You studied all of this bullshit for him."

She knew from her conversations with Ben's group they were talking about Jakob Venelov, the lead of Venelov Manufacturing. She remembered what he had done, what the CSO had tried to stop.

Zachary had told them that it was too late, that Venelov's agricultural and farming chemicals were already being distributed to early testers on farms around Russia.

She knew that a large region targeted by Zack for early testing was no less than twenty miles away from their current location. They had chosen it because of its unique ecology: the taiga forest met with permafrost, and yet the ancient Char Sands nearby offered one of the world's smallest deserts. It was an environmental petri dish, the perfect place to attempt to test whether or not Venelov's wheat product could grow crops even in a strange climate such as this.

And yet, something about it didn't make sense to her.

As Zack and Ben argued, she stepped forward. Eventually, both men stopped and looked at her. Meekly, she spoke, "I don't understand how Zack's product, how the Venelov Manufacturing product, could affect anything here," she said. "I assumed that it would have something to do with the groundwater, that this slime mold you added to the wheat product somehow penetrated the soil and got down to these subterranean levels."

Ben frowned, but Zack nodded. He offered her a kind smile. "That's exactly right — over time, the product *can* leach into the soil just like any other chemical. Trace amounts will start to be evident in six months, a year. But my tests proved that none of this is *detrimental* to the soil, much less plant or animal life. On the contrary, it will bolster the wheat crop it's applied to. We'll be able to grow food for populations where agriculture was never possible in this way."

"Yeah, but Venelov wanted to be the one in charge of *who* got to grow that crop," Reggie muttered.

Lucia shook her head. "That's not the point. Yes, that's terrible — it's population control in the worst way."

She saw Freddie and Reggie look back to Zack as if she had just proved their point.

"But what I'm confused about is that it hasn't *been* six months to a year," she continued. "It's been *days*. Weeks at the most. Right?"

Zack nodded. "Shipments began a few weeks ago, so we expect the crop in this region to only have been affected by the product maybe a few days ago."

"That's what has me confused. That's hardly enough time for it to penetrate deep into the soil, and much less be noticed by the environmental flags the researchers would have been watching for. That's a six-month cycle, minimum."

She noticed Julie's and Ben's eyes widening at the revelation. Julie spoke. "So whatever we are all here for — whatever the Russian government is worried about, and whatever Lucia saw and posted about on that forum — it's *not* because of Venelov Manufacturing. At least not the wheat production chemicals."

A moment passed. Finally, after a few seconds, Ben spoke again. "She's right. It can't be. At least not directly related to the wheat Zack and Venelov were working on."

Lucia saw that Victor and Ortega looked just as confused as everyone else, but Victor stood straighter and cleared his throat. "Perhaps this was not related to wheat at all," he said. All eyes turned to him. "I mean, sure, we are all here because we *assume* my boss was wrapped up in Venelov Manufacturing and trying to control the world's wheat population."

Zack glared at his subordinate, his hired gun.

Victor shrugged. "What? I'm good at my job. I do research, too. Besides, none of that is really a secret anymore, correct?"

Zack's cheeks flushed with rage at the subtle accusation, but he nodded. "You're not wrong, technically."

"Fine," Victor continued. "But Venelov Manufacturing doesn't just make products for wheat production, correct?" He waited for a few nods. "From what I gather, your old boss was heavily invested in chemicals of *all* sorts. Wheat wasn't his passion — finding a new way to grow food was. Wheat, and all the products required to produce it, from the seed to the fertilizer to the testing kits for the soil itself — was just a science experiment for him."

Ben turned and walked over to Victor, and the others pulled in a bit closer. Lucia noticed the young Russian soldier glancing around at the faces as they spoke. If she had to guess, the kid didn't speak English very well or at all. He had no idea what they were all talking about.

"What are you getting at, Victor?" Ben asked.

"Nothing specific, not yet," he replied. "Just a hypothesis. But this place is a research base. They were studying something, obviously. Whatever posting got us all here, whatever captured our attention, it originated from this place. Your scientific envoy, Lucia Vergotti, made the connection that it was somehow related to Venelov Manufacturing. But we just determined that it couldn't be related to Jakob Venelov's goal to grow *wheat*. That would be impossible at this time."

Lucia suddenly understood the line of reasoning Victor was following. "He's right," she said quickly. "I guess that was Venelov Manufacturing because of the flags we found in the soil. But Zack confirmed that they hadn't even *begun* attempting to grow the wheat product here until only a few days ago. At least growing it with the slime mold-enhanced product."

"But you said there were trace amounts of their chemicals in the soil?" Julie asked.

She nodded. "Yes, exactly. That means what we saw was not from Venelov product in wheat fertilizer or seed, but in something else."

"I don't understand," Zack said. "What else could it be?"

"You'll have to tell us," she said. "But a research station like this would have plenty of chemicals inside. It depends on what they were studying, but they would also have to have a way to flush those chemicals. To purge them from the internal systems of the infrastructure here."

"You mean drainage?" Ben asked.

She looked at the CSO leader. "Yes, precisely. They would have a drain somewhere here, perhaps multiple. Just like any other building, only this one would be pump-controlled, since it's underground. But that pump would carry everything up and out of the research station. And if I had to guess — no offense to the Russians in the room — but one of the issues we've had for a long time in this country is the lack of environmental planning during construction projects.

"Meaning I would bet a *lot* of money that the drain pumps anything and everything right out into the lake nearby."

Freddie smacked his head and nodded. "Of *course*," he said. "They're dumping a bunch of goo into the river. Some of that goo is getting sent downstream, leaching into the fields nearby. The exact same fields — "

"The exact same fields where Venelov and Zack were going to try growing some wheat," Ben said.

CHAPTER 38
ZACK

"IT'S POSSIBLE," Zack said.

All eyes in the room were on him now. He felt uneasy and shaky. This wasn't the same anxiety he had been feeling for the last few weeks — the stress of work, overload, and fear. This was something new, something he hadn't expected.

In truth, it was the very fact that he had not expected new information here that caused him almost to panic. He tried to swallow, found his throat completely dry. He forced down whatever was there, the lump that wouldn't go away. It didn't work. Instead, he felt more anxious than ever, the tingling appearing in his hands and feet until his whole body was wracked with nerves.

If what Lucia said was true...

"What do you mean it's *possible*?" Julie asked him. "You mean it's possible that the research team here was leeching something into the countryside?"

"That much we can be sure about," Zack said. "Because you're right. There's not so much as a worry about pollution in places like this. The government would have set up this research station with one purpose in mind — to study whatever it is they were studying here. Aside from the fact that this place was probably built decades ago when environmental concerns were not even a twinkle in their eye, pollution and harming ecological life would still be the furthest thing from their mind."

"What about Venelov Manufacturing products specifically?" Ben asked. "Lucia made the leap of logic from discovering that *something* around here was changing environmental factors to that something being Venelov chemicals. Why would she think that?"

Zack looked at Lucia, who responded to Ben's question. "As I said, Venelov Manufacturing probably makes all sorts of things that have nothing to do with fertilizing wheat crops," she began. "I made the connection because I knew you all were looking for Zachary Bennett because of his connection with Venelov. My assumptions were based on simply finding strange chemical markers where they shouldn't be that were no doubt human-caused."

"That's what I meant when I said it's possible," Zack said softly, trying to force his hands to stop shaking. "We know Venelov does produce other chemicals. When I started working with Jakob Venelov, he showed me some of the numbers from their R&D wing. I was using some of the chemicals they sold for other applications to produce the trigger switch for the slime mold molecule — the same one you and Julie were trying to figure out how to turn off."

"What other applications?" Julie asked.

Zack shook his head, shrugging as he tried to fumble through an answer. "Hell, it's almost limitless. Any application you can think of — chemicals used in science labs in high schools, all the way up to a special injection fluid used in what will become the newest line of EVA suits for Russian cosmonauts."

"So Venelov Manufacturing is really a chemical company," Reggie said.

"Effectively, yes. I told you before that Venelov's pet project was figuring out the causes and effects of — and solution for — overpopulation. Growing wheat where it never could be grown before was the first phase of his ultimate goal. But all of that was just one small arm of the R&D Venelov Manufacturing was engaged in. They are known as an agricultural chemical company, but that's more for legal and government assignment and organization than anything else. They're just a chemical company, a producer."

"What sorts of chemicals would they have produced that could be used in a lab like this?" Lucia asked. "Specifically, what would they have been using for long enough that it could begin affecting the chemical composition of the soil in the taiga forest nearby?"

Zack waited, trying to figure out the best route toward the answer. It wasn't an easy answer — there were a thousand chemicals he could think of that Venelov Manufacturing may have produced, a thousand things in a lab that he knew Venelov Manufacturing was capable of creating and selling.

But the answer was not simple, either. Because there could be a thousand answers, he didn't know what to say. It was very likely it was only a single chemical that had caused an environmental flag to wave, but he couldn't begin to know which one it was.

"Even if we find it, I thought you said Venelov hadn't started distributing the chemicals until a week ago?" Victor asked. "That would hardly be enough time for the offloading effect of the chemicals to leach into the fields."

Zack nodded but stared at the floor. "Only the wheat-related fertilizers and seed crop product were delivered a week to three weeks ago," he said. "If it was another chemical here, it could have been delivered at any time since Venelov Manufacturing's founding."

"But we highly suspect that this chemical has been contaminated with the slime mold you built," Lucia said. "We can't forget that key component. This whole thing comes back to that slime mold, correct?"

Zack studied the woman's face with keen interest. She was beautiful, with soft features and enough intrigue in her eyes that Zack could tell she was not just intelligent but cunning. He wasn't just looking at a woman with book smarts. This woman had earned street smarts as well, and he could see her trying to put the pieces together as she raced through hypotheses.

"That is correct," he said finally. "I've been careful to ensure the slime mold stayed where it was supposed to be, but as things... accelerated — "

"You mean as Venelov got involved," Ben snapped.

Zack looked at his older brother. "Yes," he emphasized. "As I said, as things accelerated — and after you killed Jakob in the middle of it — we

161

had to ramp up production and push forward the distribution timeline. There's a chance that some of one product got into another, and — "

Next to her, Julie suddenly gasped. Lucia turned and looked at Mrs. Bennett, now pointing at her. "It's the slime mold, isn't it? It's not just capable of being triggered by external forces — light, water, the stuff we discovered last time we were in Russia," she said. "It's also capable of self-replication."

Zack knew where she was going with this and he picked up the thread. "Yes, that's been my fear from the beginning. We needed to create something that could replicate itself under ideal conditions, only so we could increase its range. It would be prohibitively expensive to create all of it we needed in one lab, so we had to give it the ability to replicate just as a mold would in the wild. In fact, it effectively is the same sort of replication a slime mold might use to reproduce itself. A biological specimen has the same mechanisms in place as our artificial one."

"Because it's not entirely artificial at all, right?" Julie asked.

Zack nodded. "Again, that's correct. It was just an artificial mitochondria — that's what you found last time — that we added. Its energy system is artificial, but it is designed to take energy from sources a completely biological slime mold specimen wouldn't be able to use. However, its reproductive system is intact and therefore can replicate freely under ideal conditions."

Zack watched as the CSO group, Victor's men, and the last remaining Russian soldier in the room listened on. Freddie, a man Zack had not met, spoke next. "Do you think the lab downstairs — wherever it may be — had some of these ideal conditions?"

"No," Zack said quickly. "But the lab we created the slime mold in did. And there were an unknowable amount of different products in that same lab. Cross-contamination was not only possible, but probable. When I was there, working alone, I took every precaution. But later..."

"When we came in to ruin your fun," Ben said, with malice in his voice.

Zack ignored him. "Yeah, when I was no longer in the lab but had hired laboratory assistants. Chemical professionals, employees. I guess I should have known contamination was likely. But we can find all that out later. If we get outside, I can go back to one of my remote laboratories in Moscow, and together we can-"

"The only thing we're doing together is figuring out what the hell is downstairs, and what you and your terrorist organization had to do with it."

Zack looked at his brother with an expression of pained disbelief. He did little to hide the fear behind his eyes, the anxiety. Ben could read him like a book.

"This is what you've always tried to hide behind, Zack," Ben said. "You always let other people do the fighting for you. Me, my team, even Ember. You've used us as your personal security force like Ortega and Victor."

Victor shuffled in Zack's peripheral vision as he answered. "No, it's not like that at all," he started.

"Save it," Ben snapped. "The time for hiding behind others is over. The only thing we're doing together is going downstairs," Ben repeated. "You and Lucia will look for clues, anything the scientists left behind. My team and your mercenaries will find whatever it is that's been killing soldiers."

Zack knew he couldn't argue his way out of it. Even Reggie, the one person who seemed to have agreed with Zack early on, was now nodding slowly behind Ben.

"No more hiding, Zack. No more letting other people do the fighting for you."

CHAPTER 39

BEN

THE NEWLY FORMED group consisting of the CSO team, Zack and his hired mercenaries, and the lone Russian soldier, descended the stairs at the back of the room. They walked in silence down the first set of stairs onto the first subterranean level before one of them spoke.

"What do you think caused the explosion?" Victor asked. "The place looks old, and I'm sure the structural integrity is not what it used to be, but it didn't sound like something collapsing."

Next to him, Ortega shook his head. Behind him, Freddie answered. "No, it didn't. If I had to guess, it sounded like a grenade."

"The generator?" Ben asked. He was walking near the middle of the pack, once again holding Julie's hand as they progressed downward. They had left the room upstairs with more questions than answers, but at least they were together, and at least they had a plan.

They would work as a team, all of them, including the Russian man. If he had anything to offer, Zack and Lucia could translate.

Ben turned to the Russian now, walking behind him with Freddie and Lucia near. "Does your team have any explosive devices? Grenades?" he asked.

He waited for Lucia to translate the question. The Russian looked at Lucia, then back at Ben, then nodded. "Yes," she said. "He says there are grenades, some ordnance, whatever that is, and C4."

"The lights are still on, so I'm assuming the generator is still up and running," Ben said. "Is this thing that's been chasing your team something your commanding officer would have told you to blow up?"

Lucia translated, then responded. "He says yes; if the 'monster,' as he's calling it, reached the rest of his team, they would have tried to destroy it. He says he was on patrol with the man who killed himself upstairs. He saw it, in the shadows. Saw what it did to one man."

Ben's blood chilled as he listened. The hair on the back of his neck stood up. He had been in situations before where there was an unknown presence, some sort of animal or man waiting to jump out and end his life.

It gave him only a little bit of hope to know that every one of those times it had been something mundane, something fully explainable. He didn't like terrorists trying to kill him, and he didn't like members of the animal kingdom trying to turn him into food, but at least these were things that could be fully explained without needing to resort to fantasy.

This monster that was terrorizing everyone in the base might be a huge, pissed-off bear, but at least a bear was a known entity.

He thought back to what Freddie had said, what Reggie had said. He remembered the incident well, one of the last times he and his brother had been on speaking terms before Ben had disappeared and begun hopping around national parks in the US as a ranger.

Even more, he remembered the look on his father's face as the bear charged him.

Ben swallowed, inadvertently squeezing Julie's hand tighter. She stopped, slowed, and looked up at him, frowning as she silently asked the question.

"I'm okay," he whispered. "Just want to make sure you get out of this safe and sound."

He knew Julie well enough to know she didn't believe him for a moment. Sure, he wanted her safe...

But he was thinking of himself.

If it *was* a bear they were dealing with, how would he react? How would he respond? Would he freeze up, like he had when he was with his father? Would he wait that one crucial second longer than necessary before fighting back?

And if it was as large a bear as the others seemed to be fearing, what could he do anyway?

Reggie had given the assault rifle to Freddie, and Ben had not argued. He didn't want it in the Russian's hands; he trusted his own team more.

He swallowed again, listening to Lucia's translated words. "He is rightfully confused about why his team would not have simply shot the beast. Any explosives would be in their cache, which they had deposited into one of the rooms near the entrance to the cave system. But their weapons would be on them at all times, as a matter of course. He assumes we should have heard gunshots first, before an explosion."

"So he doesn't think it was a grenade?" Reggie asked.

"He doesn't know. He agrees it *sounded* like a grenade, but has no idea why."

"It doesn't matter," Ben said. "We'll find out soon enough."

He hadn't intended for the words to sound so clipped, so forced. Was he lying to himself? Was he trying to convince himself that this was the right course of action? Sure, they were moving together now, working as one unified team. Even Victor and his men had seemed to fall in line well.

So why was he feeling the unease deep in his stomach then?

CHAPTER 40

VICTOR

"GARCIA SAID there's a Biohazard Safety Level 4 laboratory on the fourth subterranean level," Victor said, leading the group down the corridor on the third level. "It's in shambles, like the rest of this place, probably because of whatever animal we're dealing with. With any luck, it's injured and hiding."

Victor didn't need to say out loud what he feared most. *An injured animal is a dangerous animal,* he thought.

"Have you explored the BSL-4 chamber?" Lucia asked from behind him.

He continued walking down the corridor on the third level as he answered. "No, we didn't have time. We just saw an airlock decontamination chamber and shone our lights through when the overhead lights were off. We didn't want to get stuck somewhere, but I took stock of what sorts of rooms we passed."

"That would be where I would start then," Lucia said. "There's debris everywhere, papers and files from all over the research station littering the hallways. But if I had to guess, the best way to figure out what they were studying down here is to go to the source. If there's any information we can glean, it will be from that lab."

Victor nodded as he led the way. He reached the spot before the stairs where they had run into Garcia. He needed to check on him to see if the man was ready to rejoin the fight or if he needed more time. He had seemed groggy and confused after bumping into them in the stairwell. Originally, he had written it off as fear, but the more he contemplated it, it didn't track with what he knew of the man. Garcia was a hunter, someone who enjoyed the thrill of taking down a huge animal as a trophy. He had a healthy respect for nature's predators, but he would never have been as terrified as he had been when Victor and Ortega found him.

They reached the room with the bunkbeds and desks where Garcia waited, and Victor turned and entered. He still held his assault rifle, and he used the barrel of it to push the door open wider. It was tighter, having shifted after the explosion, though not sealed shut like the one upstairs. He gave it a bit more force until the door was wide enough for him to enter.

He walked into the room, glancing around in confusion.

Ortega was right behind him. "What the hell? Where is he?"

Victor didn't answer. He gripped the assault rifle tighter. The man — and his weapon — were gone.

"I thought you said you had another man down here," Reggie said from behind Victor.

Victor nodded once. "We do — we *did*. He was over in the corner, sitting on the bed. You met him."

"I remember," Reggie muttered. "He was rocking back and forth like a baby. Scared out of his mind."

Victor straightened his back and turned to the others. "No, not *scared*. Considering. He's a hunter, always has been. Used to take two-week vacations with his entire family back in Uruguay, hunting anything they could eat."

Ortega watched him as he spoke.

"He went downstairs," Victor continued, "likely to try to find this thing and bring it down. It would be the perfect trophy for him. He didn't want to wait around for us and took matters into his own hands."

He looked at Harvey Bennett. The CSO man did not seem convinced.

"We're going down there anyway, yes?" Victor asked. "If he is down there, we'll find him. If he somehow snuck back upstairs and hid in one of the rooms we passed, he can't go anywhere. In that case, he can't do anyone any harm. I trust him."

"Fine," Ben said. "Let's keep moving. Whatever this thing is, it's still out there. We haven't heard any gunshots, so your guy hasn't found him either. I don't care if he wants a trophy or just wants revenge; he wants the same thing I do. He wants this thing dead."

Victor watched the scientists — Zachary and Lucia — as Harvey spoke. They both seemed to wince a bit at the mention of killing the beast. He felt the same as Harvey Bennett did — this monster was a threat to him and his team, and it needed to be eliminated. But he also understood Lucia and Zack's point of view: this was a thing to be studied. Even if it was an animal that had broken in, why had it done so much damage to the place? Why had it felt so threatened that it needed to enter every single room, crash around into every file cabinet, table, chair, and piece of furniture in sight, then continue on its way?

A bear, a boar, a wild ox — Victor had no idea what sort of animal life they could expect in this region. He was far from a zoologist, but he figured there were a handful of different large mammals that might react poorly to being caged that could have gotten inside the facility somehow.

However, he didn't know of a single one of them that could do what it had done to the people here.

What *effect* it seemed to have on the people here.

He thought back to the man who had shot himself in the head upstairs. That had been a Russian soldier, likely a good one, a man who would not be easily intimidated by something so simple as a wild animal. The assault rifles they were carrying were plenty capable of taking down even a bear. It would take a few handfuls of rounds unless someone got a lucky hit, but it was still very possible.

No, the man had acted strangely, similar to how Garcia had been acting in this very room. Why? What was it they were all so afraid of? What could scare them to their core so much that they had become different people altogether?

He didn't know of any animal — predator or otherwise — that could cause a complete personality shift.

Whatever it was, Victor knew they were going to find it.

CHAPTER 41
BEN

BEN WANTED to get down to the next level, to investigate the Biosafety Level Four laboratory. He left the room after Victor and Ortega, waiting for Julie, but Zack swiftly joined him in the hall.

"We need to talk," Zack said.

Ben ignored him, finding Julie walking out with Freddie and Lucia.

"I said — "

"I heard you," Ben said. "We'll talk once we figure out what this place is and what this is all about."

"No, we need to talk about what happened before."

Ben stopped in the middle of the hallway near the stairs, turning around quickly and staring down his younger brother. Zack's face registered surprise, his head falling backward and letting his longish brown hair fall over his eyes. He swiped the hair to the side in a practiced motion. Ben had never seen Zack with long hair. Growing up, they had both shared the same haircut: a simple military-style buzz around the sides and sometimes a bit longer on the top.

It was like looking into his own eyes. Ben and Zack both shared features of their mother and father: broad shoulders and lanky, thin frames from their Scandinavian heritage on their father's side. Hair, eyes, and skin from their mother's Mexican-American descent.

Ben had fallen into a life of outdoorsman activities, working at national parks and spending most of his life outside, and his body had thus become strengthened and tanned. However, before meeting Julie at Yellowstone years ago, Ben had rolled into full adulthood with the slowed metabolism that came along for the ride. He had gotten slightly overweight, not pushing his body nearly hard enough to maintain the physique he'd had in his younger days.

Thanks to his years of strenuous training with Reggie and the rest of the CSO, staying fit to do the work required by the group's interests had built him once again into a fine physical specimen.

Zack Bennett was not bad-looking, either. Even though he'd spent his younger days in school, earning advanced degrees and working his mind more than his body, he was in good shape. And in his relationship with Ember Clarke — another person of near-perfect fitness — he had no choice but to work hard to keep up.

Now, both brothers stood shoulder to shoulder, face to face. Ben was half a foot taller than Zack and physically imposing, but Zack didn't back down.

"I know you blame me for all of this," Zack began. "But I just want you to know — "

"*Blame* you for all of this?" Ben stammered. "Blame or not, this *is* all your fault, is it not?"

The others had stopped as well; Victor and Ortega already in the stairwell, but Lucia, Freddie, and Julie were waiting just outside the doorway to the room. Freddie was pulling the Russian soldier along with a firm grip on his upper arm, though the kid hardly looked like he was about to try to make a run for it. The look on his face told Ben he had resigned himself to his fate.

"No, Ben," Zack responded, stressing the first syllable. "You always want things to be so cut and dry. So simple. You blame me for Dad dying, you blame me for you running off and disappearing for ten years, and you blame me for everything that's happening here."

Ben worked his tongue over the inside of his cheek. He shifted his jaw, clenching it and unclenching it. He wanted to argue; he wanted to fight. He was no scientist, no chemist like his brother.

"No, I — " Ben stopped himself. It was his turn to be perplexed. He didn't know what to tell Zack, didn't know how to make his case.

But this *was* Zack's fault. There was something here relating

Venelov Manufacturing and this facility, with whatever it was the scientists had been studying. Zack had something to do with Venelov Manufacturing.

He may not have known about this place, but he knew what Venelov had been planning.

"The past is the past, Zack," Ben said. "But that doesn't mean it's stopped affecting us. You were working with a man who wanted to change the future. That's why we're here, and that's all I care about."

"Listen to yourself, man," Zack said. "When did you become so self-righteous?"

"*Excuse* me?" Ben snapped.

"No, I'm serious. When did you get so high and mighty? You used to be *fun*, the kind of guy who just wanted to be out in the world, experiencing it for what it had to offer. I always looked up to you for that. You were more than just a brother to me, even back then."

Ben didn't know what to say. Unbelievably, unable to stop it, he felt tears coming to his eyes.

Zack continued. "After Dad died, I figured you felt responsible. I understood that you wanted to get away. You never were an angsty teenager, at least not from what I remember. But you hit adulthood way too early because of what happened. Running away made perfect sense at the time. But I expected you to come back. We both did."

Ben turned his head slightly. *Don't go there*, he willed. *Don't talk about her. Not here, not now.*

"You broke her heart, Ben. You were *everything* to her. Mom just wanted to be a family again, just wanted to start healing. But she couldn't do it without you there. *We* couldn't do it without you there."

Ben swallowed, his head falling, his eyes closing. He squeezed back the tears, wishing above all else he could be anywhere else right now. He wanted Zack to stop, to take back everything, to just walk away. Hell, he would even let him. In this moment, he didn't care about making Zack answer for his injustices. He just wanted this all to go away.

And yet... there was something inside of Ben yearning for more. Some closure of a wound he hadn't realized he was still carrying, still open. Seeking closure he hadn't realized he hadn't already found.

Julie was by his side then. He hadn't noticed her walking over. She didn't touch him, just stood there, guarding.

"You have a family now, Ben," Zack continued. "I'm sure you understand even better than I do, now. But you have to know that for years I *blamed* you. Not for Dad, but for Mom. Not just running away from us, but running away from yourself. I think that's what hurt her the most. You ran away from yourself by running away from your own family."

Ben stared straight ahead, over Zack's head and down the dark, dimly-lit hallway.

Zack wasn't lying, but he wasn't completely correct.

And he wasn't wrong, either.

"Zack, let's talk about this later," Julie said suddenly. Her voice was soft, and Ben knew she was doing her best to let both men down easy. She cared for both of them, wanted both of them to put aside their differences.

Zack didn't respond. Instead, he looked up at Ben, waiting. As if asking permission.

Ben felt everyone's eyes around, staring at him, pouring into the back of his head and into his soul. Whatever they were dealing with here was going to wait, apparently. He wondered if even the beast they were looking for was listening, waiting for Ben's response.

"No," Ben said. "Keep going. This is something I need to hear. And it's also something you need to say."

CHAPTER 42
BEN

"MAYBE WE CAN MOVE this back inside?" Reggie asked. He was standing behind Ben, near Victor and Ortega at the stairwell. "We're still, uh, on the clock, if you will."

Ben shook his head. "This won't take long. At least, I don't think so."

Zack confirmed. "I just needed to get that off my chest. I've been wanting to tell you that for a long time, not because you needed it or I need it, but because the universe needed it. For some time now, I've sort of felt that they were looking down at us, waiting for us to have this conversation."

"Zack, I — " Ben started and stopped again. What was he supposed to tell him? Apologize? Accepted Zack's apology? He wasn't even sure if Zack *was* apologizing. He wasn't sure if he was ready to apologize to *him*.

"Don't worry," Zack said, rescuing him. "I don't need you to say anything. I know there's a lot more to this now, about my work with Venelov Manufacturing and the reason we're all here. We'll deal with that as we come to it. But if we're ever going to be able to deal with it appropriately, we needed to clear the air about this first."

Ben nodded, a tear finally making its way out of the corner of his eye and resting on his cheek. He was keenly aware of everyone else staring directly at it.

Still, he didn't dare move his hand to wipe it away. He didn't dare call more attention to it.

"You're my brother," Zack said. "The only family — the only *true* family — I have left. And I'm the only family you have left. That has to mean something, doesn't it?"

Ben didn't respond.

"There's something here that's trying to kill people. Hell, there's a small army of Russian soldiers who might want to kill someone. But I didn't want to step another foot on the stairs until I said my piece."

"Have you?" Ben asked, finally finding words.

"I think so, yeah. It didn't come out as eloquently as it sounded in my head. But... at least I said it."

At this, Ben smiled. "Yeah, I know how that is. We *are* family, after all."

Zack returned the smile. It wavered a bit, falling slightly on one corner, just like Ben's used to do when he was younger. He had the strange sense that he was looking into his own eyes as if he was talking to himself.

And yet, he knew he wasn't. This was a whole person, one entirely different from himself. A completely different life, completely different experiences. He had forgotten that, had ignored the fact that someone so similar to him — and yet someone with completely different aspirations, dreams, and expressions — existed.

"I know this isn't over," Zack said. "I know there's a lot we have to cover before I'll ask you to trust me again."

Ben raised an eyebrow. "Good luck with that."

In an instant, all the anger returned. Betrayal, the memory of what Zack had done, of who he had worked with. Misguided or not, his brother should have been intelligent enough to know what he was getting himself into.

As if reading his mind, Zack continued. "Trust me, I know you have every reason to believe I've betrayed you and your group. That I betrayed my own country. But you have to know that it's not black and white, Ben. It never has been. There's so much here you don't understand — you can't understand."

"Tell us, then," Reggie snapped from behind Ben.

Zack turned and faced Ben's best friend. "No, I can't," he said, shaking his head in resignation. "It's impossible, at least right now. But soon..."

"Yeah, I've heard that one before," Reggie said, rolling his eyes.

Zack returned his gaze to Ben, addressing him directly. "I get that you can't trust me about this either. But this is all part of something so much bigger than anything I can explain in the middle of the hallway. Especially with... whatever it is down there. Let's get back on track. At this point, there's an enemy we know."

"I wouldn't say one we *know*," Ben said. "But I get your point."

Zack nodded. "Thanks. Let's just get down there and figure out what we're dealing with while we're all together. It's our best bet, and it's our best option for convincing the Russian army down there to let us leave."

Ben heard Reggie's neck crack as his friend spoke. "Yeah, easier said than done."

CHAPTER 43

BEN

BEN STEPPED through the doors into the antechamber. It was built like an airlock, just as Victor and Ortega had described. Entering directly from the hallway, Ben walked into the small inset room, taking note of any and all descriptive features the room provided.

There was a door on the other side of the room, but as the room was so small, he could stand in the middle, stretch his arms out to the left and right, and touch both the hallway entrance door and the airlock exit door at the same time. There were some instructions scrawled in red paint on the wall in Russian, a sprayed-on stencil. He heard Zack reading some of the words aloud and saying something about 28 seconds.

Ben understood. This was a decontamination room, a prep station before entering the larger laboratory inside, to ensure that any dangerous bacteria or chemicals wouldn't be able to hitch a ride to the outside world. 28 seconds was probably the amount of time required to stand inside while the spray nozzles up above did their job.

And this tiny room, like almost all of the others they had entered, was also destroyed. Since there were no storage cabinets, shelves, chairs, tables, or anything of that sort inside the small space, it was difficult to see the damage, but it was evident when Ben peered closer.

Thanks to a single square light fixture above their heads, the whole space was bathed in fluorescent yellow. He saw scratch marks on the wall and on the handle that had become detached from the huge metal swinging door leading deeper into the space. The door itself was still mounted to the heavy-duty metal hinge that ran its length from the ceiling to the floor, but one side of the metal had been smashed inward as if something huge had bumped into it.

Ben looked closer at this door as he passed through into the larger laboratory, changing his assessment. It looked like something larger had banged something much smaller into it. The cavity on the door was round, the shape and size of a soccer ball.

Or a human skull.

The disarray inside the larger laboratory space matched that of the other rooms as well, if not worse. Stacks of filing cabinets sat on top of each other in smashed piles, their papers and folders spilling out of every open drawer. One of those drawers lay halfway across the room, underneath a table turned on its side. This table had a missing leg, and a broken laptop sat smashed where the missing leg should have been.

Along the exterior of the room were more tables, some of them miraculously undamaged and still in place. He saw where the researchers in this lab would have worked, sitting facing the walls as they performed whatever experiments were needed.

He saw a broken refrigerator as well; its glass shattered, one door hanging open on a single hinge. It seemed the generator that ran the lights was not keeping the refrigerator cold. There were no lights on inside the appliance.

Next to that was a standing water station, the upturned jug half full of clear liquid. Ben frowned, finding it interesting that a Biosafety Level Four lab would have drinking water, knowing that the people inside would be wearing safety suits and thus not have an easy way to bring a cup of water to their lips.

Zack stepped over. "It's an easy way to provide water for experiments," he said, anticipating Ben's question. "Water is stable, and extremely useful in a laboratory environment, and a great way to dilute solutions to test a chemicals' effects against unknown compounds."

Ben nodded, now looking around the room for any broken vials, beakers, or any scientific-looking apparatus that might contain some such bacteria or chemical. He wanted to make sure they weren't walking into a hellscape of infection, inadvertently breathing in some viral outbreak or some soon-to-be viral outbreak.

Zack was still talking, now explaining the water jug to Reggie, who had made some joke about there being a water fountain in a BSL-4 lab. Ben felt a pang in his heart as Zack's words from upstairs once again echoed through his mind. He thought of his mother, Diana Torres Johnson, and the last moment he had seen her, lying in her bed in her home.

He remembered foolishly reaching out and touching her hand as they said their goodbyes. She had been infected with a virus that had eventually become an outbreak. She had been studying it in a lab not unlike this one, working for a company that Ben had eventually discovered had far more nefarious purposes than just examining the effects of a simple virus. The virus had been inserted into a bacteriophage, artificially producing a compound that was elegant in its chemical and biological makeup but deadly in its practical application.

Ben had always suspected foul play regarding his mother's death. She was a brilliant chemist, meticulous and careful... just like her son Zack ended up becoming. She would never have allowed something like that to spill out onto her skin, or breathe it in.

He had been infected with the same virus, whether from touching her then or from before, at Yellowstone when the outbreak began. He hadn't known it at the time, but his saving grace was that Juliette Richardson, working with the CDC in a newly formed division called Biological Threat Research, had remained by his side the entire time, allowing the virus to replicate to its capacity and overload itself, spreading from one human host to the other and back again until it burned itself out in both systems. That had been the final revelation they had discovered — the deadly virus had been designed to work its way out of the host body *only* when it was placed in contact with other hosts. Isolating individuals and quarantining only led to more death.

Ben had never contemplated it much, had never spent much time dwelling on his mother's death. The past was the past, as he had told himself and Julie over the years, and as he had told Zack upstairs. But over the years, he had finally come to admit to himself the truth: if he and Julie had simply stayed back with her, simply waited by his mother's side, they all would have become infected. But the viral load would have increased to a capacity greater than its ability to maintain itself, and it would have burned itself out, saving their lives.

By leaving her then, he had signed her death warrant.

In a single moment, all the shame, regret, and anger he had felt at different times over the years since her passing returned in full force. Compounding that was the memory of the death of his father, doing his part to protect his sons.

He looked over at his brother, smiling as he and Lucia walked around the room, no doubt feeling like kids in a candy store as they recognized scientific materials and gear and prepared to dive into figuring out what the hell was going on here. They were in their element, in their zone.

And they were all in danger.

All because he and his brother had been forced into the same orbit once more. All because his brother had made mistakes.

Ben knew he needed to try to forgive, to try to understand before casting judgment. Without that, Zack might shut down and refuse to help. Ben needed to extend the proverbial olive branch.

But he didn't like it.

CHAPTER 44
LUCIA

"LUCIA, LOOK AT THIS!"

Lucia turned to the speaker — Julie Bennett — and began walking across the large laboratory room. Julie was standing near the back corner of the space, in front of one of the metal tables that had survived the damage and destruction. She saw a battered computer lying on its side next to the table, and a few severed cables poking up from behind the metal table, pressed against the back wall. She assumed this computer used to live on top of the table, and she saw the broken monitor lying about eight feet away.

But Julie wasn't focused on the broken computer. Instead, she was holding a small, clear cube. She tried to place it between her eyes and the fluorescent lighting above, obviously working it around to get a better look at what was inside.

"What is it?" Lucia asked as she walked over.

Julie shook her head. "I don't know, but I was hoping you might."

The others were mingling in the room as well, paired off or standing in small groups discussing some aspect of the laboratory space or another. She noticed Reggie and Ben talking to Zack Bennett nearby, with frowns on their faces — apparently a common look for the two CSO men — but they kept glancing at each other.

If the younger Bennett was upset like his older brother, it didn't appear on his face.

She recalled the conversation they had had on the level above. There was history between the two brothers — more so than just family drama. She knew their father had been killed in a grizzly attack when they were younger, but she had been a bit confused about the talk of their mother, Diana Torres Bennett.

Apparently, the woman had been a scientist, just like her youngest son, but had perished in the terrible viral outbreak and terrorist attack that plagued the United States about half a decade prior. She had read all of this as it had taken place in the months after the events in and around Yellowstone National Park, both interested as a concerned citizen but also professionally, as someone interested in the goings-on of other researchers and scientists.

That it had all happened at another national park had piqued her interest, but she had not given it much thought. When Lucia had begun poking into the Civilian Special Operations team and their dealings, she had been surprised to find the link between Harvey Bennett and the Yellowstone incident. She seemed to recall that both his mother and father were no longer around, but had not remembered this small detail.

Even then, it was not the only allusion to a shared history Zack and Ben had argued about above. While their mother's death — and of course, their father's — was an open wound, it seemed Harvey was upset with his brother for innumerable other reasons.

She knew they were trying to track down the younger Bennett by coming to Russia, trying to stop whatever it was he was doing meddling in the affairs of Venelov Manufacturing. She had gotten the gist of it in the Italian restaurant in Moscow, and also through the many briefings she had read that Julie had passed out.

But Zack Bennett didn't seem to know how exactly this place was associated with Venelov Manufacturing, if at all. Sure, he had admitted to the chemical compound potentially showing up in the soils in the taiga region surrounding this park and the nearby lake, but couldn't for the life of him recall a scenario where that made sense.

He had claimed not to even know of this facility's existence — a fact Lucia believed. *None* of them had known of this place, and it seemed the Russian government had long intended to keep it that way.

They were living in a conspiracy, one layered like an onion just as the levels of the space were layered above the cave that sat somewhere beneath their feet.

Each level they descended into the ground, a layer of that onion was peeled back, more secrets revealed.

More questions.

And they still had not answered the *crucial* question: what had the scientists here been studying?

There were many other questions Lucia wanted answered, including, of course, why and how Zachary Bennett and Venelov Manufacturing were related to this place. But she was also curious as to where those same scientists were now.

Had they been killed? Had this creature they were after, the one terrorizing and plaguing the other inhabitants of this facility, attacked the scientists as well?

It led to a lot more questions about the timeline. When exactly had this creature gotten inside? Had the researchers known about it? Or had they somehow left before it came inside? If so, why? That they had found a team of mercenaries, Zachary Bennett, and a group of Russian Army soldiers, yet not even a trace of any scientists or facility employees gave her the chills. It made her think they had walked into something bigger. This was more than just a situation where a stray animal had gained access accidentally.

It made her feel as though there was something about this place far more sinister than just flickering lights and the sense of dread.

Julie handed her the square prism, and she felt its cold surface. She squeezed it a bit, feeling its sides give just a touch. Some sort of plastic, or plexi composite material. It was clear, neither side of the glass fogged or scratched.

But there was something inside. She held it up, just as Julie had, using the light to illuminate whatever was inside. It looked like hair. Long, wispy strands of some sort of fur. Multicolored, ranging from rusty to darker brown, with a few tufts of whitish blonde sprinkled in.

The others were paying closer attention now, watching as Julie and Lucia examined the object.

CHAPTER 45
JULIE

"WHAT IS IT? BEAR?" Julie asked.

Lucia stared at the hairs inside the clear prism, watching as the lighter tufts of fur seemed to dance in the light, becoming invisible as they passed over the fluorescent illumination.

She shook her head. "I don't think so. The lighter ones are almost translucent. Similar to how polar bear fur looks when held up to the light, but then there are tufts of darker hairs as well tucked in."

Reggie walked over with Freddie and was standing near Julie and Lucia's right side. "They're more like bristles than hair," Reggie said. "Doesn't look like bear fur to me. Boar, maybe. But the coloring is off."

"And they're pretty long for a boar," Freddie added. "But it could be. We used to go hunting for them when I was a kid. Nasty boogers, too. They'd mess you up if you're not careful. Definitely aggressive."

Lucia thought of the animal they were chasing after inside this facility. Could it be a boar? Or a half-albino species of bear that had wandered in from outside?

She was no zoologist, certainly not an expert in either species, but she had seen enough to know a little about what they were dealing with. "Looking at this scientifically," she began, "we can deduce that we're dealing with a mammal. It's definitely fur — that much we can be sure of. Judging by the length, I would assume the animal it belongs to is large, but that doesn't really tell us much. Beaver fur looks similar, albeit a bit thicker and homogenous in color."

She handed the prism to Reggie, and Freddie leaned in as the two men now examined it themselves. Lucia turned back to Julie. "It's not enough to go on," she said. "But we can probably assume they were studying mammals here. At least one species."

Julie nodded, glancing around the room. "I'm a computer scientist, and I've seen plenty of biosafety labs from my days at the CDC. This isn't one of them. The airlock is far too small, and there is no workroom just inside. Usually there's a large space with lockers before the airlock, as well. The place where the researchers would change clothes, don their chemchurian suit, then come inside.

"Speaking of, I don't see any hazmat suits either," Lucia said.

Julie nodded. "Yeah, it could be as simple as there weren't enough to go around, so only the researcher or researchers who were currently on shift would have donned them. They could be hanging up somewhere else in the facility. But it is an interesting point — for spending so much money building this place and digging out the cave and the levels, you would think they could have sprung for a decent lab with enough hazmat suits to be redundant."

Lucia frowned. Julie was right — this place did not seem like a proper biosafety lab. It seemed... too hastily put together. As if it had been built as an afterthought.

She suddenly had an idea. "Forgetting the Venelov connection for a moment," she began, "what if this place was not built to be a laboratory at all? What if it was simply a facility meant for some other purpose altogether? We know it's built on top of an ancient cave system, one that abuts an open cavern down below, at least according to Victor and Ortega."

Julie watched Lucia's face, waiting for her to continue.

"I know it seems like a long shot, but this facility could have been constructed to make it more convenient or comfortable for whoever was down in the caves," Lucia said, continuing their earlier conversation.

"A warm bed to sleep in at night?" Julie asked quizzically.

Lucia smiled. "Right. And enough light to forget you're five stories underground."

Julie shrugged, considering. "It makes sense — it doesn't seem like it was originally designated to be a laboratory at all. I'd bet that if we had an engineer or architect here, they might be able to find a way to corroborate that claim — maybe the airlock is clearly something that was added after the fact. Maybe — "

"Jules," Ben's voice boomed from beside Lucia, interrupting her. He was still standing along the far wall, though Zack and Reggie had moved away. They turned and looked at the large man standing near what Lucia had assumed to be a wide closet door.

"Check this out. I think I know what happened to our scientists."

Lucia suddenly felt the dread return. She didn't like the ominous way Ben said the words. Or was it just her mind playing tricks on her? He had simply stated a fact; he hadn't done anything to change or alter his voice tone.

No, she felt the trepidation return because once again, she did not know what she was about to see. She did not know why this place was here, and she and Julie had all but verified that it was not, in fact, a proper laboratory for studying chemicals.

She walked over, inadvertently a step behind Julie. She liked this woman, felt at ease with her. Julie was kind, gentle, but there was an air of grit to her that Lucia wanted to borrow. The woman was brave, confident in all the ways Lucia was not. She was a scholar like Lucia, intelligent and academically trained. But she was also gifted in the very street smarts Lucia prided herself on having, though Julie's seemed more like battle-hardened toughness.

Ben pushed the closet door open, revealing a smaller room. He had already seen whatever it was he wanted to show them, so he leaned back against the wall and looked at Julie with a level gaze. "Just peek," he said quietly. "No reason we need to spend too much time in there."

Lucia held her breath, watching as Julie pushed the large door inward more. She knew now it was not a closet. The door was thin but strong, made of metal, similar to the airlock door but much wider, almost square-shaped. It also swung on heavy hinges as it opened, creaking a bit at the end.

Julie walked one foot into the room and gasped. Lucia nearly stumbled into her back as Julie stopped, her head on a swivel.

Lucia frowned, trying to see around her, and then her other senses assaulted her before she got a good view of what lay inside. The smell of rotting flesh. The tinge of iron on her tongue.

Blood.

Then she saw it. As the light from the larger room outside bathed the blue-walled room inside, her breath returned in heaves. Her chest compressed involuntarily, and she had to force herself to inhale.

"Oh my..."

Julie suddenly turned and walked out of the room, having seen enough.

Lucia formed a mental picture of what lay in front of Julie just based on the information she was getting from her nose, her mouth, and her peripheral vision. Now, however, she saw in full view what lay in the middle of the small closet-sized room.

And it terrified her.

CHAPTER 46
LUCIA

BLOOD SOAKED the walls and floor, with even streaks of dark staining the ceiling in two corners. A drain sat centrally in the room, and long rivulets of dried blood led from the corners and edges of the room to its middle.

Lucia's eyes widened, but she couldn't look away. This was a crime scene. Never in her life had she seen such a brutal display. Never in her life had she seen anything like it, at least not in person. It reminded her of some of the true crime television shows and police procedurals her parents enjoyed watching. For her, she couldn't stomach things like this. She had a hard time sleeping with images of murder, rape, and other heinous acts dancing as replacements in her mind.

Still, she took it all in, knowing it was data. Information. She was not just a passive observer, a casual bystander. She was in the crime scene, here to figure out what exactly had happened. Sure, it would have been nice to have a detective or coroner or somebody like that, but they had her. The CSO team would have their own opinions, but she was a scientist, ostensibly trained to examine situations and make observations.

Well, Lucia, what do you observe now?

It was clear humans had died here. She saw a few pieces of fabric, the bright blue of a hazmat suit — one of the same that she and Julie had been surprised not to find present in the larger laboratory space. There was the bottom section of a shoe: a rubber galosh, the kind that went up almost to the knee over a suit and provided stability and grip on a wet floor.

Wet floor.

She looked now at the floor, seeing the rivers of blood, noticing that they were thinner than that of the blood on the walls. Where on the walls it was caked, thick and dripping with cold viscosity, the floor was dry. She squinted down, wishing there was more light than the single fluorescent above her head.

Why would the walls be seeping blood... but not the floors?

She studied it, hearing Ben's voice from outside the room. "Dr. Vergotti, it's okay — you don't need to stay in there."

His voice was reassuring, but she *did* need to stay. She wanted to know what had happened here. She examined the ceiling for any water-spouts — the kind found in office buildings for fire mitigation. There were none. There was nothing on the ceiling at all except a light fixture.

On the wall behind her, next to the large door, a tiny intercom speaker inset into the wall. A way to communicate while inside the room. Sure enough, she saw a tiny black button next to the speaker that likely allowed users to converse with those outside this small space.

So what was this space for, then? The drain in the middle, a light above, no other unique features besides the intercom.

Suddenly, she had a thought. She looked down at the floor, crouching and hovering to avoid having to lay a hand on the floor. It was bad enough that her shoes had to come into contact with the remains of the poor souls who had perished inside. She wasn't about to touch the floor with any other body part. She tried to read the signals she was getting from the room, the clues left behind. The blood was certainly thinner than the blood on the walls and even the ceiling. It almost seemed pink, as if...

"Water," she said.

"What was that?" Julie's voice came from outside, and Lucia turned to face her through the open door. "Water, I said," she repeated. "The blood is thinner on the floor — and dried out — because someone hosed it all down. It diluted the blood, drained, and allowed the floor to dry."

Julie looked confused for only a second, then her head fell back with understanding. "Right... I hadn't even put it together that the blood on the floor was different than the blood on the walls. Those poor people..."

"Nothing we can do for them now but figure out what killed them, Reggie said. "And then kill it." His voice boomed from outside the room, and Lucia figured the man must have walked over after her, his much taller frame easily able to see through the door and over her head. It sounded like he was standing next to Ben against the wall.

She walked out, seeing the rest of the group — save for Victor, Ortega, and Zack, still huddled together around the broken refrigerator. "Someone tried to wash the crime scene away," she said, putting on the most confident voice she could muster. Her shoulders squared, and she looked out to the CSO group.

It was Freddie who smiled, a mischievous glint in his eyes. He looked at her, then glanced at Reggie and Ben. "What?" she frowned.

"Nothing," Freddie stammered. "You're just... when you're trying to be confident... I find it really..."

"I don't think someone tried to clean the crime scene, Lucia," Julie said, reaching forward and grabbing her upper arm. Lucia hadn't realized she needed consoling, but suddenly found herself shaking. The effect of the room had taken its toll on her, it seemed. The blood, the smell of decaying flesh, the death.

"How — how do you know that?"

"If it was a hose, if someone had been trying to spray it all down, they would've cleaned off the walls and ceiling, too. It's not like the blood there isn't obvious."

Of course. "Right... I'm sorry — I'm not — "

Ben smiled at her. "Please, no reason to apologize. You're not wrong that it looks like water caused the blood to dilute and drain from the room. It may not have been someone trying to clean up after themselves, but none of us noticed that obvious fact until you pointed it out."

"It *does* seem to be water-related," Julie said. But if it wasn't a hose, what was it? Why just water on the floor?

CHAPTER 47
BEN

THE SMELL of death had taken hold inside Ben's nostrils. He sniffed, trying to force the fumes away, but it was unmistakable. He recognized the faint smell he had caught a whiff of as they had entered through the airlock into the larger laboratory room.

It had gotten stronger when he'd pushed open the large door leading into the tiny room, and since then it had not subsided. The others seemed affected by it as well, though no one mentioned it. He took pride in knowing that everyone here was on the same page, perhaps with the exception of the young Russian soldier who cowered in a corner, ever guarded by either Freddy, Reggie, Victor, or Ortega. But the kid didn't seem to want to make a break for it. He knew he couldn't get out by ascending the stairs and exiting through the door they had all come in through.

And he didn't seem excited about descending farther into the base and finding whatever creature had taken out his friend either.

Ben stared at the young man as the others examined the smaller room and then rejoined the group in the larger laboratory space. He met the soldier's eyes, sensing the kid trying to tell him something. His facial expression was neither English nor Russian, communicating in a language that was only human.

I told you so, he seemed to be saying. *I told you there was something here.*

Ben still wasn't convinced they were dealing with anything more than just a wild boar or whatever type of bear patrolled these regions. He knew nothing of this region other than some of the geology and ecology they had studied on the flight over. But he had a keen interest in the natural world, had always been intrigued by the veritable forest that was nature and all her inhabitants.

Ben had spent his childhood camping, hunting, fishing, and just generally being outside. They had a small house, tucked away near the back of a suburban neighborhood, jutting up against a large wooded area on the outskirts of town. Ben loved reading Gary Paulsen stories, *My Side of the Mountain*, and other survival young adult thrillers.

He used to spend hours planning his own getaway, making checklists of all the gear and supplies he would need, trying to calculate the weight of each and keep it to a reasonable level. This was all before the internet, so his research included checking out books from his elementary school library and working on his plans on the bus ride to and from school.

Once home, he would hurriedly work through any schoolwork remaining and run out the back door, aiming for a large stand of trees about a few hundred yards from their back porch. His mother would call after him, making sure he had enough snacks to get through until dinnertime.

Ben had never planned to *actually* run away. It was all an exercise in preparation and preparedness. He loved Boy Scouts, the thrill of being able to make nature his partner rather than his enemy, surviving on what she had to offer. He loved the idea of it more than the actual thought of running away from his family.

It was a good family, too. At least back when he was part of it. Their family camping trips — sometimes straight out the back porch near Ben's hollowed-out tree trunk, sometimes at a state park nearby, and sometimes with scouts — meant they were together very often.

His mother, never having been a camper herself, had taken to the sport immediately. She learned to perform all the duties of kitchen patrol as if all the stumps and trees, branches she used to place pots and pans, and hang utensils from, in trash bags, was her own suburban kitchen.

His father, Johnson Bennett, had even built them a small chuckbox. Heavy as sin, but able to hold all the kitchen gadgets she could want to make their life outdoors as tasty as possible.

Ben breathed in now, ignoring the smell and trying to pretend it was that of a crackling campfire late at night instead. He remembered the wind of the chilly evenings, the weightlessness of it, unaware it was even there until it stung his cold nose.

He thought of his father's stories — truthfully only three, and only two were any good — that he told over and over again every trip. He remembered baby Zack, laughing and giggling as his mother held him on her lap, while an 11-year-old Ben pretended he was as strong as his father, chopping wood and carrying it back to the campsite.

The memory hurt, and he wasn't sure why. It's not that he hadn't thought of it over the years; it's just that he knew there was no way to go back to it. He understood time, understood how things changed, and he was generally okay with it. It was just that Zack's presence here — their conversation upstairs — had solidified the memory as one purely unattainable, purely fiction, destined to live in his own mind for the rest of his life. Zack reminded him of the better times in his life, reminded him of a time before Harvey Bennett had become the man he was today.

Carefree, intrigued, driven — those were the three characteristics he had lived by as a child and young man. Now, those same three characteristics had turned into a rash drive toward action, paranoia, and a motivation to protect his family and friends at all costs.

It was like he was living out the unhealthy version of his own personality day in and day out, and it had taken Zack's presence here today to remind him of that.

CHAPTER 48
ZACK

ZACK COULDN'T BELIEVE what they had found. There had always been a thought in the back of his mind that the researchers here — scientists, employees, whoever — had perished, either at the hand of the Russian soldiers down in the caves or by whatever it was terrorizing them.

And he had found his answer.

He had gotten a quick glance inside the room but had decided against visiting it for a closer inspection. The others could perform that duty just fine; he was queasy at the sight of blood, especially human blood.

The assumption so far was that it was, in fact, human blood, and no one argued the opposite. He heard their whispers and voices as they discussed what they had found, heard Ben and Lucia talking with Julie and Reggie. It seemed there was clothing inside the room as well: a boot, pieces of a hazmat suit, and that sort of thing.

No, Zack had no interest in checking it out for himself.

He shuddered, cowering in the corner between the refrigerator and the entrance to the room. The sooner they could get out of here, the sooner he could start to feel normal again. He was surprised the blood had this much effect on him, though he also knew it could have to do with the situation.

He had been running on empty for the past few weeks, trying to put the finishing touches on the project's next phase.

That, and making sure he had covered the Venelov tracks that pointed back to him. His old boss had been zealous, committed to his goal, and while Zack agreed with the first few phases of that goal, he had balked when he had learned of the final play that Jakob Venelov had been planning.

It was too much to explain now, too much that could be written off as unbelievable or unlikely, so he didn't try. But that didn't mean he could stop working. He needed to find out what this place was, why the Russian government had sent its army here to check it out. He knew they had sent the soldiers down to investigate the same report Lucia had found online, the same one the CSO had picked up on.

But he also knew there was more to this base than just its potential connection to the ecology and environment nearby. There was some connection to him, to Venelov Manufacturing.

Still, he didn't believe the Russian government would be that motivated to send even a small subset of their army here to investigate just that. A couple of detectives, maybe. Not armed soldiers. He sensed there was something more to the story, and he had not quite figured it out yet.

He had theories, most of them fighting against one another in his mind, causing him to lose focus on what lay directly in front of him.

He forced bile back down his throat as he thought again of the blood and decimated remains of the poor men and women in the smaller laboratory sub-room.

He stepped forward, clearing his throat. He intended to jump back in the fray, to prove to Ben and his team that he was here and was on their side. They had a right to be suspicious of him, perhaps even paranoid. He had made missteps, mistakes.

He still believed in his project, but knew it was going to take cooperation with Ben, his brother, and the CSO group to accomplish it.

Victor and Freddie looked over at Zack as he cleared his throat, as if waiting for him to speak. He had nothing to say, but he wanted to look like he was part of the team. At least more so than the Russian soldier, who was still hunched against the wall without anyone directly guarding him. Zack knew better than to think the kid could make a run for it, however.

He noticed Freddie, Reggie, and even Ben glancing over quickly at the soldier every few seconds, and Victor and Ortega were both gripping their assault rifles with one hand, the strap hanging on their shoulders.

His two mercenaries had not separated since they entered the room, whispering in quiet tones off to the side. Zack needed to catch up with Victor soon, too. He got a sense that Victor didn't like him much, that he annoyed the older mercenary, but wrote it off as professional distance.

The mercenaries were good at their jobs, and while he was still a bit confused as to what had happened to the other two men Victor said were inside the base, Zack knew that Victor didn't need his help doing his job. He'd already lost one man outside, and he figured Victor and Ortega were discussing how not to lose any more.

Zack gave Victor a quick nod as he walked near Ben and Julie. Freddie had joined Reggie again, and the pair was off to the opposite side of the room, working their way through a cabinet that had been yanked off the wall and lay right side up on the floor. Two of its cabinet doors were missing, and screws stuck out of the faces where the hinges had been connected.

Ben noticed Zack coming and stepped aside, revealing Lucia, who was deep in discussion with Ben and his wife. He waited there for a moment to let her finish, but Reggie called his name.

"Yo, baby Bennett!"

Zack bristled. He had never been called 'Baby Bennett,' and it didn't seem to be a nickname he wanted to keep around. Still, he glanced over at Ben's friend. Reggie and Freddie were both looking at him.

"Come check this out."

Zack walked over, seeing that the two men had pulled out a couple of jugs of what looked to be clear fluid. The shape of the jugs was that of a vinegar container or bleach, but he couldn't see any obvious markings on the side until Reggie twisted the jug and turned it around so he could see it.

"Look what we found, Zack," Freddie said.

Zack squinted, examining the simplistic label on the front. It was rectangular, with only a few words in Russian and a logo.

His mouth fell open. "What — what is that?" he stammered.

Reggie smirked. "I was hoping you could tell us that, my man."

Zack stared down at the logo on the side of the jug, horrified. He recognized it instantly, would know it anywhere.

It was the logo of Venelov Manufacturing.

CHAPTER 49
ZACK

"ANY IDEA WHAT IT IS?" Ben asked Zack.

They had all gathered close to the cabinets, except Ortega who was guarding the Russian soldier against the wall. The jug had passed from hand to hand, each of them examining it, sloshing around the clear liquid inside.

When Zack held it, he turned it over a few times, frowning down at it.

"It's not volatile," Julie said. "It wouldn't be kept in a jug like this, or it would at least have a biohazard marking on it. Something like that."

Julie shook her head. "Not necessarily. Some of these chemical companies get a little lazy with their labeling. If it was purchased in bulk, it could have been straight from the manufacturing plant that Venelov operates. They would not have wasted money on extra stickers."

"What's it say?" Reggie asked.

Lucia answered before Zack could. "It's just a chemical compound, written in Cyrillic letters."

"Zack?" Julie asked.

All eyes turned to Zack. He looked at each of them in turn, then down at the jug that was thrust into his hand. He turned it over, around a few times, then shrugged while shaking his head. "I have no idea," he said softly. "I've never seen anything like it. I didn't know everything that Venelov was dealing with, what all of the products he produced. You have to remember, he ran a multinational company — over a billion in revenue."

Ben didn't seem convinced. "So we should just take your word for it?" he asked.

Zack felt the hairs on the back of his neck stand up. He didn't want a confrontation now, but he wasn't scared of his brother. He didn't think Ben had it in him to kill Zack, but he knew that Ben might try to hurt him, as he had in the past.

And he wasn't afraid of being hurt. Not by Ben.

"What do you want me to tell you, Ben?" Zack asked. "I *told* you I've never seen it before. Are you going to interrogate me to find out if I'm telling the truth?"

Reggie smirked again next to him. "Is that an option?"

Ben shook his head, closing his eyes, annoyed. "Listen, Zack," he began. "We're in this together now. Remember? At least for the time being, we need to figure out what this is. Why it's here."

"I know that," Zack snapped. "So stop second-guessing me. It doesn't mean I know what it is. Trust me, if I did, I would tell you."

"What about the chemical symbol? You're a chemist, right?" Lucia asked.

It wasn't antagonistic — the woman was kind, gentle. She meant well. She just wanted to know the answer, like they all did.

He shook his head again. "I'm drawing a blank. I recognize the individual elements, but I've never seen them in this configuration. That's not out of the question, either. It's a huge compound, something wildly complex. I would need the lab manual and workspace just to compute the size of the molecule."

At this, Ben seemed a bit assuaged. Not convinced, but on his way.

Zack continued. "But I understand why you're all waiting for something from me. That's obviously Venelov Manufacturing's logo, and I don't have any reason to suspect it was forged. Why go through all the trouble to stamp the company's logo on it?"

"So you think Venelov had something to do with this research station?" Julie asked.

"Who's to say? This is just a product that can be bought off-the-shelf — or at least ordered. I know for a fact that Jakob Venelov never told me about some secret research station deep in the Kodar Mountains. But he had his fingers in a lot of things, remember? Even though you think he was only doing some nefarious stuff to grow wheat that he could control, he was also running a company, one that had been passed down to him for at least two generations."

Ben nodded. "That checks out — at least passes my gut test. I want to know what it is, though. Is there a way to test it? I don't know, pour some out on the table and see what it does?"

"We don't have suits, protection," Victor began.

Zack stopped him. "That shouldn't matter. As Julie said, this stuff was put in a jug that looks like it could have been sold in any big box home improvement store. Besides that, it's obviously been shelf-stable as long as it's been here. I don't think there's anything to worry about."

He held the jug up, examining it in the light. For all he could tell, it was full of water. "Lucia, see if there's anything else we can use as a reactor. There's water in the corner, of course, but there might be something else in the fridge. I want to know what this chemical reacts with and how. I don't think there's any reason to worry, but I'd prefer if it were just me in the center of the room. Everyone else can stay against the walls."

Quickly, as if he had commanded it, the group dispersed to all four separate walls, leaving Zack near the cabinet toward the center of the room. He walked over and flipped over a metal table, dragging it closer to the center of the room. He saw a drain cover there, happy to see that if things got out of hand, at least the chemicals could be washed away.

Well, assuming we can find more than just a half-jug of water, he mused.

Satisfied everything was in place, he set the jug on the table and waited for Lucia to return. All she had found was the rectangular prism they'd been examining earlier, clear, with tufts of fur inside. In her other hand, she held a cup of water she had retrieved from the bucket in the side of the room.

He shrugged. "I guess that'll have to work," he said.

Carefully, he pried open the plastic lid on top of the jug. He pulled it away, but nothing happened. The liquid inside sat stagnant, unmoving.

Using his right hand, he pulled some of the fumes toward his nose, inhaling slightly. It had a strong odor, a scent that wafted easily into his nostrils and began to fill the air around his head.

"I really hope this stuff isn't potent," he said. "It smells awful."

He was about to continue when he noticed Lucia's eyes growing wide. He looked up at her, shocked and confused.

She stared down at the jug, then back up at Zack. Finally, with a shaky voice, she spoke. "I know what this is," she said. "I recognize that smell."

CHAPTER 50
BEN

THE GROUP LEFT their posts along the four walls almost as quickly as they had found them. The majority of them rushed forward toward Lucia and Zack, but Ben was pleased to see that Victor stayed along the wall, guarding the Russian soldier. It seemed he and Ortega were the consummate professionals, and had worked out some sort of arrangement to take turns guarding their captive.

He still planned to debrief with the pair of mercenaries to determine what exactly they expected from this Russian soldier. They couldn't exactly kill him in good conscience; he had not tried attacking them. The kid was scared, evident in his eyes and on his face, but his jaw was set, and Ben could see him trying his best to look hardened and unflappable.

On the flip side, Ben didn't want to just turn this guy over to his counterparts downstairs and in the nearby cave. There was a reason the Russian soldiers were holed up in the cave and had not wandered into the facility, and Ben had a few guesses as to why. Most likely, they were also being harassed by whatever creature had killed some of their men and threatened Victor.

Furthermore, Ben suspected they were here to examine the caves themselves. While they had parked outside near where Ben had left their vehicle, the Russian soldiers seemed to have gone straight down to the caves directly. He got the sense they had not arrived here much earlier than when Ben's team had arrived and had made a beeline for the bottom level.

Whatever they wanted, it was in the caves.

That was his working theory, at least. But Ben knew one thing: he did not want to trifle with the Russians. They were armed, dangerous, and most likely looking for something to kill. Turning over the Russian kid to the Russians might seem like an olive branch to him, but he knew the paranoid military force would not see it that way. At the very least, they would want to bring Ben and his crew in for questioning. That would never lead to any good.

They walked toward the table as Ben waited to hear Lucia's explanation.

"I don't remember the name of it," she said. "Honestly, I never even used it, but someone else in the lab I worked in during my postgraduate studies did. They were on a completely different project than I was, so I didn't interact with them much. But they used it as a sort of saline solution, I believe."

"Saline, like salt?" Julie asked.

She nodded. "More specifically, a salty brine that caused ice to melt faster. This stuff isn't saline, but it works the same way, only faster."

Ben watched Julie's face. She was puzzled, like they all were, but seemed to be working it out in her head. He saw her eyes dancing left to right as she examined the jug in Zack's hand, looked at the small white plastic in his other.

Suddenly her eyes shot up and met Ben's.

"Ben, what if — " she stopped herself, suddenly realizing she was really talking to the whole room. Was what she was about to say private? Was she scared of something?

He urged her to go on.

"What if this place was built *after* they discovered something in the caves down below?" Julie asked.

Ben frowned. "After? You mean like they found something in the caves they want to study, so they built this place up around it?"

Julie nodded. "I've been working it over and over. This place apparently empties right out into the cavern, right? That cavern may have had a steep vertical entrance, but it was completely destroyed and replaced by this facility. Why do that? Why build something so quickly, so hastily, just to study the cave?"

"Because they weren't studying a cave," Reggie said. "They were studying something *inside* the cave."

"Exactly," Julie said, snapping her fingers. "This laboratory was on the same level as the larger cavern out there. And it's also the only level large enough to really bring up something of any size and house it. That smaller room back there, the one where all the people... well, you know."

Ben nodded for her to continue.

"And then this chemical — it's meant to defrost something quickly. Why not just use heat? Why not just hold a torch under something you want to defrost quickly, or use something like a microwave — a low setting that effectively cooks something by vibrating the water molecules?"

Lucia smiled. "Because this particular chemical is meant to do it in a gentle enough way that it doesn't disturb the cellular biology inside. A microwave would vibrate the water molecules too violently. Using heat alone would cause whatever was being melted to defrost too quickly because the ice crystals inside would melt too quickly. It would destroy the sample."

There was a long pause, and then Zack spoke quietly. "Not sample. *Creature.*"

They all looked at him. He looked around, then continued. "Isn't it obvious now? Lucia, you found tufts of this thing's hair. That back room, the drain on the floor? It's not for *blood*; it's for *water*. This chemical Venelov Manufacturing produced? It was injected into the creature to cause it to melt safely enough they could examine it before *and* after it defrosted."

Another long pause, and Victor then spoke up from against the wall. "I don't think they got around to examining it."

Lucia's smile vanished. "He's right," she said, horrified. "Whatever this thing is, it was frozen, quite literally, in a block of ice that melted and drained away the blood that was on the floor when — "

She cut herself off, but Julie continued for her. "When it woke up and killed everyone in the room."

Ben swallowed.

How the hell could that be true?

He looked at everyone else, knowing they were thinking the same thing. "We don't... we don't actually *believe* this, do we?" Reggie asked. "You're talking about some creature that's been frozen in a block of ice for God knows how long and it just... *woke up*?"

Ben shrugged, stepping closer to the table so the front of his legs were now touching it. It was cold and did nothing to help the chill that had already run through him a moment ago. "Guys, we can't afford to throw out *any* possible scenarios, *any* possible outcomes. We've got two scientists here capable of figuring out what exactly we're dealing with. Even more of us are capable of helping, of uncovering the clues. We need to put our heads together, to figure out if there's any reasonable way this can be true. But right now, I'm not seeing any better alternatives."

There were nods all around the table. Even Ortega seemed to agree.

Zack began talking, trying to think out loud, but Ben was focused on the Russian kid near Ortega and Victor against the wall.

The Russian locked eyes with Ben, and there was no more hardened grit to him.

All he saw was fear.

CHAPTER 51
VLADIMIR

VLADIMIR WATCHED the Americans with interest. They had caused him no harm, but he didn't trust their judgment. There were two others, mercenaries he guessed, who didn't seem to be American but had taken it upon themselves to guard him as they marched throughout the facility.

He wanted to spit, to force the bad taste of this place out of his mouth, but he didn't want to call attention to himself. They were all gathered together, huddled around a table in the center of the room, discussing this or that.

He understood little English — a few words here and there, mostly — but they didn't know that. He had few cards left to play, and language was one of them. As poor as his English may be, if there was any information he could glean from these people before reconnecting with his team and commanding officer, the better.

And that was just what his plan was.

Vladimir intended to steal away when the opportunity arose. He wasn't sure when that would take place, as the pair of mercenaries taking turns guarding him seemed to be very well-trained and keenly interested in ensuring he did not slip away.

But Vladimir was young and fast. He may not have a weapon, but he had speed and agility on his side. He had sized up the two mercenaries as soon as they had approached him upon entering this laboratory room. One was older, the leader of the pair, and one was slightly younger but shorter and squatter. He had no doubt they were fit, a requirement for their line of work, but he had no plans to wrestle them. If he could get away without them noticing, he would be able to run the remaining hundred feet or so to the cavern entrance and find his team.

Of course, he would have to get past *it* first.

Whatever it was that had killed his teammates and no doubt the other patrol was still down here somewhere. He didn't know if it was a hunting predator, like some sort of cat, or more of an opportunistic one, like a bear or a wolf. It didn't matter — he knew who was predator down here and who was prey. He had no interest in becoming its next meal, but he knew better than to think he could run faster than it.

He still had not seen it, had not formed a fully clear picture of what it looked like.

But he knew what it was capable of.

It was a monster, and monsters were capable of all sorts of heinous things.

He remembered the Russian myth he had heard, knowing the parallels were just coincidence but still not able to assuage the fear coursing through his veins. He remembered his mother telling him stories at night, a strange tradition, and smiled at the thought. For whatever reason, young Vladimir had loved scary stories — they had helped him sleep.

Against her better judgment, his mother had told him stories of creatures like the Domovoi and the Leshy, the kinds of things that would cause children to stay up all night, their sleep plagued by nightmares.

But not young Vladimir. He had loved every second she had told him the stories — perhaps because he had loved every second he had spent with her. His father had died before he was born, and his mother had raised him and his three younger siblings. Two of those siblings had died from a fever that had ravaged their region when he was only 10 years old, and it had nearly broken his mother. But she was a strong woman — stronger than anyone he knew — and had made it her life's mission to raise happy and healthy children.

Vladimir loved hearing his mother's voice, no matter what she was talking about. The scary stories had become a nightly tradition, and one of those stories was the first time he had heard of the *chort*. A creature — a devil — from ancient Russian folklore, the chort lived in caves and came out at night to hunt nearby villagers and farmers. But it did not eat them — instead, it dragged them back to its cave, injured but alive, feeding on their souls. It was a haunting and terrible reminder of the dangers of being alone at night.

His entire life, Vladimir had known the chort to be fictitious, a figment of some old storyteller's imagination. Passed down from generation to generation to scare children into staying safe and sound in their beds at night, and as a warning against becoming a drunken fool, stumbling around in the dark, Vladimir had never put much weight into its reality. He was beginning to rethink that, even though he knew it was impossible.

And yet... this place was plagued by *something*. Some creature. Had this facility been constructed by those intending to study that creature? If so, how were they contained prior to its breaking free? How had they caught it in the first place? He didn't want to believe that — that a creature from so long ago had come back to prove its own existence — but truth be told, Vladimir did not know what to believe anymore.

He had heard the group talking about water and ice, two English words he recognized. He wasn't sure of their context, but he thought he also heard the word 'bear.' Perhaps that's what all this was — a bear who had somehow gotten into the facility and was now scared out of its mind, willing to kill to get free once more. That would make sense — a predator backed into a corner always fought for its life.

But he had seen the way it fought, the calculated way it crept toward its prey and then moved swifter than you would have thought something of that size could move. It didn't seem like a bear, but what did he know?

Pulled back to the present, Vladimir watched as the two mercenaries discussed something to his left. They were still holding their assault rifles, a make he didn't recognize. They had taken his, and one of the Americans was holding it over her shoulder now.

Now he had no hope of trying to recover his weapon, but that was the least of his worries. With any luck, the two mercenaries guarding him would continue pulling their attention away, seeing him less and less as a threat. He hoped that moment was soon. He was standing closest to the door they had entered from, only an old broken refrigerator designed to hold individual microbial environment containers next to him.

He watched as one of the mercenaries pulled away and started toward the table. The other was watching the action over there, the voices suddenly cut short as they all discovered something about a jug of clear liquid they had been discussing. And then, a chorus of voices as everyone began talking at once. The final mercenary turned his back to Vladimir, and he knew this was his moment.

CHAPTER 52
BEN

"HE'S RUNNING!" Reggie shouted.

Ben looked over and saw the young Russian soldier dart out of the airlock and into the hallway just as Reggie finished yelling.

"He's making a break for it!" Victor yelled.

Ben looked at Ortega, the mercenary who had been guarding the Russian, and saw a look of shock on his face, quickly replaced by one of disappointment.

He knew how the man was feeling in an instant. He had one job, one objective. He and Victor had been trading off guarding the Russian — something none of them had spoken about but had done on their own accord. He was a trained soldier as well, a professional operative, and he had failed his mission.

Ben was frustrated, but didn't fault Ortega or Victor. They had all been consumed by the revelation that whatever was on the table had somehow caused the creature to melt and apparently come back to life.

It was a hell of a revelation, one Ben wasn't sure he still believed, but the evidence was stacking up in its favor. What else were they to believe? And the Venelov Manufacturing chemical in the jug Reggie and Freddie had found only corroborated that evidence. Lucia and Julie, both scientific-minded, as well as Zack, had plenty of opportunity to argue and offer an alternative suggestion, but no one did.

Now they were faced with another issue, another serious concern. The Russian soldier had run away.

Ben knew where he would go — he claimed to have more soldiers down in the caves, which meant he was probably going to reach the end of the hallway and into the cavern system before they had a chance to start chasing him. Still, Ortega had taken it upon himself to chase after the young man, darting out of the laboratory room and into the airlock, his assault rifle up and ready.

"Don't shoot him!" Victor yelled.

He started after Ortega, but Reggie shouted for him to halt.

Reggie was ignored, and Victor disappeared after Ortega and the Russian soldier.

This was not good. Not only had the Russian gotten away — not only was he putting them in danger if he came into contact with the creature in this hallway — but now they were split up.

Freddie and Reggie started toward the door, but Ben held up his palm, halting them. Reggie rested his fist against Freddie's chest. Ben could see in Reggie's eyes he wanted to disobey Ben's order. Anger was splashed across his face.

"It's okay," Ben said, trying to keep his voice calm. "Nothing we can do about it now but stay together."

"He's *right there*," Reggie said, emphasizing the last two words. "We can stay together, we just have to chase after him."

"No," Julie said firmly. "Let him run. Let Zack's guys go after him. If they don't get to him, at least we won't be split up around this space."

"We *won't* be splitting up all over the base," Reggie snapped. "We'll be split up in *one hallway*. The kid's obviously going into the caves, trying to find his men."

"And what if there *are* no more men?" Ben asked, his voice sharp and tinged with command. He had no hierarchy in his organization; he was not in charge of anyone implicitly. But he was the de facto head of the CSO, and the others had learned to lean on his judgment, for better or worse.

Still, he needed to appear as confident as possible. He was shaken by the revelations they made in this laboratory, even more so by the words he and Zack had shared on their way down here. But he was most shaken by the weight of leadership. They were all leaning on him, even Julie.

And it had been Julie's idea to *not* split up. Ben had agreed, for once allowing himself to be convinced to distrust his gut and go with his wife's. He had felt confident about it earlier, but now he was second-guessing that opinion.

If they had only split into two large groups earlier, half of them could already *be* in the caves, sniffing around and prepared to intercept this guy.

No, he thought, arguing with himself. *Then we would just be two halves of a whole, fractured and separated.* The Russian force in the caves was still an unknown. There were at least four — now reduced to one — but claims had been made that there were up to a dozen men total.

He remembered the two black SUVs parked outside. Certainly capable of carrying a dozen men into this place.

He suddenly felt the eyes of everyone in the room on him. Zack and Lucia to his left, Julie, Reggie, and Freddie in front of him, still around the table. Freddie and Reggie had stepped closer to the airlock door and entrance to the room, but they were clearly awaiting Ben's orders.

Slowly, with as much confidence as he could feign, he shook his head. "No, Julie is right. We have to stick together. We made that choice upstairs."

"*You* made that choice upstairs," Reggie snapped.

Ben tilted his head, glaring at his best friend. "You want to do this now?"

Reggie didn't respond. The standoff seemed to last for an hour, when in fact only seconds had passed. But they were long, drawn-out seconds, when Reggie finally nodded once.

"We'll move into the hallway, but let's do it together. We're not in a hurry — let Victor and Ortega chase after him. They're not our men, so they're not our responsibility."

From his side, Zack mumbled. "They're *my* men."

Ben glanced at his brother as if daring him to move toward the door. He even motioned at it with his head. "Be my guest, little brother."

Zack didn't move.

"That's what I thought. Get your heads back in it," Ben said. "We are a team, and we're going to stay that way. There are too many unknowns, too many variables. We're starting to uncover what happened here, and I intend to finish that. We don't need whatever the hell kind of monster is prowling this place getting in the way, and we certainly don't need to go on a wild goose chase in a freaking cave full of angry Russians with guns."

No one argued. Lucia looked scared, his wife concerned. Reggie and Freddie were passive, maintaining their stoic expression they had learned from field and active duty. He didn't have to guess what they were thinking; he already knew. They wouldn't be upset with him necessarily, but they certainly didn't like backing down from a fight. As smart as they were, they were still soldiers, still bent toward action.

Ben felt the pull as well — he had made a career of running into the fray, of getting himself in trouble and hoping for the best.

But he had a daughter, a family. The last thing he needed to do was run into a firefight in the dark without a weapon.

"Alright then," he continued. "We move slowly, toward the caves. No talking, no noise. We've got at least two known enemies, but one of them is going to be a better hunter than all of us combined. If you so much as smell anything out of place, give a quick, quiet hiss. Reggie and Freddie will run point, weapons up and ready. Got it?"

More nods came from around the room.

He took a deep breath, then let it out. *It's as good a plan as any,* he told himself.

But as he started toward the airlock door, following behind his two teammates, he couldn't help but second-guess himself as well. He was not a planner, was not prone to strategic thinking and technical maneuvering. Everything felt too calm, too organized. Just because they had had an exciting minute didn't mean moving slowly and carefully throughout the rest of the base and into the caves was the right call.

But he steeled himself, forcing his mind to push those thoughts away. He noticed Julie suddenly by his side.

Together they stepped out into the corridor once more.

CHAPTER 53
FREDDIE

THEY REACHED the end of the hallway, and Freddie watched as the concrete support structure they had been walking through transitioned to rock. The ceiling was reinforced concrete for an extra ten feet, while the walls gave way to cold, hard stone. Mother Nature had done over the course of millennia what had taken men only years, but Freddie trusted Mother Nature's work far more.

As his feet found their grip on the slippery rock floor when they entered the cavern system, Freddie felt himself let out a breath. He felt relieved, surprising himself. He wasn't exactly a spelunker or a cave diver. But there was something oppressive about the subterranean concrete facility they had just spent time in. It felt as though nothing could hurt him here. He knew it was a farce, knew that he was in just as much danger as he had been, if not more, but there was something soothing about the natural stone and breath of the cave.

And that breath was certainly evident. From deep below, past the turn in the main cavern they were in, the earth itself seemed to be breathing, sleeping soundly. Its breath formed a slight breeze that flew upward and out, pushing the hairs away from Freddie's forehead. He had been in caves before, knew the phenomenon well, and it added to the feeling of comfort as he strode forward, the Russian assault rifle ready in his hands.

The others fell in line behind him. Reggie was just behind his left shoulder, with Ben and Julie standing behind him. They walked in front of Lucia Vergotti. Victor and Ortega had stopped and waited for them at the entrance to the caverns, not having found the Russian soldier and not wanting to continue onward without the safety of the larger group. Zachary Bennett had fallen to the back of the group, his face still registering shock at discovering his company's product inside the laboratory room.

Freddie tried to make sense of what he had seen and what they had said. Apparently, the chemical was some sort of liquid that helped gently reanimate cells without causing the ice crystals to crush them.

Reanimate.

That word had hung in his head until this moment. He had pushed it aside, not realizing his subconscious was dwelling on it until right now.

Reanimate.

Could that be true? Was it possible that the liquid could actually *reanimate* dead life?

He shook his head slightly as he marched through the well-lit tunnel. Whoever had built the structure above had strung up single-bulb light fixtures and bolted them to the stone. He wasn't sure how long these lights trailed, perhaps all the way to a secondary entrance, a cave near the lake, perhaps.

No, it wasn't reanimation, he reminded himself. The creature — whatever the hell it was terrorizing this place — had been frozen in ice. At least that's what he thought Lucia had been referring to. Some sort of animal, long thought extinct, had defrosted inside that laboratory room, woken up, and killed everyone around.

Still, it didn't make sense. He knew better than to think an animal could be frozen in ice for any amount of time and somehow wake up after being defrosted. Sure, the chemical component could potentially lessen the effects of the sharp, jagged ice crystals bursting the cell walls inside the creature, but life was more than just a bundle of cells.

Homeostasis was required, both in the overall temperature of the creature and in the pH of the blood. He knew his seventh-grade biology well enough to know that major organs — heart, lungs, brain, whatever else might be inside a creature like this — could not be frozen for any amount of time without losing its ability to interact with every other organ required for life.

Unless...

Before Freddie joined the Civilian Special Operations team, he had read about their exploits. He had read about Harvey visiting Switzerland to help a woman whose husband had been murdered by a mercenary group hired by a company focused on doing something similar to what seemed to be happening upstairs and in the laboratory behind him. He had read that Ben and the woman, upon investigating the company's headquarters building hidden high in the mountains of Switzerland, had discovered a macabre experiment attempting to mount a human brain inside a gorilla's skull cavity.

But it was more than just an attempt — it had actually worked. Both creatures — human and ape — had required sophisticated scientific implements to keep both bodies preserved during the course of the experiment. It had obviously been a success, proving once more that medical advancement had hardly stopped advancing.

But was he seeing the same thing here? This wasn't a creature that had been frozen using the latest medical and scientific techniques and equipment. It happened accidentally, organically, frozen thousands of years ago.

Lucia had guessed that this was some previously extinct species. Sure, a chemical compound had helped defrost the creature and allow it to function, but how exactly had that happened?

Freddie was so intently focused on chewing on the problem of how there had come to be a creature from thousands of years ago roaming the halls and killing humans, that he had nearly missed the turn into another hallway. He felt Reggie pulling his arm, a slight grip and tug.

Hold, he was saying. Reggie, also trained by the US military, had no need to use his voice. He and Freddie could communicate silently without calling attention to themselves.

He looked up, then around at why Reggie had called a halt, not thinking much of the large cavity he had started walking across. He brought his gun around, but Reggie was already in front of him, holding out the sniper rifle.

But there was nothing to shoot at. Instead, Freddie's peripheral vision had done him well once more. He hadn't missed anything in his peripheral vision. It was just a pile of rocks. Just an empty, earthen void of stone and boulders.

"What's up?" Freddie asked.

The others stopped as well, but the latter half of the group couldn't see around the bend Reggie and Freddie were standing in front of. He eyed the space, and Freddie flicked on the gun-mounted flashlight and pointed it at the pile to get a clearer view of what Reggie had noticed.

"This pile of stone wasn't here before," Reggie said.

Freddie frowned, still watching the stone but eyeing his friend. "How do you know? You weren't down here before?"

Reggie shook his head, then pointed. "See the char on the ceiling? On the floor? There was an explosion. Whatever it was brought down a whole section of stone from the ceiling, blocking this passageway."

Freddie's eyes widened then. Indeed, he saw exactly what Reggie was talking about, and it was unmistakable.

"Well, I'll be damned," Ben muttered from behind Freddie. He stepped forward, past Freddie and Reggie, and began investigating some of the small piles of rubble at the far edge of the pile. He picked one up, turned it over, and with an index finger, wiped black soot off the bottom of it.

He sniffed it. "I'm no expert, but this was definitely explosives. C4? Maybe a grenade?"

Reggie walked over and began investigating as well. He confirmed what Ben guessed. "I think it was a grenade. Most likely the cause of that explosion we heard and felt upstairs."

"So these Russians — wherever they are — closed off a whole section of the cave? Why would they do that? And why this one? Reggie turned and looked at Freddie, then back at Ben. The others gathered in the main corridor, waiting.

"Isn't it obvious, bud?" he asked. "They're obviously terrified of the same thing everyone else is scared of. And I bet they got the sucker. If it's not underneath all of this rubble, it's stuck somewhere on the other side of this pile."

Freddie nodded. "That checks out," he said. "They probably had the thing backed into a corner and threw a couple grenades to either kill it or close it off from the rest of this space. Seems like it worked, too."

They hadn't heard any strange sounds, any gunfire, or any shouts since the explosion. He wanted so hard to believe that the Russian army team here had successfully taken out whatever had been terrorizing the people down here. But as he locked eyes with Ben, he knew that hope wasn't going to get them through this.

Ben spoke, nodding slowly at Freddie as he addressed the rest of the group. "Maybe they did, maybe they didn't. But when they blew this thing up, it definitely sealed off the door upstairs. We've already guessed that there's another entrance somewhere around the lake. It might be where the Russian soldiers exited. Or they might be in here somewhere waiting for us. Hell, they could have failed, as well. Could be that damned creature is in here waiting for us too."

Freddie knew Ben was right, and everyone else did as well, as no one argued.

"Unfortunately, the mission hasn't changed," Ben said. "We're still in this together, still trying to figure out what happened here. We keep moving forward, pushing deeper into the cave. With any luck, we'll pop out up top in broad daylight free and clear, and we can have..."

"That sounds nice," Reggie said, smiling. "Did anybody bring any stuff for a picnic?"

CHAPTER 54
VLADIMIR

VLADIMIR AGAIN RAN like his life depended on it.

He ignored the fear seeping into his mind, the constant reminder that he was, in fact, running for his life. As he passed the single door at the end of the hallway where he had hidden before in the dark, he couldn't help but wonder where the beast was now.

The Americans behind him would now be much quicker to shoot first and ask questions later. Sure, they may have given him the benefit of the doubt upstairs, but down here — especially after he had made a run for it — he knew he wouldn't be able to argue his point.

He ran through the open doorway that led into the cavern system, hardly noticing that his men's supplies and gear were gone. He knew they would have begun working toward the entrance, the exit of the cave they had scouted two days ago on the eastern side of the lake.

Their mission here had been to investigate the facility, protect any assets they had found within, and ensure no one else came to poke around. As such, their commander had ordered half of their team to scout the area around the lake, looking for any other entrances to the underground system.

Information about the cave and the facility were sketchy, but Vladimir's commanding officer seemed to know a few rumors about the place. He had claimed that it was built on top of the massive cave structure, featuring myriad mazelike corridors and huge caverns. There were many entrances dotting the region, high up in the Kodar Mountains and down here at ground level around the lake. He told them there had been stories of the ancient people who lived here, stories of living in the caves and using them as shelter for ages.

No *modern* information existed, however, as whatever geologic surveys that had been done during and before the construction of this base had long since been lost to time.

But the team that had scouted around the lake had discovered another access point to the cavern system. Large enough to walk through, they had entered the cave and followed the largest of the passages its full length, aiming southwest, hoping it eventually coincided with the corridor Vladimir was in now.

They had succeeded, reporting back to their commander that there was, in fact, at least one entrance that was usable. It hadn't been a challenging task, either — whoever had built this place had made the cave entrance a sloping, filled-in road. Wide enough for a vehicle to pass through with slick, stone floors, they had even mounted light fixtures along the walls that were powered by the generator.

That team would be heading back down to that entrance now. Vladimir passed an offshoot and saw a pile of stones and rocks that had tumbled down, blocking that entrance. As he ran, he wondered if this could be the reason for the explosion they heard earlier. He thought he saw marks along the ceiling, black scars where smoke residue had landed and stuck.

But still he did not stop. He ran until he felt his legs were going to give out, though he knew he hadn't traveled far. In truth, he was exhausted, had been before he had made his break out of the laboratory in the facility. The others were now armed with his own rifle, which his commander would not appreciate. But he knew better than to stop and wait for them, see if they would be so kind as to return his weapon and not kill him on the spot.

Vladimir had read between the lines, had made some assumptions about their mission — the *real* mission. For whatever reason, his government had gotten spooked by something. They had known something was here, that whatever it was needed to not only be covered up, but to be protected so others — *outsiders* — didn't find it.

Those outsiders were chasing him now, the very people his commanding officer had been sent down here with the team to protect against.

Vladimir didn't know who the people chasing him were, nor did he care. He had heard their voices, trying to piece together what they were talking about, but his poor English prevented him from understanding fully. Although two of them spoke Russian well enough to converse, Vladimir was not interested in volunteering more information than what he thought was necessary to keep himself alive, and the Americans had not seemed to want to press the issue.

He entered a long, curving stretch of tunnel that seemed to descend at a slight grade, giving his legs a respite. The ground was uneven, and although the rocky gravel and stones littering the floor in some offshoots had been removed from this main corridor long ago, he felt as though every step would be his last, that he would land in a small pothole, flip head over heels, and break his ankle.

He forced himself to slow down and focus on his footfalls. It seemed as though the lights were dimming, but he knew it was a trick his eyes were playing. He needed to get to the end, to his team.

He felt their presence, as if he was going to crash into one of them just around the bend. But the bend continued, making what seemed like a full circle, even though Vladimir knew it was more likely a huge, mile-long quarter turn. The single bulbs mounted to the walls were his saving grace — the generator had been performing admirably, and it seemed as though the machine had decided to cooperate.

He was grateful for that. He had never been afraid of the dark, never one to be scared of things he couldn't see. Lately, however, he had been questioning that lack of fear. While he had assumed the stories his mother used to tell him as a child were the reason he had no fear of places like this, what he had seen in the last hours was truly beginning to fight against his confidence and bravery.

The bend shifted to the right sharply, with two smaller offshoots squirting to the left and directly in front of him, but they were smaller, no more than four feet tall each. Likely ancient waterways that had long since dried out, he ignored them and continued moving to the right, following the lit passageway.

Eventually, these lights would end just as the scout team had reported, but by then they said there should be enough light from outside reaching down here. He looked forward, seeing the lights as far as the corridor traveled, wondering if he was even getting close to the end.

He passed another offshoot, this one larger. He continued running, now moving at a jog but still not daring to slow for fear of the Americans hot on his tail.

And then he heard it.

A low, guttural groan. Something large, beastly.

He froze. His mind screamed at him to keep running, to keep moving. His body wasn't listening, as if it had a mind of its own. He was fighting with himself, trying to decide whether he should continue or stay still, try to hide in the shadows.

His eyes flitted left to right, looking for anything he could hide in. There was only the old round tube, darkly beckoning to him, covered in shadow. But it was the same tube the noise had come from, and he didn't dare stick his head in it.

Where, then? There was nowhere else to hide, not even a nook or edge along the smooth rock cave wall.

The growl picked up, now a low rumble. He tensed, feeling the hairs on the back of his neck stand up. He wanted to scream, but knew it would be the end of him.

He decided to keep moving, but slowly, hoping he could move silently away from the creature hidden in the shadows. He stepped with one foot, then the other.

He made it five feet, letting out a breath. Still, he was silent, not making a sound. His confidence returned, and he dared a glance back over his shoulder. The corridor was empty. He let out a longer breath now, to get back in. "Breathe," he told himself in a whisper. "Move forward."

His foot caught against a dip in the cave floor, pushing his body forward and over his knees. He couldn't stop himself. He fell hard onto the floor, and his head smacked against the back of his hand, making a loud slapping sound. His body ached, feeling as though he had broken bones.

But it was not his bones he was worried about.

It was the scraping sound behind him, the sound of something approaching slowly and carefully.

He gulped, trying to pull himself up to his feet once more. The scraping sound grew louder and faster. He turned his head for another look back at the corridor behind him.

His eyes grew wide, and he fell backwards once more.

CHAPTER 55
FREDDIE

FREDDIE WALKED NEXT TO LUCIA, who had sped up to join him as they descended deeper into the cave system. He didn't argue. Though she was unarmed and untrained, he couldn't help himself.

He liked this woman... a lot.

They had only just met, but she seemed as taken by him as he was by her. And it wasn't just physical attraction for him — he was stunned by her scientific mind, by her ability to formulate solutions to problems he couldn't even begin to comprehend.

He had always had a passing interest in science, but never had the brainpower to see it through. Growing up in the country, hunting, fishing, and working outside, he had fallen into the stereotype of a typical hick or hillbilly. Joining the Army sealed the deal — his southern accent and drawl had convinced his friends he was just a simple grunt.

He knew he was more than that, but he'd never had the chance to prove it until joining the CSO. There, science met with force to solve problems the United States government deemed unnecessary or not worth their resources. Meeting someone like Lucia was a dream come true. He wasn't sure how or when, but he wanted to see her again when they got through all of this.

If they got through all of this.

They were walking down a curved pathway that descended deeper into the subterranean space. There were lights strung up alongside the walls, the same lights that had lit their way so far. They continued on both sides, a single bulb in a fixture bolted into the rock and connected with long lines of extension cords.

Not up to code, but Freddie knew this wasn't the sort of place that was going to be inspected.

Directly ahead, Freddie saw the path bend to the right, a sharp ninety-degree angle. He slowed, and the rest of the group slowed behind him. They had decided to walk after finding the blown-up passageway just at the edge of the facility. If the Russian soldier had kept running, he would be long gone by now, but they were relying on finding the rest of his team as well. They had written off any hope of trying to find the Russian kid alone, and since the mission was to investigate what was going on down here, Ben and the others had deemed it necessary to find the Russian soldiers' commander and force instead.

All that could be done by walking, not exerting too much energy and running like a bunch of crazy people through a dark cave.

The floor was uneven here, potholes carved out from standing water that had dried up long ago. He kept moving, now shuffling his feet more than stepping, trying to avoid tripping and looking like an idiot in front of Lucia. He was pleased to see that she had begun moving more carefully as well, only placing her feet when she knew the way forward was steady.

They turned, then stopped.

Freddie's mouth fell open. Reggie nearly bumped into him, feeling the cold steel of his rifle scope dig into his back.

"What in the world?" Reggie mumbled.

Freddie took a precarious step forward, but Lucia and the others did not follow. He stopped again, trying to squint and force what lay ahead into focus.

"It's a body," Ben said.

Freddie confirmed, the shape finally coming into focus enough to understand what he was seeing. Once again he walked forward, now standing about fifteen feet away.

It *was* a body, but it had been massacred. Completely ripped in half, blood pooling in one of the very potholes Freddie had to step over.

The others began talking at once, their voices low, some even whispering. Victor and Ortega flanked the scene, each standing alongside one wall of the corridor, the shadows cast by the glowing bulbs above their heads creating long, eerie shapes that danced over the macabre scene.

To Freddie's left, an arm. To his right, a foot. It seemed as if the guy had been sent through a guillotine over and over again, each time lopping pieces of his body off and tossing them aside.

What the hell can do something like this? This was the work of no bear — even a full-grown grizzly could not perform such a piece-by-piece dissection. The torso was severed, but its upper half was sprawled face-up, the head still cruelly intact, the eyes staring up at Freddie.

"I guess we found our boy," Reggie said.

The voices stopped, and everyone fell silent, examining the murder scene. Freddie knelt down on one knee as he tried to piece together what had happened. Clearly, the same creature they thought had been killed or blocked behind the passageway up above was free, and it had done this.

And clearly, it was something Freddie did not want to see in person.

If it could do this to one man, he couldn't imagine what it could do to their entire group. They were still largely unarmed, with the sniper rifle and assault rifle being the only weapons they had. Victor and Ortega were armed as well, but seeing the destruction here, Freddie wasn't entirely sure that bullets would take this thing down.

He watched as the torso and head, with one single arm attached to its side, shifted beneath the shadows and light bouncing around as the team moved into the cave.

Freddie squinted harder, trying to re-create the battle — as one-sided as it may have been — in his mind. The shadows glancing over the poor soldier's face and closed eyelids seemed to shatter and dissipate, each becoming longer, twisting wraiths. Victor and Ortega had slid sideways, trying to get a better view, while Reggie, the two women, and Zack all took up positions over his shoulder, looking down.

He leaned forward still, trying to inspect the damage. Strangely, the man's face was unmarked by scars or cuts. Like the other Russian soldier upstairs on the top level, the wounds had been mostly around the waist and legs. Freddie assumed this meant the creature had struck with its claws straight out, rather than reaching up for the soldier's face. This seemed unlikely — most predators, when cornered or attacking, would aim for the eyes or throat, a natural evolutionary tactic that nature had provided such creatures.

He was busy trying to recall all of the predators he knew of that could possibly do something like this but drew a blank. Once again, he thought of a full-grown female grizzly or male.

No, this was the work of something other than a bear. He was sure of it.

He was leaning far over the man's head, examining the shadows and lines on his face. They seemed to be moving, they seemed to be —

Suddenly, the soldier's eyes shot open.

Reggie shouted, and Freddie fell backward on his butt. He pushed away involuntarily, his boots not finding purchase on the slick rock floor.

He stared in shock. Each eyelid blinked slowly, on separate schedules.

The mouth fell open, and what seemed like a guttural sigh escaped the Russian soldier's lips.

CHAPTER 56
ZACK

"WHAT... THE ACTUAL..."

"It has to be — "

"I've never seen anything like it."

The voices all came at once, and Lucia could not differentiate between them. She had reverted to thinking in her native tongue, Italian, and the English sounded like gibberish now. Slowly, one sentence at a time, it all began to make sense.

Not what was happening, of course — *that* was still as strange a thing as she had ever seen — but at least the words were making sense. She listened as different members of the group, including Ben, Julie, Reggie, and Victor, all muttered responses as they looked down at the dead soldier.

The poor young man had been ripped to shreds, literally scattered around the cave floor. She noticed a leg off to the right and had been watching the torso while Freddie examined the kid's face.

And then it began to move.

Not like the movement of a human dying or in pain, but like the movement of a thousand ants just beneath the surface.

When the man's eyes snapped open, each blinking one at a time on their own tempo, she had nearly fallen over in shock.

Never in her wildest dreams had she ever imagined seeing something like this. Something so... horrifying.

But it *was* happening right there, right now. Freddie regained his composure and crawled back over, still on his knees but using his hands as leverage in case he needed to pop up and run. Lucia was right beside him, her hand resting on his shoulder as he crouched over the soldier. She tried to force herself to watch from an observer's standpoint — from a scientist's perspective, removed from the action. Yet it was right there, right beneath her feet.

It was as if the arm could reach out and —

The hand wiggled, and she shrieked.

"What the actual — " Reggie began again, finishing the sentence with an expletive that was drowned out by Ortega, who was now cursing loudly in Spanish.

Reggie walked over and pointed the end of his long rifle down at the man's forehead. "I'm going to end this, whatever the hell it is."

"No!" Lucia shouted.

Suddenly all eyes turned to her. She didn't look down but suspected that even the Russian soldier on the ground was now staring at her.

"You understand what's happening?" Zack asked softly.

She paused, then shook her head. "No. Of course not. I've never seen... never seen anything like this." Her words fell out slowly, stuttered, but she pushed through it. She was formulating a hypothesis as she went. "But the soldier was clearly attacked by... whatever it is that's in here. Something tore the poor man apart, possibly spreading some sort of disease to him in the process."

Julie spoke next. "You think this is some sort of... bacteria? A virus?"

"Impossible to say for sure," she said. "At least not yet. Zack, is something like this possible?"

If anyone could understand the epidemiological effects of something like instantaneous viral transmission, it would be Zack or Julie, both with backgrounds in biology and the sciences. Julie had worked for the Biological Threat Research division of the CDC, while Zack had more recent experience in biochemistry and microbiology.

He worked his jaw side to side a bit before answering. "At this point in my life, I'm willing to say anything is possible. Although this... seems to be closer to the impossible side of the spectrum, but after what we've seen..."

"If that thing infected this guy after he killed it, how is he alive now?" Reggie asked.

"I don't think he is," Lucia said. Once again, everyone stared at her. "I mean, we all saw him move. We also saw his eyes open and his mouth open and shut like he was trying to speak. But that's just what humans happen to look like when they are moving around and speaking, right? It's literally just a series of muscles contracting and releasing. Underneath the skin — wherever this infection is living — it could be that it's interfering with his muscles. It could be that it's trying to work out how to make its host work."

"Make its host work?" Reggie asked incredulously. "You mean like some sort of sick zombie thing?"

"As Zack said, anything seems to be in the realm of possibility these days, given the right environment and planning. Whatever these scientists were working on here, we know they had a litany of tests that happened long before we ever set foot in this place. Sure, this creature was probably dead before it was frozen, countless eons ago. And we know that a litany of manufacturing chemicals were used to help re-liquefy the contents of its bloodstream and serums, as well as preventing crystallization in the ice around its individual cells."

"So that creature is running around, killing people, but it's not actually... alive?"

She nodded. "That seems to be the most plausible explanation. All we know is that there is something here — something large, extremely dangerous, and capable of brutality, either purposefully or not — *and* that it is capable of transmitting some sort of infection that spreads incredibly fast in a host."

"A host that was very recently alive," Zack muttered.

Lucia wasn't sure why Zack had to bring up the poor soul who had trudged with them through the complex once more, but suddenly she understood. "Exactly," she said. "This thing — the infection — can't jump hosts unless that host is able to provide the proper environment. That's how all disease vectors work, essentially. A virus doesn't jump from a tree to a dog, and usually won't live long on an organic surface. This man is very much dead, unfortunately, but his body — the host —

is still fresh enough to provide a proper vector and breeding ground for the disease."

Ben and Julie had worked their way down to the bottom end of the torso, still inspecting it as they listened. After a moment, she spoke again. "So we've got some sort of infectious disease running around in a creature that is very much dead," Lucia said. "It's not feeling anything. It's not alive, not technically. It's simply a host — a body that was thawed after being dead for some unknown number of years. It could be 10,000, it could be 100,000. It doesn't matter. The creature was probably extinct long before humans ever set foot in these mountains. The point is, it was a well-preserved body — a perfect host for this disease to move in and claim it."

Reggie chuckled. "I find it incredibly hard to believe that some... *bug* could come crawl inside something like that and figure out how to work its eyes, ears, nose, and mouth. Much less its hands and claws."

He seemed spooked by the whole thing, and Lucia saw that his eyes were dancing back and forth, up and down the hallway, as if waiting for it to reappear.

She smiled, trying to reassure him. "It's certainly dangerous, and certainly something we'll need to watch out for. But it's not exactly as you say it is. This creature is no longer alive, it's just as dead as it was before. The bug — the infection, as we are calling it — got inside of it and used it as a host, but it doesn't know what's what. It's just working as a unified whole, all of its cells commandeering those of the animal, and moving things around randomly."

"Randomly?" Zack asked.

This time, everyone turned and looked at Ben's younger brother.

"No," he began, shaking his head. "I don't think this is random at all. Sure, I agree with Lucia that we're dealing with something we've never seen before, and that it's just a random occurrence that it found a way to latch onto this creature as a host, but whatever it is — a virus, bacteria, or something else — it has a goal. *Every* life form, no matter how small, has one purpose."

Everyone stared, waiting for the punchline.

"Reproduction. Survival."

"What are you saying?"

Zack continued. "If this thing feels like the only way to reproduce and thrive is by killing us and passing it on, then that's what it's going to do."

CHAPTER 57
ZACK

ZACK STOOD TO THE SIDE, near Ortega, against the cave wall. He couldn't believe what he was seeing. The Russian soldier was twitching, convulsing on the ground as the infection inside plagued him. He knew the soldier was long past feeling pain, and while he had the most untimely and gruesome death Zack had ever seen, it was over.

He was dead, unable to feel, think, or breathe.

But it was hard for Zack's mind to convince him of the truth, for him to believe it. The young Russian man looked, for all intents and purposes, as though he were still alive, flapping around with just a single arm and no lower half. The back of his head cracked against the stone floor with a sickening crunch, if not causing an actual fracture, then certainly causing a bruise, had the man's blood still been coursing through him.

But his blood had been nearly completely replaced by whatever this disease was, whatever this infection could be.

But what?

In all his professional career, in all his experimental experience and work, both with legitimate companies and those with a more sinister purpose, Zack had never seen such a ravaging disease. He remembered the story about the woolly bear caterpillar's ability to freeze solid for a season, knowing that Mother Nature found incredibly interesting ways to seek survival, including being able to withstand insane temperatures, both hot and cold. He knew that there were entire colonies of microorganisms living at the bottom of the ocean under immense pressure and directly above superheated vents, boiling with geothermal activity. He knew that tardigrades, the small 'water bear' creatures that lived in just about every place that was wet, could even survive in the absolute zero environment of space.

And he knew that hostile takeovers of one species by another were not just possible, they were common. There was the wasp that burrowed into the abdomen of ants, eventually taking them over and using their bodies as their own. He had read accounts of other creatures with other symbiotic relationships, some not so beneficial or mutually beneficial.

But this was something else entirely. He had heard rumors of Haitian zombies, the originator of the zombie myth. Could this be what he was seeing? Could this man have been infected by some sort of bacteria that caused the cells to reanimate, if only to do the bidding of the very organism that was controlling it? Or could some sort of chemical compound coat...

He stopped himself. *A chemical compound.*

He had been thinking along the lines of all of the known organic and inorganic compounds he had studied since university. All of the compounds he had used in the lab, created under a microscope.

But what he had not been considering was a compound that he might have helped create.

Could it be possible? Could something like that really work?

He heard a voice and suddenly realized it had been talking to him. He looked up, glancing at his older brother.

"Any ideas, Zack?" Ben asked.

Zack frowned, then realized the question had been asked after the group had been discussing something. Zack had been lost in his own mind, in his own thoughts.

But it didn't take a genius to figure out what they had been talking about. All eyes were on him, but the subject was the same — how in the hell did half of a Russian corpse suddenly reanimate on the floor?

He nodded. Everyone waited. Then he frowned. "Ben, I need your word."

Ben matched his gaze, his voice lowering. "My word about what?" he asked tersely.

"I need to know you're not going to hand me over to the Russians. Those soldiers were looking for *me* — I need your word that you won't just give me to them."

Ben was about to speak, but Reggie cut him off. "Speaking of those Russian soldiers, how about we keep moving? We can walk and talk, people."

Zack and Ben both nodded in unison, turning to face the same direction, the one leading farther into the cave. In the distance, Zack thought he saw the lights ending, the single bulb fixtures no longer spaced every 20 feet. It was another half-mile down, but it was a straight shot. If he had to guess, it seemed as though this entire corridor had been dug out by Mother Nature herself and with the help of a crew of workers.

"Sounds good," Ben said, addressing Reggie. He walked side-by-side now with Zack. "I can't give you my word, Zack," Ben said.

"Why not? You can't do this! You can't just -"

"Do *what*? Make you answer for your crimes? Make you answer for everything you've done so far? You might not be Jakob Venelov, but you *were* working with him. You're an accomplice in this, Zack."

Ben's words were biting, though Zack understood full well why he believed them. They weren't entirely untrue. "I understand," he said, lowering his voice so only his brother could hear. "What if I told you I could make this all go away? That I could come clean, at least explain myself?"

"Explaining yourself and making this all go away are two completely different things, little brother."

"Agreed, but I *can* do both. I need you to trust me, though."

"You've already asked us to trust you multiple times. I'm not sure we've got enough trust spread around the lot of us for it to be enough. You still haven't answered my question: if this is all part of some bigger plan, some big game Venelov was playing, what is it? Why couldn't you tell us before?"

Zack winced. "I... still can't tell you, at least not here."

"Why not?" Ben leaned into the words.

"Because... it's not safe. But trust me, Ben, I know what I'm doing. I've always known. I didn't work with Venelov — he worked with me. He thought I was working for him, but it was exactly the opposite. It's just that our interests were aligned for the time being. But when you killed him... it forced my hand. He was going to initiate everything, but *I* had to then. It all fell to me, and there was no way out of it, not without finishing what he started."

"What *you* started."

"No, that's where you're wrong, Ben." Zack kept walking, but now he was looking over and up at his brother, trying to plead with him to understand. "I know you want to believe that I'm just a bad guy, that I was working with Venelov like we were some terrorist buddies. But you couldn't be more wrong. Sure, I bought into his overzealous belief that he could *actually* control the world's population. But have you ever stopped to ask yourself what it would be like if he could? If he did everything he said he was going to do, and it worked as well as he said it would?"

Ben squinted down at him. "Did it?"

"It's too soon to tell, but I believe it's possible, yes. But that's not the point. Venelov was getting into things I didn't agree with, methods that led to an end that didn't justify the means, in my opinion."

"We *are* on the same page about that," Ben snapped.

Zack could tell that the others had gathered tightly around them, not as a way of protecting the group, but because of their interest in their conversation. *What the hell,* he thought. He knew it was all going to come out at some point — any secrets shared here would not last the day without the rest of the CSO group knowing.

But it wasn't the CSO Zack was worried about.

He glanced around, then back at Ben. "Look, I'll tell you *everything* soon. But right now, all you need to know is that the plan I thought I was helping him with was only a small portion of his overall plan."

"The slime mold," Julie said, her voice a mix of interest and curiosity.

Zack nodded. "Yes, exactly. I helped build the slime mold and its artificial mitochondria, and all the stuff you discovered the last time you were in Russia. All that is true, but that is the extent of my dealings with him. I have plans... " He stopped himself, keenly aware that everyone was waiting for him to finish.

His mercenaries, his paid bodyguards, walked a few paces behind the group, acting as if they were in their own little world, but Zack knew they were listening as intently as the rest. "Anyway, I have another plan. One that Venelov didn't know about, and one you guys have no idea about. I can assure you, too, it's completely out of left field, something so bizarre I can hardly believe I'm attempting it."

Ben and the others waited, but Zack was not ready to reveal what he had been working on for so long. "Look, brother, we're on the same team. Ultimately, it's something that's so hard to explain that I didn't want to do it. I understand now that I must, but it's still so implausible it's going to take me time. I need to get things prepared, need to get things ready."

Reggie snorted. "You mean, like putting together a slideshow presentation?"

Zack side-eyed him. "Yeah, exactly like that." Reggie's smile faded immediately.

"Got it," Ben said. "I've seen enough strange stuff in my day to believe there's all sorts of other weird things I wouldn't believe if someone just told me. I hear you. Sometimes things are easier when you have some visual cues to go off of, some information you can show us."

"Yes, exactly," Zack said. "So — "

But his words were cut off by the sound of gunfire suddenly erupting from farther down the passage.

CHAPTER 58
BEN

SHOTS RANG out from all directions. The cave did a terrible job of informing them where the noise was coming from, and Ben felt as though he had stumbled into a small room with explosions happening in every corner. His eyes told him the truth, however. They were about a quarter-mile away from the firefight, and it was difficult to see clearly through the dim light of the corridor.

The bulbs that had been strung up and bolted to the walls ended about 200 feet in front of where they were now, so the cacophony happening beyond was a strange dance of shadows, flashes of light from muzzle fire, and eerie shapes.

Through it all, Ben thought he could see more light — natural light — illuminating the space behind the scene. It would still be broad daylight upstairs and outside, and Ben wondered if he was looking at light spilling in from outside.

If so, it meant there was indeed an exit in this direction. Unfortunately, it also meant their only hope of escape was somehow working their way through the mad mass of soldiers, gunfire, and whatever the Russians had begun shooting at.

Ben didn't need to guess what that was. He couldn't see it, but he knew they were fighting the same beast that had been crawling and prowling around down here.

The same creature that had destroyed the poor Russian kid,

unarmed and helpless as his limbs were plucked from his body, his torso torn completely in half.

Ben shuddered as they picked up the pace, now running directly toward the fight. He hadn't explained his thoughts to anyone; no one had spoken. They had all just started running. Even Lucia, a woman he had identified as a bit more hesitant, was running beside Freddie.

He knew the two had a thing going, he and Julie had heard as much upstairs. He wondered if she was borrowing some of the large man's courage, some of his bravery, as they all ran toward the fray.

Part of him was happy they had all decided to stick together, satisfied that their team had become one. It would not have been his first motivation, but he had been wise to agree with Julie.

They were stronger as a team.

And yet, they were running toward armed soldiers, all scared enough to be firing their weapons at something.

Ben focused on small flashes of light as he ran. At this rate, they would reach the area of the standoff in about half a minute, and he wanted to get a read on just what they would be walking into. If any of the Russian soldiers decided to look up, they would see his team coming — mostly unarmed, but a force to be reckoned with — battle-ready American men, crazed women, and armed mercenaries running toward them, all wide-eyed and terrified, running the exact wrong direction.

He hoped none of the Russians would take any shots at them, but he figured they had enough excitement to deal with.

His goal was simple: figure out what the hell they were doing. With any luck, they wouldn't turn their guns on the unknown group. Ben typically hated relying on luck, though he knew that in most situations, luck played an unfortunately large role.

The Russian team seemed to be firing on their own men, most of them spaced around the sides of the corridor as his own team had been upon coming down into the caves. A few, their backs to Ben, stood centrally in the corridor, firing downward. He heard screams between the bursts of three-round shots from the assault rifles, knowing men were hitting other men.

What had them so riled up that they had lost all sense of sanity and security, and had devolved into insanity? What had them so confused that they had decided shooting each other was the best option?

The answer revealed itself soon enough. They had traveled another hundred feet, and then now saw the dark, heavy shadow of the object of the men's ire. The thing they were shooting at was large — impossibly large.

It looked like a bear, but hunched over and sitting on all fours. They had guessed it was some sort of bear or boar, and both of these seemed to fit the impression Ben got. However, this was larger than even the largest bear Ben had ever seen. It stood easily five or six feet tall, hunched over on all four legs. It was thinner, too, and Ben suddenly understood how it could have fit through the narrow doors leading out of the laboratory room and airlock.

Every few seconds it would lurch upward, awkwardly, on one or two back legs, whirling around as the shots slammed into its torso and body. The beast roared, but the sound like the guttural moan they had heard from the Russian soldier, broken and decrepit. It didn't seem to fit the immensity of the creature itself; it was as if someone was piping in the sound of a dying cat on top of a silent movie taking place in front of Ben's eyes.

He understood a bit more now about what was happening — this creature was also infected. Whatever had plagued the Russian soldier had been given to him by this very creature, either passed through the strike of its claws or some mixing of serum, blood, or saliva. He knew the creature was not *alive* but simply playing host to the terrifying demon inside of it — a bacteria or viral infection.

Something otherworldly, apparently. He had never seen anything like this.

The others were shouting, the sounds mixing with the Russian soldiers' voices and gunshots. He heard Reggie's screams as he fired his own bursts of single-fire rounds from the sniper rifle. Any other man Ben would have doubted, but if anyone could run full-bore, full-tilt, *and* fire a sniper rifle scopeless and hope to hit his target, it was Gareth Red.

Ortega and Victor were firing shots as well, three-round bursts that seemed to be centered on the beast in the middle, though two Russian soldiers fell, the ones standing near the center of the corridor. Either from shots from behind out of his team's guns or those of their own team, or a lucky blow from the beast's wild, frenetic dance, Ben did not know.

Another fell to the left, against the wall. This one had been tackled by a shadow, the beast itself still hidden from the light. They were approaching close enough to warrant attention from the Russian soldiers and Ben suddenly felt vulnerable without a weapon.

Too late now, he thought as they continued the charge.

CHAPTER 59
BEN

ONE BY ONE, the Russian soldiers fell.

Ben and his group crept forward, no longer running, not wanting to disturb the battle and accidentally get clipped by a stray round — or one sent their way on purpose. He and the others halted along one wall, knowing they were in full light of the hanging bulbs yet no one had seemed to notice them yet. He hoped to keep it that way.

Two soldiers directly in front of him — perhaps fifty feet away — fell with screams as the beast rushed forward and simply smashed its huge head into their chests. Ben heard the sickening crunch of bones, sternums, and collarbones cracking and disintegrating beneath their skin, somehow even over the assault rifle fire.

He got a good look at it then. It was, for lack of a better word, a *beast*. He had never seen anything like it. It stood nearly six feet tall while hunched over, and while he had seen it run on its hind legs, it had never stood straight up like a bear. He wasn't sure if it was able or not, and if not, due to the infection inside of it not understanding precisely how to use its host's limbs.

The flashbacks came hard and fast. He couldn't get the picture of the mother grizzly out of his mind. He pictured Zack cowering by the tree, his father bravely rushing forward with his rifle. The memory had been seared into his mind, and though he had pushed it away time after time for the last fifteen years, it was as vivid and detailed as he remembered.

But this creature was clearly no bear. Even in the throes of war, the mother grizzly had had a sense of grace about her. She hadn't killed his father on purpose — hadn't destroyed his family out of some evil intent. It had simply been nature versus man.

And man, that day, had lost.

This creature in front of Ben now was everything *but* natural. There was no descriptor available Ben could use to give credibility to what he was seeing.

The beast's head turned, facing his group. Its eyes were dead, hollow. The glassy orbs seemed to stare right through Ben. Could it see them? Had the bacteria or virus inside spread enough to prevent the optic nerve to send signals to the brain?

He knew there was no way the thing was actually *seeing* them. This infection was operating on some deeper connection, some hive mind inside its host that simply crashed around until it connected with something organic.

Something alive.

The beast itself may have died long ago, but *something* inside of it was still very much alive.

Even now, Ben could see the two Russian soldiers it had crashed into groaning in agony on the floor. But they weren't dead — far from it. They held their stomachs and chests, covering the scratches and cuts with both arms. Their guns lay helpless on the stone floor, useless against the undead creature.

Ben knew then the truth of it. This thing had wreaked havoc throughout the entire base, possibly even venturing outside and murdering the soldier they had found whose blood they had found there. At some point, it had gone back in, either through the main entrance door or finding another entrance to the cave it was in now. At some point, it had moved throughout the facility, blind, deaf, and unable to know where it was, simply moving on instinct, controlled by an invisible demon that plagued its insides. Ben knew that this was why the rest of the base had been destroyed — this creature had smashed through any room with the door open to it, accidentally creating a disaster scene; it looked as though a bomb had gone off nearby.

The beast's head turned back to the few remaining Russian soldiers firing at it. Its body was bleeding in the few spots where there was enough blood to still fall out. Its heart wouldn't be working, of course, but the creature had died in such a way as to be preserved by the ice, so the once again liquefied serum still coursed through its veins and poured out with the help of gravity.

Huge, gaping holes had appeared in the beast's side where chunks had been blown away by rifle fire. New bullets hammered into the beast on two sides of it even now, but still, it didn't falter.

It walked in a strange calm, lumbering way. Its feet were awkward, like an adolescent teenager. They were long, reminiscent of the feet of an ancient reptile, but covered in fur. Most of that fur remained intact, but huge patches had been sheared away or fallen off. It was dark brown and seemed to shimmer a lighter color when exposed to light, but appeared equally as dark when in the shadows.

Its head was the shape of a bear's, but with an elongated snout ending in a reptilian mouth full of huge, razor-sharp teeth. Arms and legs looked the same, four total, and there was a small knob for a tail on its rear end. To Ben, it appeared like some sort of pig-bear-reptile hybrid. If it was a creature that had lived deep inside these caves, staying underground for most of its life, it made sense that it would have mammalian and reptilian features. He wondered if it was even somehow amphibious, originally starting its life deep in one of the watery ponds below the earth, crawling out onto land as whales and other prehistoric animals had.

There was nothing in the animal kingdom's taxonomy explaining what this was, at least not to Ben's knowledge. Perhaps a bone or two had been found over the years, but Ben knew how rare it was to find fossilized remains of any animal. If this was a transition creature — one that had existed between two more popular genuses — it could be that they were looking at the *only* creature anyone would ever find. But his scientific mind was quickly shut off and forced back into the present as the creature lunged once more.

Two more Russian soldiers — the last two standing — were hit head-on by the creature, its paws swiping and leaving deep, open gashes across their chests and thighs. Both soldiers stood fast, bravely aiming down at the creature's head, assuming that was how it could be killed.

They were wrong.

Since the creature was just a sack of meat and bones controlled by a microscopic organism inside, it didn't feel. It didn't hurt. It didn't hunger, or thirst.

It simply killed.

Both Russian soldiers fell to the ground, sprawling out and leaving their bellies exposed. The creature tore into them with its mouth, tearing flesh and uniform and fabric. One died immediately, the other poor soul unfortunately crying deep sobs as the creature dug.

Ben watched as the final Russian soldier pulled something off of his belt, barely missing the pile of intestines that had spilled out to the side.

"Get back!" Reggie yelled suddenly.

The creature stopped, turning as if trying to see them.

Apparently, it could hear or sense their presence. That made sense — even though the ears would not be working, it was possible Reggie's voice — literally a pressure wave — had crashed into the outside of the creature's body, vibrating it and allowing the organism inside to know there was another threat nearby.

Now Ben understood why Reggie had yelled. The small metal orb bounced a bit, landing just beneath the creature's body.

A grenade.

CHAPTER 60
FREDDIE

"EVERYONE OKAY?" Reggie asked.

Freddie frantically searched through the pile of bodies. Most of them had simply dived for cover, but Freddie had been pulling Ben backward and bumped into Lucia, who had been standing directly behind him. When the grenade exploded, there had been nowhere for the pressure wave to go but straight up and down the corridor.

He had left his feet, knowing that the blast had scared him into jumping, but feeling as though the explosion had been far larger than it had been, pushing him through the air.

And then landing directly on top of Lucia.

He heard her groan beneath him, his left arm resting across her chest. He pulled it up quickly, then pushed himself to his hands and knees, bumping someone behind him who cried out. He ignored it, focusing only on the doctor lying beneath him.

"Are you — are you okay?" he stuttered.

She was rubbing the back of her head and had bruises on both of her elbows, but otherwise seemed intact.

Slowly, she nodded. "You didn't have to land on top of me," she said softly.

Freddie smiled. "That blast was *insane*. If I wasn't standing right in front of you, you might have burned to a crisp. Or disintegrated. Just... *poof.*"

She rolled her eyes and smirked back at him. "Well, aren't you just the knight in shining armor?"

She allowed Freddie to pull her up to her feet, and together they stood, surveying the damage.

The creature that had been attacking the Russians had also likely saved their lives. Most of the grenade blast had been focused beneath the monster, which had blocked the explosion. As well, it had been drawing the Russians' attention toward itself, their attacks focused on downing the extinct creature.

Freddie had locked eyes with one of the Russian soldiers just as the animal had burst forward and crushed the man, pinning him against the wall for a moment as he died. Freddie shuddered as he recalled the scene, the horror.

Still, none of those guns had turned toward his group, and for that he was thankful.

Somehow, miraculously, the CSO team, Zack Bennett, and his mercenaries had all come out of this unscathed.

"What the hell is that?" he heard someone groan.

Freddie glanced over, recognizing Reggie's voice and looking toward where pieces of the monster lay scattered on the stone floor of the open corridor. This section of the cave looked like a large, rounded chute, and he figured it had been blasted out of the bedrock by whoever had built this space. There were offshoots of this cavern, leading to the maze-like subterranean cave complex, but it seemed whoever had constructed this facility had built some sort of underground road they were standing in now.

But it wasn't the architecture of this corridor that had caught Reggie's attention. Freddie frowned, watching where his friend was pointing. He squinted, at first not understanding.

Then he saw it, and his heart sank.

One by one, all of the Russian soldiers that were previously dead on the floor began moving, pulling themselves around in their twisted, sickening states. One of them, a man whose guts had been pulled from his insides and strewn onto the stone floor, not unlike the younger Russian soldier that had been brutally attacked farther up the corridor, seemed to be in pieces.

Yet his head jerked around awkwardly, twisting and cracking bone as it did.

"You've *got* to be kidding me," Ben muttered. Julie was next to him, inspecting both of them for superficial wounds, but she stopped, staring as well.

Freddie saw Ortega push forward, his weapon drawn and ready, but Victor intervened and got in front of him, using a hand to push his gun down.

He shook his head. "There's no point," Victor said. "They're not alive, remember? Those Russian soldiers were trying the same thing, trying to attack that thing by aiming for its head, its vital organs. It failed, and you will fail if you try the same thing on them."

"But we *have* to try," Ortega said under his breath.

"The only thing that's going to take them down is explosives. As disgusting as it sounds, whatever's infected them moves extremely quickly and isn't affected by gunshot wounds, because the infection is microscopic. It will just regroup. The host has to be blasted apart for the thing to be able to stop moving."

Reggie chuckled. "Wasn't the case for our little Russian buddy upstairs," he said. "Seems like the little bacteria — or whatever the hell it is — just contracts muscles over and over again. I bet it can even make an Addams Family hand out of one of these guys."

Ben shook his head, and Freddie watched as the team reconvened, shaking off their cuts and scrapes from the grenade blast. Lucia worked her jaw, trying to clear her head and popped her ears, but Freddie noticed she wouldn't move farther than a foot away from him. He straightened his back, squared his shoulders. He wasn't about to argue with that.

"So what do we do?" Julie asked. "We can't just... leave them here."

Ben turned to Victor. "Did your men bring any explosive charges with you? Anything we can use to handle this?"

Victor turned and looked at Ortega, then back at Ben and the rest of the group. Freddie noticed he locked eyes with Zack before speaking. "Yes, we did. More than enough to take this entire corridor and bring it to the ground on their heads. We've got grenades, C-4 in our packs.

Back outside, one of my men had a Claymore. He's no longer alive, but we can retrieve his — "

"What you have is more than enough. We don't need to bring this entire place down. We just need to make sure these soldiers are well-buried. *None* of this can get out. Whatever this is — this infection — it has to stay in the cave."

Victor stared at Ben, and Freddie waited for the man's response. After a few seconds, it came. "Agreed. This has to stay here. All of it. If the Russian government finds out what this is, they'll tear this place apart, then come looking for us."

"And the disease will spread," Zack said softly.

Two of the Russian soldiers began crawling forward, using their hands as levers. Their bones were broken, but it didn't seem to slow them down. Their faces were contorted in a mask of rage or fear. Freddie couldn't tell the difference, and the muscles on the men's faces twitched as they approached the group.

Freddie noticed that the rest of the team had taken a step back, their eyes fixed on the approaching soldiers. He saw Ben motion to Victor and Ortega, who moved forward to place the explosive charges.

Freddie turned his attention back to the soldiers, feeling a sick sense of dread in his gut. He wondered how many more of them were out there, infected and crawling toward them like this. He knew that they couldn't afford to take any chances, and that they needed to get out of here as quickly as possible.

As the soldiers crawled closer, Freddie raised his weapon, the assault rifle he'd taken from the Russian upstairs, taking careful aim at the closest one. He felt a surge of adrenaline as he squeezed the trigger, watching as the soldier's head exploded in a shower of blood and bone fragments. The second soldier continued crawling forward, undeterred by his companion's death.

Freddie fired again, this time hitting the soldier in the chest. The impact knocked the soldier backward, and he fell to the ground, unmoving. Freddie let out a deep breath, feeling a wave of relief wash over him.

It was a small comfort, knowing that they had made it through the massacre alive. But he knew that their troubles were far from over. The infection was still here, waiting to spread to anyone who crossed its path.

And if they didn't find a way to stop it, it would continue to ravage everything, including them.

CHAPTER 61
VICTOR

VICTOR STEPPED over the pile of Russian soldier parts and dodged an infected arm that swiped out at his legs. Ortega followed closely behind him, likely unsure of Victor's plan.

That's okay, he thought. *He'll figure it out soon enough.*

The others watched on as Victor walked delicately through the maze of infected soldier bodies. Most of them simply writhed in place, the bacteria or virus inside bubbling just beneath the surface but otherwise unable to move their host.

"What are you doing?" Harvey Bennett called over to him.

Victor didn't respond. Instead, he held up a brick of C-4 explosive, hoping that would satisfy the CSO team. Zachary Bennett ran forward, coming to stand next to his older brother. "Victor, how much of that stuff will it take?" he asked.

Victor stopped, kicked the head of one of the Russian soldiers crawling on the floor to redirect it, then responded. "Probably all I have," he said. "I'm no engineer, but this place is old. Probably not kept up very well."

Light from the cave entrance, another 200 feet distant and downhill from their spot, cast all the clamoring soldiers on the floor and the standing men and women in eerie shadow. The bodies scraped and pulled against the slippery, slick surface, but they were far too slow to be of any danger to him or Ortega.

Ortega pulled his own pack around and pulled out his charges. The explosives were sticky, capable of adhering to almost any surface, though the smooth, slippery walls in this place would prove to be formidable. Even if they fell to the floor, however, the effect should be the same.

The entire place would come crashing down over their heads. Fissures, slowly cracking open over millennia of wear and movement, deep inside the earth, would appear and grow. It was very likely that it would cause the entire cave system to come down on top of all of them.

All of them, of course, except for Victor and Ortega.

Victor nodded to Ortega, who began sticking the C-4 onto walls, high enough that none of the Russians could accidentally swipe them off. If they adhered properly, they wouldn't be going anywhere, but that would take some time. While Ortega worked, Victor worked his way back around the group of soldiers and over to where the CSO team stood.

He stood close to Ben and his brother; his eyes focused on the rest of the group. He had respect for the two soldiers among them, Reggie and Freddie, and immense respect for Julie and Lucia, the two women who had proven quite useful in their expedition so far.

But he had no need for most of them.

In a flash, he took two quick strides, closing the distance between himself and Freddie, swung his assault rifle from its perch on his shoulder out in front of him, and fired two quick shots, directly into Freddie's gut.

The shots were deafening, and the CSO group stumbled backwards. Victor continued moving, reaching Freddie as the man stared down at the two open wounds in his stomach. Blood was pouring from them already, and Victor saw a trickle of the stuff start seeping from the corner of the man's mouth.

He stretched a palm out, steadying Freddie, then ripped the Russian assault rifle out of his hands. "I'm sorry," he said softly, genuinely meaning it. "I didn't come here to kill anyone, but I can't help but take advantage of an opportunity when I see one."

"Victor, what are you doing?" Julie shouted.

Ben and Reggie had rushed over to catch Freddie as he fell backward, which helped Victor even more — the only other weapon in the group, the sniper rifle Reggie had been carrying, was still on the floor on the other side of the cave, having fallen out of the ex-Army sniper's hands after the first grenade blast.

Reggie didn't seem interested in picking it up. Only seconds would pass before him, Ben, or one of the women would realize what had happened and that Victor was no longer a friend.

But he was already in motion, tossing Freddie's assault rifle across the pile of Russian soldiers and the slain monster that littered the cavern space, over to the side of the passage that led to the exit.

He darted forward again, grabbing Dr. Lucia Vergotti's arm and yanking her with him. She yelped in surprise, but he didn't slow down.

He saw Ortega still working with the C-4, now planting the charges that he would be able to remotely detonate with the press of a button. He started running, still holding the scientist's arm, and leapt over the same infected Russian soldier he had kicked earlier.

He planted his feet and jumped over a large hunk of the dead animal. Dr. Vergotti was running as well, likely unsure why but not daring to fight back, and the pair landed just on the other side of the fray.

"Keep up!" he yelled to her. "Hurry!"

CHAPTER 62
LUCIA

SHE HEARD the others yelling now, though she still felt shell-shocked from the surprising blast of Victor's gun. Two shots fired directly into Freddie's gut. She had shrieked — at least she thought she had — and fallen backward, hitting the side of the cavern wall hard. She had nearly fallen over, catching herself only as the sound dissipated and the shouts replaced her foggy brain.

Lucia watched in horror as Victor came for her next. He held the gun out in front of him, just as he had before he had shot Freddie. But instead, he grabbed her. It was rough, hostile, and he yanked her with him back into the disgusting pile of human and animal bodies.

Ortega was still doing whatever it was he would have been doing, sticking bricks of some explosive to the cave walls. He had planted three charges, two on one side, and one on the other so far, and seemed to be planting one final charge.

Victor hauled her through the cavern, dodging humans and animal parts as he gripped her. He pulled her along as he did, stepping through the maze, but she was no more interested in allowing one of these infected hosts to touch her than she was in letting Victor take her.

"Where — what are you doing?" she stammered. He ignored her, the others continued shouting behind her.

Victor suddenly swung around and fired three shots into the ceiling above the other group's heads. She shrieked, turning around just in time to see Reggie lowering the sniper rifle he had been holding. She hadn't realized he had gone to grab it, but it seemed Victor had anticipated this.

"Set it down, or your entire team dies right here, right now," Victor snapped.

"You leave us in here, it's already a death sentence," Harvey snarled.

"Victor laughed. "A *death sentence*? Hardly. As I told Freddie, I didn't come here to kill you or anyone else. I was simply looking for a way out. It seems opportunity has provided one."

"A way out?" Julie asked, her voice shaking with rage. "*We* are your way out — what do you hope to accomplish by leaving us here?"

Victor had pulled Lucia through the pile of bodies and stood on the opposite side from the group, waiting for Ortega to finish. He did only a few seconds later, coming to stand on the other side of Lucia. He grabbed her upper arm, and Victor let go, now holding his rifle out with two hands.

A shot she knew he would not miss.

"Leaving you alive down here is my way of proving that I *didn't* come here to kill you all. But I do need her."

He knelt down, keeping the rifle out and focused on the leaders of the CSO group, but grabbed something off the floor with his other hand. Lucia was horrified when she noticed what it was.

A human hand.

Stained with blood and inside a dirty sleeve, the hand was moving, writhing around with the infectious disease. The fingers cracked and bent, awkwardly and abruptly. She shuddered. It was right in front of her face, and she couldn't help but get the feeling that this thing was somehow... alive.

But she knew better — they had already verified that this was just the macabre side effect of whatever disease wracked the inside of this host.

Victor smartly kept the thing held out in front of him far enough that the sharp fingernails couldn't scratch his face or body, making sure to keep his skin away from the Russian soldier's own by holding the remains of the man's uniform sleeve.

"And... I need *this*."

Lucia started to understand what Victor was getting at. Thankfully, he continued.

"Ortega?"

Ortega nodded, as if he understood what Victor wanted him to do.

Victor turned and addressed the CSO group and Zachary Bennett once more. "My sincerest apologies — I was hoping we could do this in a more formal way, but boss — Zachary — I must inform you of my *imminent* retirement."

Zack frowned, motioning with his hands that he had no idea what was happening. "What are you talking about? Retirement?"

"As I said, opportunity struck. This is a gold mine, you know that, right?" Lucia got the sense the question wasn't rhetorical as he spoke. "This may look disgusting, like some evil incarnate, but I see money. I see technology. A future for warfare, for terrorism — for anything someone who pays enough money wants."

"You're going to *sell* that thing?" Julie asked.

"Time for talk is done," Victor snapped. "This isn't like the movies — no long speech from me." He turned to Lucia, looking into her eyes. Surprisingly, she saw his eyes shift, softening. She found only warmth and generosity there now. He looked down at her as if to say, *I'm sorry.*

She didn't understand, other than the fact that this man had lied to all of them, had betrayed them the entire time. But she got the sense that he was wrestling with his own demons and being truthful.

This was an opportunity, and he had decided to take it.

There was no going back now, for better or worse.

Victor nodded once more at Ortega. Ortega turned back around while holding Lucia and together with Victor walked backward, both men aiming their assault rifles at the CSO team, just in case any of them decided to make a run for it.

Lucia glanced back over her shoulder, seeing that Harvey's arms were up, palms out in a gesture of surrender. But his face was lined with hardened rage, his eyes narrow, his mouth just a thin line.

Behind him, Reggie had rushed over to Freddie and was administering aid to his friend. He had already begun wrapping his own shirt over the two bullet wounds in Freddie's gut, but blood pooled around his hands.

Julie and Zack stared back at them in shock, a feeling Lucia shared.

Ortega dragged her down the corridor, and the light of daylight soon began splashing against her face. She felt the air change, a heavier, thicker air like that of maritime wind, and she thought she saw green grass in the bright white space peeking out around a corner.

It was then that Ortega pressed the detonator, causing all of them to fall forward. She caught herself, but Victor helped her up. She turned back, seeing only dust and debris flying toward her. Most of the heavy pieces of stone and rock landed, rolled, or slid to a halt, while smaller pebbles reached their location, still rolling downhill. Dust in the wind battered her face, and she had to turn away.

When she finally looked back, all she saw was darkness. It was at that moment the tears began to fall.

CHAPTER 63
FREDDIE

THE BLAST FELT a hundred times more powerful than that of the grenade. Thankfully, the charges that had been placed were directional and had been positioned in such a way that the ceiling and walls of the corridor had taken the brunt of the damage.

Still, Freddie squeezed his eyes shut, knowing that the pain he was feeling from being shot by Victor was nothing compared to the pain he was about to feel from the huge explosion. And yet... all he felt from the explosion was heat, pressure that pushed his body and slid him eight feet up the corridor.

He opened his eyes and blinked a few times to push away the dust as disintegrated stone and smoke settled. He tried to understand what had happened. He was sure the ceiling had come crashing down on top of him, and he was now pinned beneath a huge boulder. But the boulder groaned.

"You owe me big time for that one, big guy," Reggie muttered.

The pain in his gut returned, but it was no longer searing, lancing heat from the hot lead but more of a terrible throb. It was the worst pain he had ever felt, but his confusion about being alive seemed to dissipate some of it. He glanced to his left, then did a double take. Reggie's face was right there.

Close enough to kiss.

But the other man didn't seem interested in kissing. He pushed off of Freddie's body carefully, trying not to upset his wound. During the scuffle earlier, Reggie had acted quickly, removing his own shirt and turning it inside out, then pressing it tightly against the bullet wounds. He had muttered something about one of them being through and through, the other still inside his body. If they acted quickly enough, they might be able to get it out.

If the blood loss didn't kill him first...

But Freddie was awake and lucid. That was a good sign. He turned to Reggie, who was now crouched next to him, examining his own stomach.

Freddie's heart sank when he saw the huge blossoming wound in Reggie's own gut.

Reggie looked up, his eyes wide. "No worries here, bud," he said quickly. "This is *your* blood."

Freddie tried to smile, but winced instead. Reggie patted him on the shoulder, squeezing hard enough to cause a bit of pain there. It was brilliant, actually — it made Freddie's bullet wounds feel a bit better.

"Unfortunately for you, this ain't the end. Once the bleeding stops, you'll ride or die until we get out of here. I don't like the idea of you leaking, but we'll be able to keep you in one piece until we get back to the city."

Freddie heard most of the words and understood them only a bit, but nodded anyway. Reggie had jumped on top of him right before the explosion, saving him from any pieces of stone or rock that might fly their direction and protecting the wound.

He tried to open his mouth and thank his friend, but Reggie stopped him. "I know you want to whisper sweet nothings to me, but save it for later. You'll need your strength to get outta here, since I ain't about to carry you over my shoulder."

Freddie smiled again, this time working through the pain.

"Is he okay?" Julie asked, standing next to him. Freddie saw that she was covered in white dust but looked otherwise unscathed. Ben and Zack, who had been standing closest to the blast, both had a thousand cuts and scrapes on their faces. Both men had fallen backward but seemed only bruised, not broken.

Regardless of Victor's betrayal, Freddie had to admit that Victor had told the truth — he *hadn't* wanted to kill them.

Freddie nodded weakly, feeling Reggie and Julie grab his arms and help him up. He was unsteady at first, his legs feeling like they were made of jelly, but he managed to find his footing.

"We need to move," Ben said, looking around at the collapsed corridor. "Who knows how much time we have before this place comes down on our heads?"

"He's right," Zack added, coughing as he tried to clear the dust from his lungs. "We can't stay here."

CHAPTER 64
BEN

BEN WATCHED the dust settle above the pile of rock. Miraculously, the entire cavern had not come down on top of them. He wondered if this corridor was, in fact, an old road — something cut out of the original cave system meant to allow easy access to wherever they had found the frozen creature in the block of ice. The rocks at the top of the pile revealed a gaping hole in the ceiling. A cavern or crawl space existed just above their heads, and the floor of it had fallen down when Victor and Ortega's bombs went off.

It was now a massive pile of stone blocking their way, but because of the open space that had existed above, it still offered them a way out. Ben could see trickles of sunlight peeking through near the top of the pile.

It would be an arduous climb, but it would only set them back an hour or two.

"You seeing what I'm seeing?" Reggie asked.

Ben turned to his best friend. The man's hands and chest were completely covered in blood — Freddie's. Ben looked over at Freddie, seeing that the man was awake and talking, wincing through the pain of his two bullet wounds. Julie and Zack were attending to him, but he seemed to be doing okay, hobbling between them, testing his weight to see if he could walk.

"I see it. I don't know if it's going to work, though."

Reggie frowned, then looked at Freddie and back at Ben. "Yeah, that's gonna be a bit rough on him."

"That door upstairs — that was the only other entrance or exit that I saw."

"Yeah, but it's sealed shut."

Ben shook his head. "Sealed *almost* shut. It's a heavy door, but it's still a door. Just because the metal got pinched after that explosion down here doesn't mean we can't get it to budge. We didn't really try."

"It's still a long walk," Reggie mumbled. "Going to be hard for him."

"He'll make it. Still better than trying to climb over this pile of jagged rocks and squeeze through the hole we are hoping is there. And the car's just outside that door upstairs. Plus, Victor said his other man had more explosives with him."

Reggie's eyebrows raised.

"I know what you're thinking," Ben said, noticing that Julie, Zack, and Freddie were now listening in, standing nearby awaiting Ben's opinion. "Yeah, he's going to be a problem if he's still alive. Victor said that animal attacked him. We've seen what happens when that thing scratches you. If it got into his bloodstream..."

"We're going to have a pissed-off, infected mercenary to deal with."

"True, but there's only one of him," Reggie said.

"Only one we know of," Zack added.

Ben nodded, chewing it over. They could spend time moving the rocks, making a hole big enough for all of them to fit through, but Freddie would still move slowly. They could split up, sending Reggie or Julie out ahead of the group to stop Victor.

That wouldn't do. Not only was he committed to their goal of sticking together at all costs, he didn't trust Victor or Ortega to stay true to their mission — to not kill them if confronted.

No, they needed to get to Victor and Ortega as soon as possible, or Ben was sure Lucia would be long gone. The woman deserved better, and though Ben got the sense Victor was not going to torture the woman, he already knew full well that Victor would do whatever it took to get what he wanted.

If Victor wanted Lucia's knowledge or scientific mind...

None of the rest of his team peppered him with questions, all silent, waiting for his response.

No, they needed to move quickly, all together. That meant working back up through the base, moving quickly but carefully to avoid the last mercenary they knew was still alive. If they could find him, or the pack he had come in with, they might be able to find a grenade or more C-4. A grenade might work, but an explosive charge would *certainly* do the trick, blasting a hole in the front wall of the facility large enough for them all to get out.

He looked around, suspecting that everyone already knew what he was going to say. "We need to move upstairs. My assumption is that Victor and his men came in the same place we did, which means their exit vehicles are going to be up there as well. They might be hidden in the trees somewhere since we didn't see them on the way in, but they didn't know about this exit from the caves just like we didn't.

That means they'll have to move uphill to try to get back to the lake and the same entrance we are heading toward."

Everyone nodded, and Zack offered a word of advice. "Victor's not a killer. I hired him to be private security. He's not a murderer... he's going to make sure Lucia is safe."

Ben turned on his younger brother. "*Safe*? Safe would be leaving her here with us, not trying to blow up the entire place on his way out. *Safe* would be not kidnapping her."

Zack's face fell.

"Frankly, I've had enough of your bullshit, Zack. You keep telling us there's 'more to this than meets the eye,' but judging by what meets my eye, it seems like your hired guns didn't even trust you enough to stay loyal."

Zack's jaw clenched, but he didn't speak.

"I'm half considering leaving you down here to rot, little brother."

Zack looked up at him then, eyes wide. They weren't pleading, but searching.

"You know I won't, because I'm actually a good man. But if you so much as look at me or my team the wrong way, if you even hesitate when we need your input..."

Ben hoped he didn't have to finish the sentence. He wasn't about to kill the only other family member he had left on this earth. At the same time, he wasn't exactly thrilled about his brother's constant betrayal.

But was it truly a betrayal?

Zack was an idiot, a brilliant scientific mind lacking street smarts. He had done what he thought was right, even convinced himself that Venelov was working toward a goal that aligned with Zack's own.

Was Ben too different? They both got their stubbornness from their mother, but even their father had a strong sense of justice. He would do whatever it took to make things right — even at the expense of his own life.

Zack looked once more at his younger brother, finally realizing it. "I can't," he said.

Zack and the others looked at him strangely.

"I *can't*, because you're me. You might be misguided, but I've been there. More times than I care to admit. I can't in good faith threaten you with anything, because I know I won't be able to see it through. As much as I would have loved to turn you over to these Russian assholes, you and I both know it wasn't going to happen. I just hope that when the time comes, you won't betray us."

"I won't. You have my word, for whatever that's worth."

Ben looked at his younger brother and felt as though he was seeing him for the first time. "It's worth a lot, Zack."

He reached out and grabbed Zack's hand, but his younger brother pulled the larger man down and wrapped him up in a tight hug.

CHAPTER 65
LUCIA

LUCIA HAD STOPPED FIGHTING BACK. It was no use. Both men were stronger than her, and together they were formidable. It would be impossible to run away. The only reason they were keeping her alive was that she was still with them. She was positive if she made a break for it — if she somehow was able to get away — Victor Ortega would simply turn around and shoot her dead. They knew she was just the easiest way to achieve their goal.

Without her, it wouldn't be much trouble for them to go back, kill everyone else, and take Zack Bennett instead.

She didn't know if the others were still alive, if the cave had been brought down on top of them or not. From her perspective, it seemed as though after they had shot Freddie, after they had blown the explosives, the entire place had been turned into rubble, once again just a pile of rocks inside a cave in the mountain.

She hadn't heard any shouts or groans. But they had pulled her away quickly enough so that she hadn't been able to get a good look over the pile of stones as the dust had cleared.

But she knew enough: she knew the status quo had changed.

"Where are you taking me?" Her voice was even, measured. She understood what was happening, she had the street smarts and experience to know what this was. Still, any information she could glean from this interaction could potentially help her.

Ortega muttered something in Spanish, but Victor answered her. "Away from here."

She snorted, cursing in Italian. "Yeah, I got that. Where, exactly?"

Victor stopped then, still holding the Russian soldier's hand, and she noticed the plague inside of it began moving again, sensing a change in its environment and reaching out for sustenance. She shuddered; it was gross.

"Wouldn't you like to know?" Victor snapped. "I wasn't lying before — you are going to help me with my upcoming change in career."

"I will *never* help you."

Ortega spat, but Victor eyed her cautiously. "I did not know you have the strength in you, Dr. Vergotti," he said gently. As he spoke, the hand he was holding writhed and twisted. "I am usually a fine judge of character, but I must admit, did not expect you to put up much of a fight."

"This is no *fight*," she said, her voice resigned. "You know I cannot fight you. I simply want to know where you're taking me."

He studied her for a moment, then answered again. "If you're wondering if I will torture you, I will not. That's not something that interests me. I think you understand the gravity of the situation, however. You will either help me, or you will die. I am not a killer, but an opportunist. And if there is no opportunity, I am not opposed to killing."

She chuckled again. "It sounds like you *are* a killer, then."

It seemed she struck a nerve. She saw a flash in Victor's eyes, rage boiling just beneath the surface. Just as quickly as she had seen it appear, it vanished. "I am *not* a killer. Sure, I was, once. Sure, I fought for my country at one point. I am good at that, was good at that. But I have changed. I am not interested in death and destruction, despite what you may think of recent events. I simply want what is owed to me — I simply want to be done with all of this, to quietly retire in peace."

Her eyes widened. "If you want that, why not get it? What's stopping you?"

He turned and glanced at Ortega, who was busy studying the horizon. The man would not look at Victor or Lucia, and she wondered what he was thinking.

"Money," Victor said softly. "Is that so hard to understand? It's *always* been money, the source of so much pain and suffering. The source of so much joy and happiness. As a young man, I had none of it. As a grown man, I had just enough.

"But I spent my life fighting for other people — sure, killing them when necessary. But I truly have changed, and all I want is to go my own way, put down these weapons, and rest."

Finally, Ortega looked over at Victor and smiled. "He wants an island. Paradise. Some of those little drinks that have umbrellas stuck in the tops. *We* want that."

Victor smiled back, and Lucia thought she sensed something more between the men. Were they more than just partners? More than just associates? More than just comrades?

"I don't want to own the *entire* island — though that would be nice. I just want enough money to sit in peace. To read books. To explore the world behind a screen. I've had enough of the real thing — now I just want to sit somewhere quietly. Unfortunately, that requires money. Lots of it, if I expect to live longer than ten more years."

Lucia nodded as he explained. "A fine goal," she said, hoping a small olive branch would help bridge the gap. "But not like this. They're going to come after you, if they lived through that. They won't stop until — "

"Until what? Once you help me, I *will* let you go. As I said, I'm not going to torture you, and you have my word none of my men will, either. I just need your help figuring out how this — " he held up the grotesque severed hand and waved it around, "can help get me there."

"You're going to sell it?"

"Not *it*, but what it can provide. What it can *become*. These Russian soldiers were not sent here because they were trying to protect their own, trying to save whatever researchers and scientists were here. They were sent here because their government wants one thing above all else — leverage. And that leverage is best provided in the form of weapons."

He took a long breath. "And those weapons are provided by science. By things like this. You are going to help me figure out how this can become a weapon used in the field of duty. I don't know what this thing is or why it is, but you do. Or you can find out. Once you do, combined with the infection inside of this thing, I will be able to package it and sell it to the highest bidder."

Lucia stared at Victor, staring at the hand he was holding. She didn't want to admit it, but everything he said was true. She knew the Russian government would pay a huge sum for a ready-to-go chemical weapon like this — something that could not only defeat their enemies without losing a man but something that would turn those enemies against themselves.

It was biological and chemical warfare at its finest.

And unfortunately, Victor was more right than he thought. She had a very good idea of *exactly* what this infection was.

CHAPTER 66

BEN

THE CSO TEAM and Zack raced upward through the facility as fast as they could.

Although *raced* was not the word Ben would have used. They had to proceed cautiously, ensuring that Freddie didn't reopen his bullet wounds and injure himself further. The shirt Reggie had tied around his waist had gotten soaked through, so they had discarded it in favor of one of Zack's pant legs, which he had cut off and offered.

Zack raced ahead of them now, with Ben and Julie following behind, and Reggie holding Freddie up with a hand over his shoulder.

In terms of situations Ben had found himself in, he had to admit, this was one of the better ones. They were all mostly intact, and while Lucia had been kidnapped, he felt confident that Victor wouldn't harm her.

He was more concerned about what Victor would do with this infection. Whatever the hell it might be, it seemed like something out of a science fiction movie.

He also knew it was just the sort of thing a government — or another unscrupulous operator — would be interested in purchasing, and he knew Victor would make out like a bandit. He would make a killing selling the technology.

In a time where chemical and biological warfare threats were everpresent, the intrigue alone would cause the bid price for the technology to soar. And the fact that it worked extremely well, apparently, meant that the price would inflate to impossible numbers.

And yet, someone, somewhere would want it. They would move heaven and earth to acquire the technology inside the Russian soldier's hand that Victor had stolen. And Lucia, he thought, was exactly the key Victor needed to unlock it. She would be able to study it and reverse engineer it quite easily, Ben was sure.

With her help, Victor could synthesize the compound, provide additional tests, and then sell the research and product as one perfectly packaged weapon to any terrorist organization or Third World country wanting to get ahead.

Or, as Ben was all too aware, to a government like his own, willing to stoop to that level in order to keep ahead of the competition. It needed to be destroyed, all of it. He felt confident the entirety of the serum and infection contained in this very facility, with the exception of what Victor had stolen, needed to be destroyed as quickly as possible.

Since it seemed the infection only spread through the sharing of bodily fluids, he was confident Victor wouldn't accidentally let the infection run rampant. Victor would have to drop the hand and allow some critter to eat it for it to have a chance at latching onto a new host. Victor would not be so careless, however.

Ben worked ahead of the group, coming to each open door and poking a head in, trying to ensure nothing would jump out at his group as they ascended.

The stairs felt narrower now, as if the place was starting to constrict. Ben felt like the characters from the first Star Wars movie, stuck in the trash compactor.

Except the snake-like alien creature they had been trapped with was a known entity. He didn't love snakes, but he would have much preferred one to the threat they were facing now.

Anything was better than this infection.

CHAPTER 67
BEN

THEY PASSED the laboratory on the levels of the facility. The door leading into the airlock was still open, and Ben glanced in as they passed. The place was still in disarray, the only thing seemingly in place was the upturned table they had turned over and sat in the middle of the floor.

The bottle of manufacturing solution was still sitting on top of it. He heard no sound and let out a breath. If Victor's other man was still here, he was not in this room.

But they found him only thirty seconds later.

They had taken the stairs up to the next level and passed by two more doors that were still open. In front of the third, they heard the sound of shuffling. It was a strange sort of scraping sound as if someone was trying to walk without lifting their feet.

Ben was still leading the group. He stopped, halting everyone in the hallway as he gripped the sniper rifle Reggie had given him. He had only fired such a weapon at the range before, with Reggie laughing the entire time as Ben tried to dial in the settings and sight the targets from a quarter-mile away.

He had missed every shot.

But this was not a shooting range, and his target was not a quarter-mile away. There was no wind here, and no sunlight to worry about.

He held the weapon tightly, double-checking that it was loaded. Reggie had yet to fire the thing since finding it outside the base, but had informed Ben there were only two rounds available. They hadn't been able to find more ammunition.

Though the rounds were massive, Ben knew all too well what little damage two of these bullets could do against an infected host. He steeled himself, waiting behind the open door, then turned and peered inside.

Victor's man, Garcia, was there, standing in the middle of the room. Ben couldn't tell what the room's intent or purpose was, but he noticed the same disarray he found in all the other rooms, though it was slightly less in this one. There was a desk against the far wall, and a lamp that had fallen off of it. Two small filing cabinets were set on the wall to its right, but they were still standing.

Victor's soldier either didn't notice Ben turning into the room, or the infection had already spread enough to overtake the man's nervous system.

Ben reached in and pulled the door toward him. He winced, hoping it wouldn't make a sound. If they could simply close the door and keep moving, they wouldn't have to —

The door shrieked, and the mercenary whipped around, his neck cracking as his head tried to move toward the door before his feet started in that direction.

Ben saw the wobbliness in the mercenary's knees, saw the man still there, his face twisted in agony, trying to fight against the infection. His left hand was shaking, his right was contorted in a twisted group of fingers that looked like he was trying to throw something.

The infected human pushed toward the open door, and Ben couldn't help himself but stare. He was mesmerized by the twisted, agonized expression on the man's face, seeing blobs of something just beneath the skin bubbling and moving, as if there were thousands of tiny beetles undulating under the skin of the man's face.

He shuddered, wondering what it must feel like to be going through this while alive.

Ben lifted the sniper rifle, unsure of what else to do. The man stopped, but the infection inside him tried to continue pushing his body forward. It was man against nature, only this time the man was losing.

Ben wondered how long it would take — it had only been maybe an hour or two since the man had come in contact with the infected animal that passed the infection on to him. He wondered if it would move more slowly since his wounds had not been deep.

What had Victor said? Only a scratch? Ben couldn't even see the scratch now. It must have been incredibly small, microscopic. He remembered Victor's attitude toward this man — he had acted as though it were not real, as if it had not happened.

"Take him out," he heard Reggie say in the hallway.

Ben didn't respond. He did lift the sniper rifle up, aiming directly at the man's head. He wondered if this man was still human enough to know what was happening, to know that he was going to die in this room.

"It won't do anything," Zack was saying.

"It will slow the bastard down," Reggie argued.

Ben's finger pulled the trigger back, feeling the resistance. Another twitch of the muscle and the man's entire head would disappear.

Ben had killed before out of necessity, but this felt different. This felt somehow wrong. He second-guessed himself, almost faltering and lowering the rifle once more, when the man's eyes suddenly cleared.

He stared at Ben, his expression still twisted and pained, but there was a lucidity there Ben hadn't seen before.

The man's mouth moved and twitched. Ben watched, fascinated. Finally, after a few false starts, the man muttered two words.

"Do... it."

CHAPTER 68
VICTOR

"I SEE THEM!" Victor yelled.

Ortega didn't respond. Instead, the man ran forward a few steps, looking to get behind a scraggly, stringy bush nearby for cover. Victor pulled Lucia closer to him, eliciting a shriek from her as he yanked her arm and placed her body between him and the rock outcropping in the distance.

After leaving the caves, they had walked alongside the lake toward the southeast. Victor had hoped to get back to the line of trees that extended around in a wide arc, staying hidden as they ran back up toward the mountain they had descended before entering the facility. As he looked south, he saw that mountain looming in the distance, about a mile away.

The huge pile of boulders and stones, interspersed with concrete walls and ceilings, sat about a half-mile away. It blocked his view of the destroyed hut he and his men had hidden behind before coming here.

He shuddered, wishing he had never come here.

Still, he had everything he needed to ensure success. This was a new era, one where technology reigned supreme. But throughout all eras of human history, science *was* technology. He could use this information — Lucia's knowledge coupled with whatever infection was inside the hand he was still holding — and reverse engineer it.

He would be able to sell not just the theory, but the product, to whoever paid him the most.

It was the missing piece. Over the course of his career, both in the military and in private security, Victor had slowly built a network of people who would help him accomplish this final goal. He had connections to black markets in every corner of the globe, and he had trusted associates with whom he could set up observations and auctions for this new technology.

He was no fool — he had no interest in trying to do everything himself. It was the mark of a naïve man to attempt to sell prototypes and technologies on the black market without protection and without experience. He would build a team, paying them well, ensuring that he was the one pulling the strings, in control.

But none of that would do any good if he was taken advantage of, if someone swooped in and stole the technology out from underneath him.

Lucia fought against him, sensing that this was her chance to escape, but he held fast. He had two wrists in his hands — one from a Russian soldier who no longer existed, and one from the scientist who would provide his retirement plan. He wasn't about to let either go.

Ortega was already aiming down his sights, targeting the group that had emerged from the front of the facility.

They had somehow blown the door open, likely by using a grenade from one of the fallen Russian soldiers. He was impressed once again with Harvey Bennett's resilience and adaptability. He watched as the large man emerged, his wife Julie in tow. He saw Freddie next, walking slowly using some long object as a crutch.

He felt Lucia struggling harder, doing her best to pull free. He sensed she was about to fight to the death, doing whatever she could to break away. He turned around just in time.

She had reeled back and was preparing to kick him directly in the crotch, judging by the way her foot hung out to the side. Her leg swung around and forward, but he shifted to the side and let her kick him in the thigh instead.

It hurt, but it was nowhere near as painful as it would have been had he not caught on.

He dropped her hand. She looked down, surprised. Then he swung with his free hand and swiped across her face, palm open, slapping her hard on the cheek.

He heard Ortega's weapon firing now, but he was already locked in his own battle with Lucia. She was small, and thus easily able to slip away from his first grasp. He barely missed her collar, and the Russian wrist he was holding wriggled free.

It flopped to the ground, and Victor gasped. His eyes widened, but he looked at the hard-packed dirt near the shore of the lake, taking in the jagged rocks and uneven terrain surrounding it.

He looked down, watching the wrist and hand writhe around, the infection inside of it excited to explore its new location. He ignored it, realizing it wasn't going to go anywhere quickly. Sure, it might be able to pull itself along on the ground, but the bacteria or virus inside of it was not smart — it had no idea which way was forward, or where it was trying to go in the first place. Sure enough, he watched it for a second as he struggled with Lucia, seeing that it wriggled around but didn't move much at all.

Three more shots from Ortega, farther away. He glanced up, noticing that Ortega had moved behind a large tree that offered much better protection than the bush.

Victor squinted, trying to see which of the CSO people had a weapon — he knew Ben would have attempted to find weapons and outfit his team upon leaving the blast site, but he didn't see a gun in either Ben's or Julie's hands. Perhaps Zack or Freddie was hiding behind a boulder now, aiming toward them?

Lucia twisted around and yanked Victor's fingers free of her shirt. He heard it tear, felt the rip as it revealed open skin from her shoulder down to her wrist, and he found himself left holding her empty sleeve. He whirled around, and was met with a smack in the face.

"Get away from me, you monster!" Lucia screamed.

Victor stumbled back, holding his cheek in pain. He looked back to see Lucia running toward the water's edge.

CHAPTER 69
VICTOR

VICTOR'S EYES stung with the impact.

He stumbled backward, his foot catching on a rock, and nearly backpedaled into the lake. The sandy shore did little to help his footing, and he swung his arms around in wide circles, trying to right himself.

Lucia had the opportunity to turn around and run, but she didn't. She stepped back five feet, putting enough distance between Victor and herself that he wouldn't be able to surprise her by darting forward to grab her again.

It was a smart move, but he knew the smartest move would have been for her to run over to the CSO team.

Why wasn't she?

He frowned, finally regaining his balance but still blinking away tears. He rubbed the side of his face, his hand coming away slick with blood. She must have dug her fingernails into his skin, peeling away strips of flesh. It was deep, and the pain only intensified as the chilled air caught the open wound. He worked his jaw, trying to elicit more pain response from the delicate area but finding it too excruciating to help.

Ortega fired two burst rounds, and he saw the rounds pinging against the now-open door, hanging on one hinge, as well as the rocks around it. There was no one at the entrance, but he saw a shadow moving inside.

Good, Victor thought. He still had his own rifle slung over his shoulder, and a full magazine with an additional few clips clipped to his belt. Ortega had gone through half of one magazine already, but he too was well-equipped. They could make easy work of the CSO team by keeping them at bay, slowly pushing toward the front door of the facility.

He winced, suddenly feeling a shooting pain run from his cheek all the way through his body. It was as if someone had stabbed him in the side of the head with an electric rod, and he tensed. The convulsion only lasted a split-second, but it startled him enough to have to blink away and regroup.

Ortega prepared to fire again, now coming out from behind the tree and approaching the open space between their spot by the lake and the front of the facility. Victor kept one eye focused on Ortega's progress as he watched Lucia in his peripheral vision, interested in why she had not made a break for it.

He sensed she was afraid Ortega might turn on her, might shoot her in the back as he realized their prize had broken free. The pain lanced through him again, causing him to convulse repeatedly for a few seconds.

What the hell is happening?

He pressed against his cheek again, realizing that the blood had only begun pouring out of him faster. His entire palm was slick with red. But it was just a cut — just from a *slap*. Had she been wearing a ring? Some sort of blade that dug far deeper than he thought possible?

Ortega turned now but continued moving toward the facility. He lined Lucia up in his sights, and Victor watched through blurry vision as Lucia's own eyes widened. He didn't try to stop Ortega.

This is what you get, he thought. *If this is what you want...*

He heard the sharp crack, the single gunshot.

It caused more confusion. Ortega had been shooting *three*-round bursts, but this shot seemed to echo, as if it was from farther away.

Ortega fell. Victor whirled around, facing his partner and friend, noticing that Ortega was clutching his throat. His eyes were pure white, panic on his face.

A spurt of blood met the tree trunk behind him, immediately covering it with liquid from his carotid artery.

Reggie.

Victor realized his mistake — Reggie had sprinted away with the sniper rifle, hiding in the rocks.

Victor realized that Ortega was dead only a few seconds after he saw Ortega's eyes staying open. Another shot rang out, removing a portion of Ortega's skull.

Only then did Victor act. He rushed forward, trying to get out of the line of sight of Reggie's sniper rifle. He knew that Reggie was a trained sniper who was holding a weapon that he knew how to use well.

Proof of that was lying next to the tree.

He stumbled and tried to run, but the ground seemed to be shifting as he did. He tried to stand straight, tried to find his feet once more, but even then, it felt like his head was swimming.

Was he drunk? He felt as though he had just slammed five shots of tequila and had been sitting down all night and just gotten up to leave. He was seeing double, triple.

Lucia was still there, looking at him, her head cocked to the side. It was as if she was studying something.

He looked down, blinking furiously as he tried to force his eyes to focus, to see something.

But it was gone, missing.

He had been wrong.

The wrist — the Russian's hand — had, in fact, gotten away.

No, that wasn't it.

He looked back to Lucia and saw her standing closer, no longer afraid of him.

Then he saw it. In her hand, she held the soldier's own.

Even through his blurry vision, Victor's eyes beginning to fail him, he knew it was writhing, wriggling as it tried to break free of her grasp. And even from here, he could see the bright red imprint on the fingernails.

She hadn't smacked him across the face with her *own* hand, he now realized. She had cut him with the diseased claw he had been holding.

And she had infected him with it.

CHAPTER 70

LUCIA

LUCIA WATCHED Victor stumble around with fascination, though the scene was horrifying. Her scientific mind couldn't help but be intrigued.

She had screamed again when Ortega was shot twice, the second time ending his suffering with a spray of blood that landed on the white bark of the tree trunk behind him.

It was a shame, really. She sort of liked Ortega and Victor. They seemed like good men, or at least decent men.

But decent men didn't kidnap people and threaten them to get what they want. They didn't do the things Victor and Ortega did. So while there had been a moment of turmoil, her conscience was clear after Reggie removed the top portion of Ortega's head.

But her eyes were still on Victor. He was moving toward her, trying to do something. It was unclear what the man was after, or if he was even still considered a man.

What she was watching was something inhuman.

She understood the infection a bit more now, knowing what she did about it. Her conclusions still needed to be tested and proven out, but it was clear Victor was not being infected by something natural. This was no bacteria or virus. This was something completely different, something synthetic, created in a laboratory not unlike the one they had left down below.

Created by humans.

Sure, their purpose had been entirely different, but this was the downside of scientific experimentation. Without careful study and controlled experiments, havoc could be unleashed quite easily.

That havoc was now ravaging Victor's insides, the disease spreading wildly and taking over his voluntary functions. He seemed to be in pain, his face contorted in agony, though she wasn't sure if that was just a side effect of the tiny molecules casting their nets and overriding his involuntary muscle twitch response.

She watched on as he moved toward her, nearly stepping on the wrist of the fallen Russian soldier she had once again dropped on the ground. She hadn't wanted to touch it at all, but it was the only weapon she knew of and the only one within reach.

A disgusting, unfortunate weapon, but one that had done its job.

She had noticed the soldier's dirty fingernails, sharp and protruding outward from the man's fleshy fingers, saw them twitching as Victor held it while pulling her along earlier. She hadn't planned it; it was not as though the events had been premeditated. It was an opportunity, one she knew she needed to take.

Victor had said he himself was opportunistic, the kind of man who jumped at the chance when one was provided.

Lucia had never known that she, too, was this way, but she was happy to have fixed that.

She shuddered as she recalled the terror of swiping the wrist across Victor's face, of feeling its fingernails, not her own, digging into his flesh and pulling away skin. She had wondered if it would be enough, if Victor would become infected.

There was no way to know, and she had smacked him with it because it was the only weapon around, but the scientist in her had wondered immediately what the effect would be.

Apparently, the compound inside the severed hand was dissipated not just throughout bodily fluids — blood, saliva, etc. — but had latched onto and around skin cells, organs, appendages, and, clearly, fingernails.

This made sense, she now realized. Victor's other soldier, the one who hadn't spoken but had been seated on the bunk bed inside the dormitory room where they met Victor and Ortega, had been rocking back and forth as well.

She knew now it was the early stages of disease, that the man's own immune system had probably been fighting off the invasion, that his cuts were so slight that he may have won the fight.

She wondered if the body was still in there, crawling around as the host for its microscopic disease.

Even now, the hand of the Russian soldier was on the ground writhing, still alive with the stuff. She didn't know enough about it, but she wondered how long it would take to dissipate, to use up the resources found in the cell structure of its hosts before dying out.

She also knew she didn't want to chance leaving it here to spread. If an animal found it...

"Lucia!" her mind was pulled back to the present as Freddie's voice reached her from across the clearing.

She turned, ignoring Victor now and focusing on Freddie's progress. He looked to be in pain still, but Zack Bennett was helping him along.

She saw Reggie near the SUVs where they had parked so many hours ago, saw him walking toward Ben and Julie.

CHAPTER 71
FREDDIE

HALF of the group gathered together by Lucia. Zack and Reggie, along with Freddie, had made their way over to her spot, where Zack had helped Freddie down to the ground, resting his back against a tree.

Lucia noticed that his wound was beginning to seep through the cloth they had used to wrap it, and she knew that it would only be a matter of time before it grew infected. Hopefully, they could be done here soon enough to pile back into the SUV and get him some help.

All said, she knew it wouldn't be life-threatening if they could get the wound cleaned and treated properly in the next few hours. They had stanch the blood flow, and aside from the dirty lead possibly still inside, he would not be in any danger.

Zack strode over to Lucia, where she watched Victor — or what he had become — still clawing around at the air in front of him. In a wide-open space such as this, it seemed the infection inside him did not know where to go. If it could hear their voices, it still couldn't pinpoint their exact location. Victor made horrible grunting sounds as his mouth moved up and down, but it seemed the infection had set in and completely taken him over.

She remembered the soldier they had bumped into, one of Victor's men, upon leaving the facility. He had been able to make sound, even forming them into words. Though his infection had been slower, likely even more gruesome than the rapid onset of Victor's own infection, it had been clear that there was still human left inside the man's brain.

She looked back at Victor now, safely fifteen feet away, awkwardly crunching over sandy snow near the lakeshore. She wondered if he was still in there somewhere, if he was still capable of thought. Was he plagued by inner demons? What sorts of thoughts could a man like this possibly create? Would the infection change even the wiring in his brain enough to change his thoughts?

Her scientific mind raced with possibilities. As gruesome as it was, it was something she had never seen before — an infection that moved *so quickly*, multiplied so rapidly inside a host that it had completely overtaken it in less than five minutes. In addition, she had never seen a parasitic relationship such as this. Usually, these sorts of infections existed only in smaller specimens, not an entire human body.

But she knew all too well not to discount nature's capabilities. She knew all too well not to underestimate its power.

"It's rather disgusting, isn't it?" Zack asked.

She glanced over at Zachary Bennett, confused. Apparently, he did not know. Or if he did, he was still pretending as though he had nothing to do with this.

"It's scientifically fascinating," she responded, her words clipped. "But... do you understand what we are looking at?"

Zack nodded quickly. "Of course. It's an infection, either bacterial or virus-based, latching onto a host and multiplying using the host's own cellular structure as a vehicle for —"

She cut him off. "No, Zack," she said. "That's not what it is at all."

He frowned. "But —"

Freddie chuckled, and both Lucia and Zack turned to him. From the corner of her eye, she noticed Ben and Julie making their way to them. She also noticed Ortega's lifeless body hunched over on the snow in front of the tree where he had died. She tried not to focus on the half of his brain she could still see poking out.

"What's funny?" Zack asked Freddie.

He continued chuckling, growing into laughter. Then he stopped short. "Oh, it's just that — wait, really?"

Both Zack and Lucia stared down at Freddie quizzically.

"Interesting. I just thought for sure you'd be able to figure this out. If anyone."

Zack's confusion grew, and Lucia watched as his head moved back and forth, looking first at Victor, then at Freddie and Lucia. "I don't understand. You guys know something I don't?"

"I wouldn't have guessed it, but yeah," Freddie continued. "I thought it was obvious by now. You know what's affecting him, right?"

Zack paused.

"You saw that jug of chemicals we found in the lab. It's got a Vanelov Manufacturing logo right on the side of it."

Zack's eyes widened. "I had nothing to do with that! As I said, Venelov was involved in a lot of production and manufacturing for agricultural endeavors. That the Russian research employees here were using a de-icing chemical made by Venelov doesn't mean that I —"

"Venelov Manufacturing was using chemicals in the taiga fields nearby," Lucia said. It wasn't a question.

"Yeah, but that doesn't mean those chemicals got into the research station!"

"The fact that I discovered what you all were doing — *and* the Russian government discovered it — means that the chemicals leached out farther than you would have hoped."

Freddie added on. "Yeah, so we know it's possible that your chemicals didn't stay where they were put. Isn't it possible that your chemicals also co-mingled back at the manufacturing plant?"

"We already covered this! I don't understand why that would —"

Zack cut himself off just as Ben, Julie, and Reggie arrived. His eyes darted back and forth again, and a look of realization appeared on his face.

Lucia nodded. "Zack, I'm afraid it wasn't just Venelov Manufacturing chemicals that helped aid in the spread of this infection. It was your work directly."

"What you mean by that?" Ben asked, joining the group.

"I think it's pretty clear that Zack's science project jumped out of its cage," Freddie said. "Stuff spreads pretty quickly, as we know already. And to my knowledge — though I'm no scientist — I don't know of anything else that could possibly do this to people." As he spoke, he motioned with his head toward Victor, the man's limbs all moving independently, bones cracking as they bent around in twisted configurations.

Zack's head fell to the ground. "I don't believe it's true."

"You *have* to believe it's true," Lucia said. "Because you're the only one who can stop it."

"If it's the slime mold," he stammered, "if it's *really* true, I don't know — I'm not sure how to kill it. There is no way to control this one remotely. These aren't equipped with artificial mitochondria — they can't be, since we didn't produce this strain in the lab. It's obviously evolved on its own."

"Still, you're the only one here who can possibly fix it."

Ben stepped forward and grabbed his younger brother by his collar, pushing him backwards.

"Hey!" Zack yelled. "I want to help! I can fix —"

"We've got something else to talk about, little brother," Ben said, his voice a mere growl.

CHAPTER 72

BEN

"HARVEY, leave him alone! We were just discussing—"

"This isn't about the slime mold," Ben said. He whirled around and sneered back at Lucia and the others. He wasn't upset with them, but he could no longer contain his rage. He turned back to his younger brother and continued berating him.

"I *trusted* you," he began. "Finally. Against my better judgment, I *believed* you. I didn't think you were in on this. Didn't think you had a hand in—"

"In *what*? Ben, slow down."

Ben felt his younger brother twist a bit in his grip, but the younger man didn't try to break free. It wasn't that he wasn't trying to fight him or contradict him. It was as if Zack truly didn't know what Ben was going on about.

He released him but pushed him back against the tree. Zack hit the trunk roughly but steadied himself with his hands. "Ben, stop *losing your mind* every time something doesn't go the way you want. Lucia and I were just discussing the slime mold. Yes, I created it. And yes, it's in the de-icing chemical they used on that creature. And yes, it's infecting—"

"*This isn't about the slime mold,*" Ben said.

Zack stared at him strangely. "You've got to be kidding," he said. "What, then, is this about?"

Ben motioned to Victor. Reggie had joined the group with Ben, but he had quickly walked over to Ortega and picked up the man's assault rifle, swapping it out for the sniper. He was now regarding Victor, ensuring that the infected mercenary didn't get too close to them.

"Him. It's about him."

"Victor?"

All eyes except for Reggie's were on Ben. He nodded. "Did you know?"

Zack suddenly looked afraid. "Know *what*? Ben, we were working together on this. Stop withholding information. Just tell me—"

"Withholding information?" Ben snapped. "I am not the one withholding information. This man and his team were working for you. You hired them."

Zack nodded. "Yes, I did. We've already established that."

Then he turned to Lucia. "You told us masked men broke into your house. Went through your belongings. You had gone out for a bite to eat, which was the only reason you weren't home at the time."

Lucy's eyes widened as she listened. "Are you saying...?"

"I am," Ben said. "It was *Victor* who broke into your house. Or his men under his command."

Zack shook his head, appalled. "I *never* ordered that. I asked Victor to keep an eye on Lucia, but I never — how do you know that, anyway?"

"We called your old flame, Ember. None of us had service down there, but she called back while we were inside, left a message. We had told her to look into it, to try hacking international police and Interpol records, just to see if there was a match on the facial recognition. Turns out, there was."

"She was able to find Victor?"

"One of his known associates. Not Ortega, but possibly the guy who just lost his head back downstairs. She said it was a pretty confident match, too. And since you just confirmed you told Victor to keep an eye on her..."

Zack tried to back up, but met the tree trunk once again. He was shaking his head, stammering. "Ben, I know I've asked a lot of all of you.

But think about it. Victor didn't just try to kill *you* in there — he tried to kill *all* of us. To leave *all of us* there to die.

"And you heard what he said. He wanted an out, a way to retire in peace. He couldn't leave any of us alive if he was going to do that. Especially not me."

Ben had already considered this, of course. But Victor could also have been playing them to the very end. Perhaps Zack had ordered Victor's men to break into Lucia's apartment. What would that change? If the man's ultimate goal had been to find a way to leave his enterprise profitably, with enough money to buy an island somewhere, what would it matter that he had betrayed his boss's orders?

Everyone paused, even Zack. No one spoke.

This is it, then, Ben realized. *This is the moment they are waiting for.* He realized the next words out of his mouth were going to be followed by his team, without question. He was their leader, whether he liked it or not.

Whether he was prepared for it or not.

All along, from the very beginning, he had wondered if he would be capable of making calls like this. Did he trust his brother or did he not? Had Zack betrayed them all once more, or was he telling the truth? Did it even matter?

If left to his own devices, Zack might simply be untrustworthy out of nothing except sheer incompetence. Zack wasn't an evil person, nor was he politically motivated. He was a scientist, a man simply wanting to find the answers to the world's questions.

He looked down at the ground, then back up at his kid brother before speaking again.

The truth was important, but Ben finally realized that it was nothing compared to something else.

Something he'd wanted for a long time.

"Okay, little brother," he said. "I believe you. Not because you've made a case, but because I *want* to. I *choose* to."

"I promise I'll — "

"No," Ben said. "No more promises. No more requiring us to trust each other. I *believe* you, because you're my brother. I've made that choice. I'm done fighting."

CHAPTER 73

BEN

FREDDIE WATCHED the exchange with interest. His side was still killing him, quite literally. But it helped to have the distraction from the pain. Reggie had packaged him up well, but he needed to get the remainder of the lead out of his torso before it leached into his bloodstream and wreaked havoc.

Still, this infection was worlds better than the infection he saw Victor suffering from.

After Ben's and Zack's heated exchange, tensions had been high, but Julie had stepped in and helped to lower them. Reggie looked like he was about to turn and take off Zack's head next, but to his credit, he kept his new weapon pointed towards Victor.

"You got any ideas about what to do with him?" Ben asked Zack, after they'd finished their conversation.

"Well, considering it's from the slime mold I helped build, I'm guessing that the solution is quite simple."

Freddie frowned, matching Ben's expression.

"You discovered it yourself, Julie," Zack continued, addressing Ben's wife now. "The stuff we made in the lab, we attached an artificial mitochondria to it, basically trying to boost its ability to interact with foreign chemicals."

Julie nodded knowingly. "Water, specifically," she said.

"That's right. The slime mold we made is triggered by water. The one we made is basically inert until it comes into direct contact with dihydrogen oxide, or H2O. It's simple, elegant, and works perfectly to keep things contained until the agricultural community using it needs it."

"*Mostly* contained," Reggie spat.

"Mostly contained, yes," Zack said. "But this one, without the artificial mitochondria, probably still will have a similar reaction when in direct contact with water. However, it will be the exact *opposite* effect. Instead of going from minor to active, multiplying rapidly, it should trigger it to shut down."

Reggie walked forward a few paces and pressed the end of his rifle into Victor's chest. The infected man immediately snarled, one of his eyes bending halfway around its socket while the other shot upward. His arms and hands reached forward, as if trying to grab the rifle out of Reggie's hands.

But Reggie kept moving. He picked up speed, keeping the gun between himself and Victor as he pushed the infected mercenary backwards.

Victor's feet hit the water first, his skin protected by the combat boots he wore. Still, Reggie pushed. He launched Victor backwards, the man falling and flailing wildly as he did.

He hit the water on his side, then disappeared beneath the surface. He came up a second later, the slime mold inside now fully awake and searching for any handle to pull itself out of the lake.

"Let's test that theory," Reggie muttered.

"What are you doing?" Zack asked. "It was just a theory! This needs to be tested and —"

"This is what we call 'field testing,'" Reggie snapped.

"What's the downside?" Ben asked Zack.

Freddie watched Victor in the water, splashing around and attempting to walk. It was clear the man had no control over his motor skills any longer, and he looked like a drowning toddler, reaching out for help. Still, his eyes rolled around haphazardly, his jaw opening and closing as his mouth took in huge amounts of water.

"I don't know," Zack said. "I can't even begin to guess. We need to —"

"Too late," Reggie said, shrugging as he cleaned off the end of the rifle in the water.

There was nothing left to do but watch. To see what would happen. If Zack's theory proved correct, this would be the end of Victor.

If not...

The CSO team all turned and watched as Victor splashed around in the shallow water. After about a minute, the splashes became less violent. He had clearly taken on at least a gallon of lake water, but it didn't seem to be drowning him. It was evident that he was being controlled by the host inside his arms and legs, with each microscopic organism controlling a muscle cell, parts of his skeleton, and his neurological system.

Finally, after another thirty seconds, Victor lay still. Reggie waded into the water, coming to Victor's feet. Freddie heard the sucking sound of mud as Reggie splashed toward the mercenary.

Using the same rifle he had picked up from Ortega, Reggie poked at Victor a few times. Finally, he shrugged. "Seems dead to me. Human *and* mold."

Ben nodded, smiling. "Sounds like we have our kryptonite, then."

EPILOGUE

THE CSO TEAM had not had a way to get water to the pile of boulders and research facility themselves.

But they had a way to get someone *else* there, who *did* have water.

It had been a risky call, but ultimately the right one. Ben had worked at national parks in the United States, but he knew that Kodar National Park had been built around the model of US parks. For that reason, he was confident the park hosted a branch of the nearest local forest department fire team.

He didn't know the protocols they would follow in Russia, but it didn't matter. With Reggie's help, the team used the remainder of the explosives and grenades to light the dry grasses and trees around the facility on fire. The blaze lit up a half-square-mile of space, and with some strategic placement of fallen logs and branches, the team gave the forest fire a route to follow.

Directly into the foothills to the south of the base.

That area had been strategic for two reasons. First, it contained the densest assortment of brush and grasses that would burn, and it was also isolated from the rest of the taiga forest around them.

Ben called in the fire, stating that he and a friend had been hiking up here when they'd seen it.

The fire department had responded faster than Ben thought possible, no doubt due to the fact that they rarely saw much action in this region.

The fire was put out quickly and efficiently, thanks to the use of an airtanker flyover.

One that dropped an entire load of water on the base.

Ben and Reggie assumed it wouldn't be a perfect solution, but it was the best they could do — the base was effectively locked up tight after Victor blew the lower cavern entrance, and Ben and Reggie blew the doorway closed they had previously used a grenade to open.

A massive, charred boulder now sat directly in front of where they had entered the base previously.

While they worked, Julie, Zack, and Lucia had taken Freddie to the nearest town, seeking help and medical care. Since their phones worked once more, they had kept in contact with one another, and Zack had driven the SUV back to pick them up a few hours later.

After all that, Ben was sitting in the tiny back room of a local clinic, watching as an ancient nurse who had to be over a century old worked her shaky hands over Freddie's wounds.

She spoke a few words in Russian, but neither Ben nor Freddie understood.

He winced in pain as she stabbed him with some metal implement.

"Ouch," Freddie said.

The stern old lady simply made a *tsk* sound with her lips, and kept working.

Ben smiled. "Sounds like she's not happy that you hurt yourself."

"I didn't hurt myself!"

"Tell her that; she seems to be convinced that you're the enemy here."

He laughed. "Yeah, well, the only Russian word I know is *sladkiy*."

Ben frowned, but the nurse suddenly stopped, then smiled.

Freddie's eyebrows rose.

"What's that mean?" Ben asked.

"It means... *sweet*. I think she — "

The Russian nurse revealed a set of teeth that somehow seemed older than the mouth they were in, and Freddie's face fell.

"I think she's got a crush on you, bud," Ben said, laughing harder. Freddie rolled his eyes.

"Too bad. I was going to tell Lucia — "

Freddie's words raced together, a smashed run-on sentence. "What? You were going to tell Lucia something? What were you — "

"Relax," Ben said, still chuckling. "I'm not going to tell her anything. I was just messing around, trying to figure out if it was this kind old nurse or Dr. Lucia Vergotti you were more interested in."

He watched his friend. Freddie swallowed, his eyebrows moving up and down as the woman worked to pluck the bullet from his insides. She kept smiling at him, through rotten teeth.

"I, uh," he began.

"It's okay," Ben said. "I'll let you tell her."

He stood up to leave, the nurse once again frowning at Ben. He waved, then wished Freddie the best.

Outside, the girls, Reggie, and Zack waited in a makeshift lobby. They were in a town of fewer than 300 people, and most of those people worked in the fields and on farms around the region. The road this clinic was on was the only road in town.

And 'town' was severely lacking in the restaurant department.

"I'm starving," Ben said. "You guys find anywhere to eat?"

Reggie smiled. "Yeah. There's a nice little place nearby."

"Oh?" Julie asked. "How far?"

"About three hours."

Ben groaned. "Fine. I guess we'll grab something that looks safe from that little store nearby."

There was a small corner store — the kind that sold everything from cracked feed corn to boiled eggs and premade sandwiches — but it certainly had not looked appetizing.

Now, Ben was ready to change his mind.

"I'll go with you," Zack said.

Ben stopped in the doorway, turning to face his younger brother. He was prepared for a quick trip, just himself, while the others waited together and planned their exit from Russia. He had not expected anyone to come along.

"Please?" Zack asked. "I got bored sitting here, and besides — we've got a lot to talk about."

Ben nodded. "Fine. But I'm exhausted. Can it wait?"

Zack stared. "Not really. It's the sort of thing you're going to want to hear as soon as possible."

AFTERWORD

If you liked this book (or even if you hated it...) write a review or rate it. You might not think it makes a difference, but it does.

Besides *actual* currency (money), the currency of today's writing world is *reviews*. Reviews, good or bad, tell other people that an author is worth reading.

As an "indie" author, I need all the help I can get. I'm hoping that since you made it this far into my book, you have some sort of opinion on it.

Would you mind sharing that opinion? It only takes a second.

Nick Thacker

ABOUT THE AUTHOR

Nick Thacker is a thriller author from Texas who lives in Hawaii. In his free time, he enjoys reading in a hammock on the beach, skiing, drinking whiskey, and hanging out with his beautiful wife, two dogs, and two daughters.

For more information and a list of Nick's other work, visit Nick online:
www.nickthacker.com

 facebook.com/AuthorNickThacker
 twitter.com/NickThacker
 instagram.com/TheNickThacker

HARVEY BENNETT THRILLERS

Harvey Bennett Thrillers

The Enigma Strain (Book 1)
The Amazon Code (Book 2)
The Ice Chasm (Book 3)
The Jefferson Legacy (Book 4)
The Paradise Key (Book 5)
The Atlantis Artifact (Book 6)
The Book of Bones (Book 7)
The Cain Conspiracy (Book 8)
The Mendel Paradox (Book 9)
The Minoan Manifest (Book 10)
The Napoleon Job (Book 11)
The Embers of Siwa (Book 12)
The Epsilon Event (Book 13)
The Cerberus Protocol (Book 14)
Harvey Bennett Mysteries — Books 1-3
Harvey Bennett Mysteries — Books 4-6
Harvey Bennett Mysteries — Books 7-9

*For a full list of novels by Nick Thacker, visit him online at www.
nickthacker.com*

Printed in the USA
CPSIA information can be obtained
at www.ICGtesting.com
CBHW021752030724
11073CB00010B/570

9 781959 148340